To:

1.

Best regards to an
lover.

Etta Pruett Martin

Molly Anderson

Molly Anderson

THE SAGA OF A PIONEER WOMAN

Etta Pruitt Martin

PHOENIX INTERNATIONAL, INC.
2005

Copyright © 2005 by Etta Pruitt Martin

09 08 07 06 05   5 4 3 2 1

Designed by John Coghlan

Inquiries should be addressed to:
Phoenix International, Inc.
1501 Stubblefield Road
Fayetteville, Arkansas 72703
Phone (479) 521-2204
www.phoenixbase.com

Library of Congress Cataloging-in-Publication Data
Martin, Etta Pruitt, 1915-
  Molly Anderson : the saga of a pioneer woman / Etta Pruitt Martin.
     p. cm.
  ISBN 0-9713470-9-3 (pbk. : alk. paper)
  1. Widows—Fiction. 2. Women pioneers—Fiction. 3. Single mothers—
Fiction. 4. Texas—Fiction. I. Title.

PS3563.A7238M64 2005
813'.54—dc22
                                                    2004030925

CHAPTER I

As David Anderson walked down the rutted streets of Nashville, Tennessee, one afternoon, he noticed a sign recently tacked to a stone building. At first he simply walked ahead, but his breathing quickened as he came closer to read that the states of Coalhuila and Tejas of Mexico were open to settlers. It stated further that all people interested in acquiring a certificate, or script, in that land outside the United States should apply without delay.

To David this seemed to be the answer to his dream, of owning a plantation like his father in Virginia. On the other hand, Molly, his wife, might refuse to leave her childhood home. He also thought how dangerous it would be to take the family into a foreign country, imagining all of the obstacles they might have along the way. He took a few steps forward, stopped, pushed back his hat, and scratched his head. Suddenly he turned toward the sign. He cleared his throat, swallowed a couple of times, and opened the office door.

"Well, Mr. Anderson, I've been hoping you would come," Sterling Robertson, who fronted for the Nashville Company Colony, said. "We need one hundred families to agree to buy land in the Nashville Company Colony in Tejas, the state we call Texas. I just came from there a few days ago. Already Tennessee families are living there. The land is cheap and the country is beautiful."

"Yes, I've heard that, but I'm afraid that my wife, Molly, won't want to live in a different country," David replied. Yet, after listening to the men who stood around talking of such a great opportunity to buy cheap land west of the Mississippi River in the country of Mexico, David could not resist. So, without thinking further, he signed a certificate to buy land in a country he had never seen. He shook hands with Robertson and walked out.

He felt a slight twinge of guilt as he rode home on Traveler, his horse. *How would Molly react to his decision to move to a new country? Did he act too hastily in signing the certificate?* He knew that in order to be fair to Molly he must tell her immediately about his plan to leave Nashville.

To be sure, she did object to the idea of going to a foreign country and plainly told him, "David, I will not live in a country without protection of the United States government. You can go if you want to, but me and my sons will stay right here."

At once she regretted saying such things. She slowly turned, wiped her hands on her apron, and quietly walked into her kitchen. She felt remorseful that she let loose her temper. She knew David to be a kind, loving husband who wanted a good life for his sons, so she vowed to say no more; at least, not at that time.

The following morning the family began preparations to go to a new home in a far different land. They loaded the canvas-covered wagon with as many household items and farming tools they could pack into or onto it.

Trunks made from seasoned cedar lumber were stacked one on top of the other. They contained clothing and a few pieces of treasured glassware securely wrapped in bed linens. Molly crammed one trunk so tightly that she hardly could close it. Nevertheless, she managed to put in the family Bible and two books that once belonged to her father.

Near the back of the wagon, fourteen-year-old Jacob and ten-year-old Willy helped David anchor two wooden barrels. One was filled with cottonseed and the other with corn seed because David anticipated an early spring planting in the new country. Then he firmly attached Molly's spinning wheel and loom on top of the barrels. He knew she considered them very important in making clothes for the family.

They hung a bull-tongue plow, so necessary in turning the sod, on one side of the wagon. On the other side they placed a broadax and another barrel.

"Before we leave we must fill this barrel with water because we won't know when or where we can find water. Jacob, I'm making you and Willy responsible to see the barrel is filled when we stop at any creeks or springs," David said.

Now, only the big high walnut bed frame remained to be loaded. It was Molly's pride and joy. It had been in her family as far back as she remembered. Still David saw no place to put it. At last he ventured to say, "Molly, I don't believe we can take that big walnut bed frame. I tried to find room, but it's too high and heavy. Maybe we can leave it at the boardinghouse. They'll take care of it for us."

"No, David, I will not leave that walnut bed behind. If we can't take the bed, the boys and me will stay in Nashville. You can simply nail it to the wagon floor to keep it steady and put the feather mattress on it. That is where we can sleep, just like we always have. And little John will sleep with us," she emphatically told David. "I've already fixed a cornshuck-filled mat for Jacob and Willy to sleep on at night." At that she smiled and added, "Of course, the boys will shove it under the big bed each morning."

In the early morning of October 28, 1834, the Andersons—David, Molly, Jacob, Willy, and four-year-old John—left their Nashville home to buy land and live in the country of Mexico. David, driving the oxen-pulled covered wagon, with Traveler tied to the back, headed directly south. For three days they went through low-lying farmland where they occasionally saw smoke rising from the chimneys of log houses and heard people calling out "howdy" as they passed by.

On the sixth day they entered a dense growth of oak and maple trees. David stopped the wagon, jumped down, and untied Traveler. Robertson had told him that bandits often came from the trees to rob travelers, taking all the supplies and even sometimes stripping the wagons of wheels and wagon-tongues.

"Molly, you drive the wagon and let Jacob help you. I'm going to ride ahead to look for the safest route. I won't be far ahead of you, so don't be frightened," David said as he mounted Traveler and rode away.

All day Molly drove the oxen, Ole Blu and Bill, in a steady gait, always looking one way and then another. They passed a broken-down wagon with the wheels and canvas gone and no supplies to be seen. Seeing that, Molly stood up in the wagon. She lashed the oxen into a fast run, desperately trying to reach David, who heard her crying out. He turned and galloped back.

"Don't be afraid, Molly," he said. "We'll be out of the trees before sundown and the going will be better. You let Jacob drive the oxen. I won't be far ahead."

David proved to be correct. When the sun went down, they saw open land ahead and camped for the night. The following day they went directly south. Two days later they saw the outline of the town of Memphis in the distance, so they camped under some elm trees on the edge of the town.

Eager to enter the city, the family started early the next morning. David rode Traveler in front of the wagon. Molly, with little John by her side, drove the oxen while Jacob and Willy followed behind. Even though it was early in the morning people were walking down the cobblestone sidewalks. Some of them waved to Molly, who smiled and waved back. Her fear and dread of going to a new country vanished. She felt extremely proud of David as he sat tall and handsome on Traveler, tipping his hat and smiling to the people.

Soon they turned west toward the mighty Mississippi River and stopped on the east bank. Jacob and Willy ran ahead where, for the first time, they saw a large ferryboat ready to take them across the river.

"Good day," the ferryman said, "for fifty cents I'll take you over the river into Arkansas Territory. How far from here do you live in Arkansas?"

"Oh! We've never been in the Territory of Arkansas. You see, we're on our way to buy land in Mexico," David answered and handed the man a fifty-cent piece.

"Goin' to Mexico, eh! A lot of folks have me take them across

the river on their way to Mexico. I guess that's their business, but
I hear there's a lot of trouble there."

David drove the oxen that pulled the covered wagon onto the
ferry. He held the reins and Molly, with Willy and John beside
them on the spring-seat, started across the great Mississippi River.
Directly behind them sat Jacob on Traveler, beaming with pride.
All too soon the family was across the river and in the Territory of
Arkansas.

"Well, I wish you God's speed and good luck in that foreign
country. Some day I may see you again," the ferryman said as he
guided the ferry back to the east bank.

Leaving Tennessee behind, they, once more, started south and
west. The weather remained fair with only a few days of clouds,
rain, and a slight drift of snow. Molly seemed to have resolved her
resentment of leaving her home behind. She began enjoying the
journey, pointing out to her sons each interesting view. Finally, they
entered Louisiana and angled south to pass through the northern
part of that state.

"Whoa, Bill! Whoa, Ole Blu," Molly yelled and halted the
oxen on the banks of the Sabine River that divided the United
States and the Mexican state of Tejas (Texas).

Instantly, David spurred Traveler into a run and stopped by
the wagon. "We're here! Look! Just look across the river! Right over
there is Texas."

Four dreary weeks had passed since they left their Tennessee
home. Although only midafternoon, they camped for the night.
They usually traveled until the sun went down behind the lands
farther west. But this was different. Tomorrow they planned to
cross the Sabine River on a small ferry they saw anchored to a big
boulder that protruded over the bank of the river. They would then
be in the Mexican state of Texas, a country completely unknown
to them.

David unhooked the oxen from the wagon tongue, allowing
them to graze on the winter grass growing along the riverbank.

Jacob and Willy gathered dry tree limbs and David built a fire. He believed a damp chill would drift down the river bottomland, especially after the sun went down. Shortly, a fire began to burn and sparks began to crackle.

"Molly, I'm goin' to go hunt game for our supper," David said. He reached for his rifle and mounted Traveler. "See that the boys don't wander too far from the wagon."

"Now, David, don't be gone too long. The boys are hungry and I don't have any meat to cook," Molly answered.

After he left she put the coffeepot, black from previous fires, on the hot coals. Soon the ground coffee beans began to brew and a tantalizing aroma filled the air.

Jacob and Willy, at once, ran toward the river to see the ferry. But they did not ask John to go with them.

"Maw, I want to go see the ferry, but Jacob and Willy said I can't go. Maw, why can't I go?" John asked as he pulled on Molly's apron.

"John, I think your papa wanted you to stay here and look after me, " Molly said in an effort to soothe him. "Come on, set over there on that big rock and watch me make corn pone for supper."

Earlier Molly noticed a makeshift hut perhaps fifty yards from the wagon. Surely no one could be living there. But around dusk a man came from the run-down shanty toward the wagon. He looked so unkempt in his buckskin clothes, long tousled hair, and beard that he frightened her. She knew David took the only gun so she looked for some kind of weapon to fight this strange man who suddenly seemed larger and more dangerous.

She grabbed the butcher knife lying near the fire and whispered to John, "Run behind the wagon. Run! Run fast!"

She looked up. She saw the man coming closer. With her right hand securely gripping the knife, she firmly stood against the wagon wheel waiting for him. She stared directly at the man.

He smiled and said, "I'm Jules Ripperdeaux. I own that ferry down by the river. Do you'ns want me to take yous 'cross the river? Well, I will if yous wait 'til mornin'. Where did y' come frum?"

"We come all the way from Nashville in Tennessee," Willy said as he and Jacob came from behind the wagon. "We crossed the big Mississippi River on a ferry. Bigger than that one down there."

"Well, a while back I poled some more folks 'cross the river. They wuz frum Tennessee." Ripperdeaux, ignoring Willy's remarks about the ferry, said, "I'm goin' tell yous jest like I told them. Git some land in Louisiana and stay here. Injuns and Mexkins don't like Anglos livin' on their land. Now, Texas's a good land but taint good fur women and chil'uns."

David, returning from his hunt and seeing a strange man at the camp, slapped Traveler into a run. When he came closer he knew he had nothing to fear. Ripperdeaux smiled and shook his hand.

Molly began to cook the rabbits David brought in from the hunt as David and Ripperdeaux sat by the fire and talked. Mainly, Ripperdeaux did the talking. He twisted his head to one side and closed his left eye. This caused David to believe the man to be partially blind.

Jacob and Willy, with looks of admiration and amazement in their eyes, silently listened. They wanted to remember every word of the thrilling adventures Ripperdeaux said he experienced.

"I wuz the captain's mate on the riverboat that sailed up and down the old Mississippi. That is 'til I lost this hand. We wuz on the *Queen Mary* jest 'fore we dropped anchor at New Orleans." He paused long enough to lift his left arm and show Jacob and Willy how he used a vicious-looking curved, iron hook as his hand. "Well, after that I didn't go back to the *Queen Mary*. But, I could've and maybe I will someday."

"Why would you want to go back? I hear there will be more people going into Mexico, and they'll need a ferry to cross the river," David wanted to know.

"I want to see my old friend, that no-good gob who made me

lose my hand." Without talking further, he turned and walked to his shack.

The family awoke at daybreak the next morning anxious to resume the way west. Willy, with the help of John, rekindled the campfire. Molly began to cook the remaining rabbit David had brought in and enough corn pone to last all day. Meanwhile, David and Jacob harnessed the oxen and hooked them to the wagon.

They had finished breakfast when they saw the sun slowly rising from above the reddish, eastern horizon. David walked back and forth, waiting for Ripperdeaux to take them across the river.

"I'm anxious to start our first day in Texas. We need to reach Villa de Viesca in the Nashville Company Colony somewhere along the river called Brazos. Robertson told me that is where the Mexican government grants settlers permission to settle. He said it's fertile river bottomland."

True to his word Ripperdeaux came from his shanty. He held the oxen's yolk. "Git goin', Bill! Ole Blu! Move. Git on the ferry! Tain't fur 'cross the river."

Then he pushed a long wooden pole to the bottom of the river, shoving the ferry into the deep water where it floated. "Boys, this is poling the ferry," he yelled. "Watch me!" It didn't take long to pole them safely to the west bank where Ripperdeaux took the chains from the wagon wheels and the oxen walked onto dry land.

David gave Ripperdeaux a fifty-cent piece due him for poling them across. As always, he smiled and thanked David. Then he muttered, "More people goin' to Texas!" Suddenly, looking directly at David, he whispered, "Yore woman, she's a pretty one. You better watch. Injuns might steal her." He said nothing else. He turned and walked to the ferry.

Molly almost became speechless when she heard Ripperdeaux mention Indians. David saw a terrified look in her eyes so he climbed onto the wagon beside her. Holding her close and brushing the hair from her face, he said, "My sweetheart, don't be afraid of this different world. I love you. Just trust me. I will always be near to protect you and our sons."

With David close to her, it wasn't long until she felt some of the enthusiasm and courage he exhibited each day. Still, deep inside her the constant fear of this unknown world remained. It was so far from the security of the United States government, the government her father fought to preserve. Yet, she faithfully tried to get rid of the tormenting thoughts that continually troubled her.

Leaving Ripperdeaux and the river behind, they started west, meticulously staying on the seldom-used path Ripperdeaux had instructed them to follow. The first twelve or fifteen miles were easy. But soon, right before them appeared a great forest of tall pine trees that stood as sentinels guarding the plants and animals within.

A herd of deer ran across the path and leaped out of sight. Squirrels, too numerous to count, scampered from tree to tree. Scores of tiny titmice ran to hide under fallen limbs. Indeed, the forest seemed alive. Bear tracks were seen all around, even on the trunk of a tall tree.

"Papa, I think the bears are after that sweet honey I smell," Willy said, looking up and sniffing the air alive with the enticing aroma of fresh honey.

Bobcat tracks were everywhere. But, perhaps, what interested Jacob and Willy most was the lone, huge track they followed until it mysteriously vanished.

"Papa, do you know what made the big tracks? Why did we only find tracks of one animal? Before we saw lots of them together," Jacob wanted to know as he and Willy ran to the back of the wagon, reached up and grabbed the suspended cover, and landed on the one vacant spot of the wagon floor.

"Son, that is a panther track; what some people call a mountain lion. Usually they go from place to place alone, except in mating season."

He glanced at Molly sitting on the spring-seat ready to grab little John and hide under the big bed to escape the panther that she now believed to be near.

"Oh! Molly, don't worry. Panthers only mate in the springtime. They must be a long way from this forest," David calmly said to lessen her fears.

Hundreds of strange signs, similar to enormous cow tracks, fascinated David. "I believe these are buffalo tracks. Ripperdeaux told me herds of buffalo, going to drink from the Sabine River, made this path many years ago. He even said that hundreds still roam the Mexican country."

Although the forest seemed peaceful, David rode closer to the wagon with the rifle beside him. He did not ask Jacob and Willy to look for fresh water. The thought that hostile Indians could be near never left his mind. Too, herds of buffalo could race through the forest eager to drink from the river.

Occasionally, he saw signs that wagons or horseback riders followed the buffalo trail. This gave him the assurance that they were going in the right direction, as most of the day he could not see the sun because of the lofty trees.

However, shortly and unexpectedly, they saw the crimson light of the setting sun. The immense forest lay behind them. When David and Molly looked back, the stately trees appeared to have been planted in perfectly shaped rows.

"This looks like a good place to camp tonight. Jacob turn the oxen and bring the wagon over here," David called out.

Even before sunup the next morning, the family started west again, but the way became more complicated. In the forest there was only one path. Here, narrow, beaten trails spread in opposite directions. Yet the trees grew shorter and the growth not as thick as most of the leaves fell in the early winter months. This gave David an advantage. He could study the land closer and choose the right trail.

All day he rode ahead. He scanned the region for signs of well-traveled roads, but saw none. Slowly, the wagon followed behind. Sometimes they went in a northern direction; other times to the south. But, finally, they always went west.

Late in the evening they saw a shallow stream flowing across the path. David waved to Molly and she forded the creek and stopped the wagon between two tall oak trees that provided a canopy for the wagon.

David took the bridle off Traveler, loosened the cinch, and removed the saddle. He slapped him on the rump, and the horse, kicking up his hooves, ran to drink from the clear water. The faithful oxen plodded close behind Traveler, eager to drink after a long hard day's travel.

David built a fire, and Molly warmed the food left from the noon meal. They all hovered around the fire as they felt chilled and said little about the day's journey. David checked the animals, and Molly put the dishes away.

"Jacob, I know you and Willy like to sleep on the ground by the wagon, but tonight I want you to sleep on the mat on the wagon floor. I see more storm clouds brewing and it may rain," David said.

Jacob and Willy did not answer. They quickly pulled the mat from under the bed, crawled in, and soon fell asleep.

A damp clammy feeling filled the air, and at times angry-looking clouds hid the moon. This did not bother Molly and John for they, at once, fell asleep.

An eerie sensation in the wind and the constant rumble of thunder caused David to stay awake. He crept out of the wagon and rekindled the fire. Sitting by the flames, his rifle near, he listened for any unusual sounds.

That day, for the first time, he saw human tracks. This gave him concern. He dozed frequently, but he did not rest. He grabbed the gun at the slightest noise.

The sleepless night ended at last. David rose to his feet, stretched his arms, and pulled back the canvas that served as a door. He called out, "It's time to get up. Molly, the fire is ready to cook breakfast. We need to start early this morning. I think we may not be far from the town called Nachogdoches."

They scarcely went a mile when it seemed night was hovering over the countryside again. Gloomy, threatening clouds rolled in as a blasting gust of wind shook the wagon. Even though they pulled a heavy load, the oxen methodically trotted forward. Traveler whinnied and reared his front hooves. Knowing he was not accustomed to violent storms, David tied him to Ole Blu.

He closed the canvas. Now, he alone sat on the spring-seat. Jacob and Willy, wrapped in warm quilts, sat on the mat where they slept. Little John, his eyes and nose peeking from under the cover, sat beside Molly on the side of the big bed.

Sometime around midafternoon the strong wind began to subside. The clouds that loomed so ominously drifted on south. Gradually, the sun came into view. The wind and sleet that sounded like huge rocks falling on the canvas top passed over.

Realizing the oxen must rest, David stopped the wagon near a patch of thorny brush the Mexicans call "mesquite." Jacob and Willy looked everywhere for water, but they found no place where the oxen could drink. So David took a bucket and filled it with water from the barrel on the side of the wagon. He managed to build a fire with rotted, twisted limbs that Jacob and Willy gathered. Shortly, the fire began to burn and throw out a small circle of flames. Molly started to cook their supper.

She roasted the quail David killed the day before and made corn pone. Nevertheless, she wished she had more to feed her hungry family. That was when she said, "David, I'm going to stew the last of the dried apples we brought from Tennessee. I know we intended to save them for a special time, but we haven't eaten since early morning. Why should I wait to cook them later?"

After a good night's sleep, David looked in every direction and saw no sign of danger. He felt it would be safe to leave the family a short while to look for fresh wagon tracks. After some time he felt discouraged but continued west. A mile farther he entered rich, rolling hills country. The grass grew so high that it reached the stirrups of his saddle. He heard a roaring sound and abruptly stopped. To him it resembled thunder resounding across the sky. But, he saw no clouds. He gazed toward the hilltop and saw a black stallion come to a sudden stop. The horse reared. Neighing, he turned to run toward a canyon, followed by a herd of spotted mares. He had never seen such horses, even in Virginia where he grew up. The stallion ran at a fast gait with nostrils flaring, muscles straining, and hooves kicking up dust. In one brief moment the horses were out of sight.

David quickly turned Traveler and headed back to the family. Galloping peacefully alone he stood up in the stirrups and whistled an old tune his father taught him many years before. He thought, *this, indeed, is a good place to live, farm, and raise sons. It's an unknown country to me. So, I must be cautious, but not fearful.*

David drove the oxen and Jacob rode Traveler as they resumed the trail west. Around dusk, they saw the dim outline of Nachogdoches. As they moved toward it, they found a clear stream and camped for the night. In the still of the evening they could hear the faint, rhythmic sounds of strange music. Songs sung in an unfamiliar language were heard above the noise of children playing and people talking as they walked to their homes.

Molly, as she always did, cooked supper. They all sat by the fire to eat, and David, again, began to describe the wild stallion and the mares following behind. About that time, to their surprise, a man riding a donkey stopped beside him. He politely removed his broad-brim hat, and his white teeth glistened when he smiled and said, "Buenos dias, Señor y Señora. Como esta usted?"

"I am David Anderson. This is my wife, and these are our three sons," David replied. He did not understand the man's words, but assumed him to be a Mexican citizen. "We have come to buy land and live in Texas."

"I am Felipe Flores. Welcome to Nachogdoches. You come to our town manana, no?" As unexpectedly as he rode up, the man turned and rode away.

Each night David recorded in a little book the date and location where they spent the night. That night he wrote:

January 22, 1835—Nachogdoches—State of Texas—Country of Mexico.

This was the first place where they would see the people of the new country. David and Molly felt a little tense, not knowing what to expect. But, they joined in the excitement with their sons.

"Now, be sure your hands and faces are clean," Molly admonished Jacob and Willy. "Don't forget to brush your hair. Goodness sakes, Willy, tie your shoes."

Little John attempted to run and hide so Molly could not wash his neck and ears. Jacob reached out, grabbed John, and sat him beside Molly.

"Young man, do not move one inch," Molly said.

At last little John jumped out of the wagon, and David, anxious to go, called to Molly, "Why is it taking you so long? We're all ready, except you, to see the town."

A few minutes later Molly stepped out of the wagon wearing a bright blue dress that fit ever so perfectly on her slender body. David stood stunned, admiring her every move. He held her close, and whirled around as if they were back in Nashville dancing the night away. He whispered, "Oh, my sweetheart. You are so beautiful."

David drove the wagon into a village very different than they were accustomed to. It did not resemble Nashville, the bustling city of Memphis, or the settlements they passed in the territory of Arkansas. Instead they saw houses of adobe brick like nothing they had ever seen or heard of in Tennessee.

"Papa, is that a big boardinghouse like the one in Nashville?" Willy asked as they passed a large, carved-stone building standing apart from the other buildings.

"Well, if it is, nobody is living there. It looks vacant to me. I'll ask when we get into town," David answered.

Along narrow streets, weather-beaten adobe houses were scattered here and there. Perhaps fifty yards farther, they came by two impressive stone houses, side by side.

"David, look over there. That reminds me of the homes of the governor and the military officials in Nashville. Can we stop and go in to see the people living there?" Molly asked.

"Now, Molly, this isn't Tennessee. Maybe the people living there won't understand our language. We'll ask when we get to the Land Office," David said.

He drove on past the big stone houses and went down the main street of the town. The log-constructed Land Office appeared to be in excellent condition. Many of the other buildings, however, showed signs of not being occupied for a long time, except by the goats that freely roamed the town.

Across the street they saw another building, the sign over the door was so dim that the words "trading post" were barely visible. A few steps beyond, another sign caught their attention. It dangled by one corner over a log house that slumped to one side. Neither David nor Molly could pronounce the name—if it were a name.

"Maw, can you read that sign?" Jacob asked.

"Well, I'm not sure. David, do you know what it says?"

"No, but maybe the first letter is a C."

"Oh! Papa, you are right. I can see it plain now. It is C-A-N-T-I-N-A, but I don't know what it says," Jacob joined in.

David stopped the wagon in front of the Land Office.

"I will see if anyone is here," he said as he opened the door. An Anglo man sat in the official chair taking a nap with his feet on the desk and a hat covering his eyes.

"Good day, sir," David said as he shuffled his feet to arouse the man.

"Come, come in and sit down," the man quickly sat tall in the chair and said, "I'm the land commissioner, Gabriel Louis. Folks just call me Gabe. Are you here to buy land? Do you have the papers you need?"

"My name is David Anderson from Nashville, Tennessee, of the United States," David replied. "I have papers permitting me to settle in the Nashville Colony. I understand it is some distance from here, so my family wants to rest a day in your town."

"Good, tell your missus and sons to come in," Gabe eagerly replied as he seldom had an opportunity to talk to Anglos.

Molly, holding little John's hand, walked in and Jacob with Willy walked behind. Gabe rose from his chair and said, "Mrs. Anderson, set down. I am glad to see you. I hope you like the town. It started many years ago as a trading post with the Indians. Then a Spanish adventurer brought in some Abolos people. These people, earlier, had been ousted from their home on the Louisiana and Mexican border."

"Are they Mexicans?" David asked.

"No, they're of French, Spanish, and English blood. They have been here ever since. Mighty good people. As you can tell by looking at them, they are industrious folks," Gabe said.

"What about those two beautiful stone houses? Do they belong to the Mexican officials?" Molly asked.

"Well, the biggest one is the home of Grace Potter," Gabe casually answered. "Grace and me are the only Anglos living here, but we like it. Her husband drowned in the Anglina River trying to save some cattle from a big flood. Now she lives here with her four sons and her slaves. In fact, she's quite wealthy." He paused then added, "Oh, the other one is where my wife, Carletta, and me live. It belongs to the Mexican government."

Shortly, two men dressed in Indian apparel walked past the Land Office. They were leading their horses carrying deer, wolf, bear, and other animal skins.

Gabe noticed Jacob and Willy staring at the men so he explained, "Those men are from the peaceful Cherokee Indian tribe. The United States government drove them from their home in Georgia. Somehow they crossed the Sabine River into Texas. Their leader, Chief Bowls, made some kind of deal with the Mexican government. Anyway, they are allowed to live in the Zavala region, west and south of here."

"What will they do with all the skins they have with them?" Jacob wanted to know.

"Once or twice a year they bring their furs in to trade for seeds, trinkets, and maybe a little coffee," Gabe answered.

"I have never seen brick houses like the ones in this town. Tell me, where do they get the bricks?" David asked.

"Have you noticed how red the soil is? Well, they mix it with straw and water in a shallow pit. Men, sometime women and children, stomp on it with their bare feet until it is at the right consistency. Then it's shaped into bricks and left to dry. They call it adobe. All the Mexican people make their homes from adobe brick. They are cool in the summer and warm in the winter. Carletta and me like them better than log houses."

Goats seemed to be everywhere. Jacob and Willy left to watch them going here and there chewing on anything they came in contact with. A young boy drove a dozen or more down the street. Gabe pointed to him and said to David, "That's Enrique. His father died last year. Now he and his mother live alone. He watches after the goats because she is very sick."

"What will the boy do if his mother dies?" David asked.

"Carletta and me'll bring him to live with us. You see, he is Carletta's nephew," Gabe answered. "He's a good boy. We'll teach him to read and write. In fact, we'll claim him as our own son."

The donkeys as well as the goats intrigued the Andersons. Men drove some of them down the street with little bales of firewood tied to their backs.

"Why do people use donkeys instead of oxen and horses like we do?" David asked.

"Those are burros not donkeys," Gabe laughingly answered. "The Mexicans never cut their bulls to make oxen of them. Nor do they prefer horses. They like burros because they are good climbers, steady and dependable. That is, 'til they get stubborn. Then, they won't move, but that doesn't matter for the Mexicans never hurry. Come, let's walk down the street. I'll show you our town."

Molly preferred to walk with her sons, so she left Gabe and David at the Land Office.

"Can you tell me what that sign over there says?" David asked as he pointed to the run-down building. "My wife and I couldn't read it."

"That is what you call a saloon. Mexicans call them cantinas. There is one in almost every village and settlement in Texas," Gabe answered when they walked across the street and looked inside. Even at four o'clock in the afternoon people were singing and dancing.

"The Mexican people seem happy," David commented.

"I like the Mexicans," Gabe replied. "My wife is Mexican, not Spanish like some people claim to be. But, I warn you, don't be made an enemy of them." That was all he said, but it created a question in David's mind.

"I've lived here in Nachogdoches a long time without trouble," Gabe said as they turned and walked from the cantina. "I've issued land grants in the Zavala Colony that reaches from here to the Gulf of Mexico. Now there are problems brewing in the country. Mexican officials are afraid the settlers will, in time, take over Coalhuila and Texas and become a self-governed country."

That statement disturbed David. It caused him to wonder if he could trust the Mexican government. However, he believed he had no choice except to follow the advice of Gabe Louis; go on to the Nashville Colony, probably a two-week journey. Gabe handed David a rough map to guide him. Then the men parted with a friendly handshake.

Although David and Molly learned much about the country and its people, they were not aware that Spain had ruled it for over a century. During that time the Spaniards intermarried into Indian tribes because few Castilian Spanish women could be found. Therefore, David and Molly did not see people resembling the original Spanish race who first came to Texas. Most of the people now had dark brown skin and eyes, but they retained the Spanish language. Government officials and military officers often swore they were of Spanish ancestry, even though most of them were born in Mexico from mothers of a different nationality.

When the Andersons left Nachogdoches in late January, a winter chill lingered over the country. They went south down the El Camino Real (the King's Road). It had been used for over a hundred years, all the way to San Felipe. Wild rye grass, like a well-kept lawn, covered the ground, faintly showing a tinge of green new growth as spring came early in southeast Texas.

David dropped the reins to let Traveler graze as he and Molly sat on the spring-seat at the front of the wagon. They talked about the time spent in Nachogdoches. Yet, not once did David mention the problem that existed between Mexico and the Texas settlers nor his thoughts that war might be forthcoming.

"David, I thought we would meet other travelers," Molly said as she scanned the broad highway. "Surely there are houses and towns along such a wide road."

"No, Gabe said we won't see another village until we cross the Brazos River. That'll be maybe another week," David answered and urged the oxen on.

"I'm tired of riding all the time. I think I'll walk a while," Molly said as she jumped from the wagon. She grabbed little John by the hand and skipped along singing, "On the bonnie, bonnie banks of Loch Lomond."

Jacob and Willy joined in. Then David's high tenor voice was heard above the others, "Oh you take the high road and I'll take the low road. And I'll be in Scotland afore ye. But me and my true love will never meet again, On the bonnie, bonnie banks of Loch Lomond."

Joyfully they continued down the old highway, laughing and singing other old Irish songs David had taught them.

That night they camped under a mass of tall trees. Evergreens were among hickory, live oak, and a tree they had not seen before. That tree was loaded with delicious-tasting dark brown nuts, which, like the hickory, supplied food for the Indians as well as the wild hogs.

The following day they went quite a long distance. The weather remained pleasant and the road easy to travel. Somewhere along the way, following Gabe's instructions, David left El Camino Real and turned west. Although he was not sure of the route, he headed into the setting sun. Night was settling in when they heard the sound of water flowing south. They unhooked the oxen and prepared to camp by the river.

When the family awoke the next morning, the river was at flood stage and had become a swift torrent.

"I'm sure the oxen can't pull the wagon across that raging water," David said.

"But, David," Molly answered, "I don't think we should stay here until the water subsides. That might be a week."

"You're right, Molly," David replied. "I think we should go south or north and find a shallow place where we can cross."

After a half day of following the riverbank north, at last they found a place where they might cross. David rode Traveler into the muddy water looking for drops or sinkholes, knowing they could be anyplace. Finally, he found a spot where he thought it would be safe to drive the oxen through. Jacob rode Traveler, and David, constantly yelling, "Gee-Haw," goaded the oxen into the water.

Because of the low west bank the water spread out and formed a marsh. Even though the oxen were extremely strong, they labored hard to walk in the soft, soggy earth. Marsh reeds all but disguised the slimy, choked channels, home to the dreaded alligators the Mexicans call "el lagarate." To be sure, alligators lived in the marsh. No more than two yards away an alligator lay stretched out in the sun, sleeping. Little John held tightly onto Molly. Jacob edged closer to the center of the wagon. Even Willy gazed in silence at the strange reptile. David wanted to calm their fears, but he also wanted to caution them of the danger of being near the alligators.

"I saw lots of alligators a long time ago when I went with my father to Florida," he told them. "I learned they lay out in the sun like they are sleeping. I don't think they eat very often." Then he added, "Remember this, we need to stay away from them. They, like all God's creatures, fight to live."

It appeared as if to compensate for the alligators, cypress, elm, and pussy willow trees grew in the swamp. Close by, also, stood the four-foot palmetto tree. Ashen-green growths, hanging from the branches of the trees, touched the ground. With no roots this phenomenon of nature, called Spanish moss, existed from the moisture of the swamp. Fearful Traveler might encounter an alligator, David tied him to Ole Blu. Ever so slowly they inched their way out of the swamp.

A short time later, they entered a dense thicket of giant hickory, walnut, live oak, and pecan trees. Around dusk, after rambling among the trees most of the afternoon, they camped for the night at the edge of a big thicket.

Early the following morning, a loud thud outside the wagon awoke David. He grabbed the rifle, opened the canvas, and there stood Traveler rubbing his nose on the wagon. Only then, he realized the day had begun as the family still slept.

Quickly, they began to prepare for another day west. Luck held, for this time only one wagon track led from the thicket. David, at last, knew they were on the right path to Villa de Viesca.

By noon the thicket lay far behind them. Before them was beautiful level prairie land covered with wild pampas, rye, and oak grasses. But, they saw no houses.

"Molly, look around us. This is good land. Maybe we'll find a place to farm like this bald prairie," David said as he waved to Jacob and Willy. "Boys, look over there. Those are wild horses just like the ones I saw near Nachogdoches."

Eight or ten mustang mares with foals by their sides ran through the tall grass, their tails held high, in an attempt to attract the attention of the stallion grazing a few steps ahead. A herd of cattle, the bulls' horns so long that they curved above their heads, contentedly grazed on the prairie grass, and calves, following many of the cows, appeared fat.

"Molly, within a year I believe we will have cattle like these," David, thrilled at the sight, called to Molly. She was caught up in David's excitement and, for a brief moment, felt secure in the foreign country.

Traveling farther west they saw where hunters had slaughtered scores of the roaming buffalo and taken all the hides. They had left the carcasses to rot in the sun or to be eaten by the ever-present vultures, the large scavengers that constantly circled above the decaying flesh that filled the air with a foul stench.

"Gabe Louis told me about the great buffalo herds, and how the Indians hunted them," David told the family.

"Papa, why do the Indians kill the buffalo?" Willy asked.

"Son, that's how the Indians live," David answered. "They eat the meat then use the bones as spoons, basins, and even arrows. The Indians never waste any part of the animal. They make their clothes and shoes, which they call moccasins, and cover their shelters with skins from the buffalo."

"Papa, do you think we will see some buffalo? If we do, will you shoot one?" Jacob asked.

"No, Jacob, I have no need to kill the buffalo. The Indians are wise," explained David. "They never kill them unless they need the meat. You see, that way the buffalo never dies out, and that means Indians can live, too. I guess the sad part is that some of the Anglos come here just to kill the buffalo and sell the hides. Gabe said they are pushing them farther west all the time."

With the stench of the rotting buffalo far behind them, they went farther west. What seemed before to be the flat western horizon suddenly became filled with numerous species of trees growing in what is called the bottomland of the mysterious Brazos River. David took the map Gabe gave him and showed Molly the words "Viesca west of the Brazos River." At last they believed they were almost at the end of the journey.

Around sundown they camped among some willow trees with branches that extended upward until the weight of the foliage caused them to reach the ground, creating a shelter for travelers.

Bois De Arc trees, commonly called bodark, grew close by. They fascinated Molly. She bit into one of the orange-colored fruits, but to her astonishment, it was not edible. There, on the east bank, they spent the night only a short distance from the ten-foot falls.

The following morning, impatient to finish the seven-hundred-mile journey from Nashville, Tennessee, they started on the last lap of the quest for a new life in a country they knew little about. The river stretched out wide at the point of crossing. Nevertheless, sandbars provided an accessible entry into the water that was clear enough to see the bottom. Scores of little fish swam by the wagon. They went back and forth as little John attempted to follow them with his eyes.

Without incident they reached the west bank. They turned south, and unexpectedly, they entered a well-traveled road along the meandering of the river, perhaps two or more miles. At the top of a knoll, among lofty trees, they saw Villa de Viesca. The settlement was named for Don Agusta Viesca, the man responsible for the colonization order granted the Nashville Colony. Here Anglo-Americans were issued grants to obtain land and settle.

The plans for the new village were laid out, on paper, in Nashville, and David studied them there. Yet, what he saw before him did not resemble the plans advertised on the billboard he had read in Nashville. He shook his head and said, "It takes time to develop and put any plan into action. So, I'll get to work and help make this look more like a town."

Molly had just stopped the wagon when the inhabitants of the village rushed out to meet the newcomers. The first to greet them were the Wheeler families they had known in Tennessee.

"Hello, Mrs. Wheeler. Hello, Ertha," Molly called to them. "How good it is to see you. My, how your children have grown. Do you remember our little John? Don't you think he looks just like David?"

"Now, Molly," Mrs. Wheeler interrupted, "everybody wants to meet you'ns and welcome you to Viesca."

One by one the women greeted Molly and pointed out their children. But she found it difficult to distinguish one from the other. Of course, they were all running back and forth playing some kind of game. All at once Molly felt warm inside. Maybe, just maybe, she would learn to call this strange country her home. Close behind Mrs. Wheeler and Ertha, came Mr. Wheeler and his son, Marion.

"David, get down and stretch," Mr. Wheeler said. "I want to show you the town. Down there under that big live oak tree is the new Land Office. Now, that twenty-foot log house is the tavern where the widder Annie Moffett and her three daughters live. She cooks for men whose families are still in the United States, or if they are not married. If there's lady boarders, they sleep in the tavern, but I haven't seen any. All the men sleep in tents by the tavern."

"I want you to meet Oscar and Tillie Mays, a fine young couple from Alabama," Marion joined in the conversation. "They have a tavern on the edge of Viesca where they cook food for the boarders, but they don't furnish lodging. The men who eat there mostly are traveling horseback, so they sleep under the trees. Others, hauling supplies north, eat in the tavern and sleep in their wagons."

Closer to the river Marion pointed out the only store—a crudely built log house. He said, "Ramon Gonzales and his wife, Celita, run the store. They usually have two barrels of sugar, two barrels of coffee, chunks of salt, and always two kegs of whiskey. Oh, now and then, they might have one or two pairs of boots some Mexican makes in Bajar."

Walking back up the hill David saw two log houses, side by side, which were not finished. Then he saw another cabin minus windows and doors.

Noticing that David did not understand about the empty houses, Mr. Wheeler told David, "The people who started to build those houses have already proved their grants and have moved to their land. But, the families in the four covered wagons scattered under the trees are waiting to choose their land and receive a grant."

David, knowing it would be a week or more before he would select his land, drove the wagon under a tall live oak tree. He unhooked Ole Blu and Bill and put the harness under the wagon as protection from the rains the men predicted would come. He hobbled the oxen to prevent them from straying and yet be free to graze. The men all stood around admiring Traveler, a beautiful bay horse with spots of gray and white all mixed together with a dark shade of red. David bragged, "I'll challenge any man to a horse race. Who will accept?"

"David," Marion Wheeler said, "wait until Jim Mason gets back. He'll take you up on your offer. At night we believe you should tie Traveler to a wagon wheel. If we don't watch close, Indians sometimes steal our horses, especially our riding horses."

After hearing that David made sure Traveler did not run free.

The men built a fire and the people brought out big chunks of venison and fat wild turkeys. When the fire burned down they hung the meat over live coals where it roasted until it became tender. Pots of coffee brewed on the smoldering ashes as women made corn pone. They put the pones on red-hot rocks above the blazing flames. Although they turned them only once, they browned perfectly on both sides. Wooden bowls of honey, fresh from a wild beehive, completed the meal.

Everyone sat around eating, laughing, and talking, telling the newcomers about their lives at Viesca.

"There is little for the men to do," Ertha Wheeler said, "except wait for the land to be surveyed. Their main chore is to hunt game for our tables. Much of the time they just sit around under the trees and whittle with their one-blade pocketknives. They let the slivers fall on the ground, never trying to whittle anything useful."

"You know, one day I thought I'd put a stop to them leavin' sticks round my front steps," Mrs. Wheeler said. "I throwed some water out the door, but that didn't bother them. They jest kept on whittling. Us women, we've got lots of spare time. This ain't like livin' on a farm. 'Course we keep busy mendin' the clothes. Can you believe there ain't no place here to buy calico or muslin?"

All too soon darkness began to settle in and the people walked back to where they slept. David and Molly, pleased with such a warm welcome, sat by their own wagon. He held her hand, and she lay her head on his shoulder, a habit she had acquired long ago, and which he loved.

He reached into his pocket and took out his record book that he used to record their journey to Texas. He said, "My dear, tonight I'm going to end the records. I don't believe we need to look farther. I think we've found our new home in a good land."

Then he wrote:

> February 10, 1835—This day David and Molly Anderson, with their three sons, Jacob, Willy and John stopped in Viesca, state of Texas, country of Mexico. We will buy land and live in this country. David Anderson—Molly Anderson. From Nashville, Tennessee, country of the United States.

They spent the first day in Viesca waiting for the judicial officer, known as an alcalade, to return. Each day David and Molly helped Jacob and Willy with their school lessons.

"Papa, can't we go down to the river and play with the other boys?" Willy asked. "Please, we won't be gone long."

David looked at Molly and smiled, but she promptly shook her head no and said, "No, you can't go until you've studied your spelling, and most of all, your writing. Annie Moffett told me yesterday there is no school in the Nashville Colony. So, I'll teach you at home. Just be quiet and study your lessons."

One afternoon David, Molly, and little John walked down to the falls on the Brazos River. They watched as the water peacefully flowed south before it plunged some ten feet over a rocky ledge. There it became a torrential stream, boisterously racing toward the Gulf of Mexico.

"The men told me that many years ago Indian tribes lived east of these big falls," David told Molly.

"Did the men say why the Indians do not live here now?" Molly asked.

"People, especially from the United States, have taken over the land and moved the tribes farther north and west. Now the tribes, particularly the Comanche and Waco, wander over the country.

They hunt buffalo and other game. Sometimes they raid the settlers' farms," David explained.

One day Jacob and Willy excitedly ran to the wagon and yelled out, "Mrs. Pharis wants everybody to come to her house and dance on the puncheon floor."

Eagerly the people, even the boarders, went to the Pharis two-room house to enjoy a night of frolic and dancing. The only instrument to be found, however, was a fiddle some man made from bodark wood. But Annie Moffett brought a cowbell, and one man had a tin pan. They used these to keep time with the fiddle. Shortly, the music began. Often it could not be heard above the laughter and toe tapping of the people, young and old.

"I'm Jim Mason," a handsome twenty-two-year-old man told David and Molly as they were standing against the wall resting before they danced another waltz. "I've been here in Texas over two years. I hear you have a horse you would challenge me in a race. I'll accept that challenge. But tomorrow I'm going west to look for a herd of buffalo. That is great sport. I don't kill them. I just love to watch them run. Would you like to bring your two older sons and come along?"

"We've never seen buffalo; only where they have been killed and skinned. We would like to go with you," David said.

"I'm a Baptist preacher," Jim added. "I hoped to build a Protestant church house, but the Mexican government forbids any church building except one of the Catholic faith. I have a league of land west of here where I want to erect a shelter and hold worship services. But, I'll have to wait and see how that turns out."

Molly did not say one word. She could not understand a country with no churches. When they left the dance, David called to Jim, "We'll see you by daybreak in the morning."

Before the sun came up the next morning, they left in a steady gallop. David rode Traveler with Willy behind the saddle, and Jacob rode with Jim. They rode about five miles. Then Jim stopped his horse, dismounted, and put his ear to the ground. He called to the others, "Come over here; lie flat on the ground."

The vibrations they felt almost equaled that of an earthquake. A herd of buffalo was charging north, gaining momentum all the time as dust filled the air.

"I believe they are no more than one mile south of here. I should tell you not to go closer," warned Jim. "Men have been trampled to death by their powerful hooves as they come by."

Before long the tremor of the ground lessened and the running herd became visible. Indeed, for David, this became a memorable day.

By the following day the sky became overcast. Swirling black clouds came in from the north. Shrieking gusts of cold wind reminded the family of the storm they experienced near the town of Nachogdoches. Only now, they felt safe from the angry outburst of nature the Texans called a "norther."

Most of the men stayed inside that day, but David became restless. He walked to the Land Office. He hoped to see the alcalade, but only Roy Pharis, the secretary, and Robertson, whom the Mexicans called empressario, were there.

Empressario Robertson, whose title meant founder of the Colony, was the man in Nashville who had encouraged David to come to Texas, so he introduced David to Roy Pharis. "Roy, I want you to know David Anderson from Nashville in the United States. He and his family are here to buy land."

"David Anderson. Ah! My wife told me about your wife and how you all danced at my house. I apologize for being absent. I work for the Mexican government so I have to stay away from home often. But, my wife never complains. One year we lived in Bexar. It's now called San Antonio. Then last year we came here," Pharis said.

"David, I know you don't understand the Mexican language. Neither could I when I came here almost five years ago. It might help you to know that a league of land is 4,428 acres. That is used in raising cattle. Farmland is called a labor, 171.1 acres," Robertson said.

"Robertson tells me you are a good worker and a man with an honest reputation," Pharis told David. "I'll be happy to help you find good land. Of course, the alcalade, the man you call mayor, will have to approve it."

"There's one thing that might bother you," Pharis added. "All newcomers must take an oath to obey the laws of the state and federal government—that bein' the state of Texas and country of Mexico. Now, there's something else. You must practice the Roman Catholic religion."

"We're Protestants, of the Baptist faith," David said.

"Something else folks don't like," Pharis, as if ignoring David's remark, said, "all marriages must be performed by a Catholic priest. Even if you are already married. If you don't, the marriage is declared void. I saw you flinch when I mentioned religions. Most people do." Then he laughed and said, "I am the ayuntomiento, what you call the secretary. I administer the oaths. Don't worry, there's only been one priest through Viesca."

"I'm glad to hear that because Molly, my wife, would never be baptized by a Catholic priest," David said. "On the other hand, she might not object to a remarriage. She could even wear her best dress. She really is a beautiful lady."

At that David changed the subject to talk of the government. "Is the rumor Gabe Louis told me really true? Are there problems between the Mexican government and the settlers?"

"Yes, it's very true," Pharis answered. "There's much unrest in Mexico. The officials are beginning to resent foreigners coming into the country. They're afraid the people will form a new state that would be governed by Anglo-Americans."

"There's been talk of this. Actually, most of the Anglos are already scheming to take over this Mexican region," Robertson said. "The Mexicans squabble between themselves, specifically during elections. Mr. Austin and me have been arguing with the officials since the last election."

David stood up and walked to the door. Pharis pointed to a map, smudged by sweaty hands, hanging on the wall with the marked location and number of acres where the colonists could settle. Pharis put his finger on a certain spot.

"David, if you want to raise cattle, this is an ideal place," Pharis said. "Oh, maybe thirty miles south and a bit west of Viesca. It's a one-league land grant with the stream we call Little River running right through it. That land is covered with the best grazing to be found anywhere."

David could not get to the wagon fast enough to tell the family about his meeting with Pharis and Robertson. He asked, "Molly, do you agree this is where we should live?"

"David, where you want to go is fine with me as long as the family is together," Molly quickly answered.

Finally, after hesitating, he told her about the requirements to obtain the land grant. To his surprise she said, "Well, if we are going to live in this country, I'll obey the Mexican law. But I don't understand this about religion. I know Ramon and Celita Gonzales are Catholic and you can't find better people. But, I think I'll stay with the Baptist Church." Then she added, "You know I promised to obey you. So, I don't think another marriage would do you any good. You know I do as I please." Smiling, she kissed him on the cheek.

Later David and Molly walked down to the falls on the Brazos River. They talked of building a house, raising corn and cotton, and growing vegetables as they sat on a boulder. David lay his head on her lap.

"David, I need to tell you something," she all but whispered. "I waited a while because I was not sure. Now I know. I'm with child."

David had not expected that. The news left him stunned but he happily reacted.

"Oh! Sweetheart, if this baby is a girl we will name her Martha, your mother's name," David quickly replied.

"If the baby is another boy, what will you name him?" Molly asked.

"George Washington Anderson," he answered without thinking further. "I believe this country will become an independent nation and our son could become president."

CHAPTER 2

Unlike the day before, the Land Office now became a busy place. The land commissioner, William Shields, whom the Mexican people called Guillamo, along with Agusta Rosorio and Manuel Valdez, the government officials who wrote the Spanish land grants, arrived in Viesca late the evening before. Then in walked Jim Mason and two other men.

"Good morning, David. I am glad to see you," Jim said. "I want you to meet the surveyor, Herman Cummuns. And this gentleman is my companion, Pablo Estrada; we work with Mr. Cummuns. Are you here to sign for a land grant?"

"Yes, my wife and I want to move to a league of land on Little River," David answered. "By the way, do you know those two men sittin' by the door? I know most of the men coming and going here, but I don't believe I remember seeing them. They don't look like the others, although I am sure they are Anglos."

"They're buffalo hunters who rode in last night. Said they wanted to rest their horses a day or two as one has a lame hoof," Jim answered, "but I think they're craving some good food at the tavern. I believe they'll be gone by tomorrow."

Mr. Shields walked over to David, shook his hand, and said, "Mr. Anderson, Roy Pharis told me you have selected a location to settle on Little River. If a man wants to raise cattle, that's a choice spot. Mr. Randolph has already received a grant for one league there. It joins the northeast corner where you'll be going. His family is in Kentucky, his home state, but last week he went to bring them here."

After that the business of negotiating the land grant began.

"What is your occupation?" Shields asked David.

"I'm a farmer and a blacksmith," David answered, "but I also want to raise cattle, the longhorn kind."

"Will you swear to obey the federal and state laws of Mexico?" Shields continued, "And will you agree to observe the Roman Catholic Church?"

How to reply on the question of religion bothered David. Yet he knew he had no quarrel with the Catholic Church. Furthermore, he believed in only one God, the God of all the people. So he simply answered, "Yes."

Then Valdez administered the oath of allegiance to the Territory of Coalhuila and Tejas (Texas). David lifted his hand and vowed to honor the oath. That cost him one dollar in United States currency.

Roy Pharis, the secretary and only member of the ayunominto (town council), recorded the document. David handed him four United States coins, the sum being two dollars.

Next came the cost of surveying that amounted to forty-nine dollars in United States money. Jim Mason, serving as translator at that time, read the document to David in English. In return, David handed out six dollars of American currency.

After that, Shields took the cowhide-bound book from the desk and entered the names:

> David Anderson—Molly Anderson—Jacob Anderson—Willy Anderson—John Anderson—From Tennessee in the United States, February 24, 1835.

Shields signed the paper and stamped the seal of the state of Tejas on the document. He handed it to David, who gave him two gold pieces amounting to twenty dollars.

That completed the transaction. David said goodbye to the officials and his friend Jim Mason and Pablo Estrada. He walked out the door, looked up, and realized that already he should have been on the way to his new land.

All morning Molly waited impatiently as she prepared food for David to take with him. Using the remaining wheat flour they brought from Tennessee, she made hard-tack biscuits. When she took them from the skillet they were a golden brown. After allowing them to cool, she put them in a gunnysack knowing they would keep several days and yet be tasty. She started to close the gunnysack, but believed it would hold more food. So, she put in a honeycomb Jacob and Willy brought in and a small bit of roasted squirrel. After tying the sack securely she put it into the leather bag with coffee and a tin can to brew coffee in.

"My dear, this is more than I need. I have my canvas tarp and the hatchet tied behind the saddle," Davis said. "You don't fret. I'll be back in no more than two weeks to get the family."

"David, be sure you find a place where there is water to build our house," Molly said. "Now, when you pass a house, stop and visit with the folks."

"I don't think I'll pass a farmhouse. A league of land stretches a long way. Besides, it's doubtful we'll have close neighbors," he told her. "I just want to find land to clear before the spring planting. Jacob, you and Willy watch after the oxen. And John, you look after your mama." At that, he hugged each son.

"Here, Molly, take this document and these eight pieces of silver. Put them in a safe place." He held her close, kissed her goodbye, mounted Traveler, and at a fast pace headed toward the prairie lands.

Molly put the wagon in order and swept the narrow floor with willow limbs. After that, she insisted Jacob and Willy have their reading lessons. Of course, little John did not want to be ignored, so he insisted she read to him. All in all the remainder of the day passed quickly.

Yet when darkness fell, she immediately began to miss David. How could she ever do without him, his kindness and love? But, after a while, she did fall asleep with the assurance he would return soon for his family.

Two days after David left to see his land, Molly decided to take the soiled clothes to the river and wash them. Regardless of a slight chill in the air, it was a pleasant day. After much coaxing, little John put on his coat and cap. Molly held his hand as they walked to the river with Jacob and Willy, carrying the soiled clothes, following behind.

Around midafternoon they walked back to the wagon, and John fell asleep on the big bed. Molly sat under the live oak tree with her head against the wagon wheel and her eyes closed, envisioning, in her mind, a happy life in the new country.

At first she thought she was imagining the sound she heard. She listened again. Then loud and clear she knew she heard Jacob calling, "Maw! Maw! Come quick. Jim is leading Traveler home."

One brief moment there was only silence. Then came the quivering voice of Jacob over the cries of Willy. "Oh! Maw, we think Papa is dead!"

The anguished sounds of her sons raced through her mind with paralyzing disbelief. Trembling, she ran to where she found Jim and Pablo. There, she saw David, wrapped in his tarp, his lifeless body tied to Traveler.

"Oh! My David," she cried out. "Jim, tell me this is not true. Tell me how you found him. Please tell me why."

All the people gathered around as Jim began to tell them what happened. "We were on our way to survey the Randolph land. When about five miles from here we saw Traveler, with no saddle, trotting at a slow gait toward Viesca."

"I knew right away there must be trouble," Cummuns, the surveyor said. "The horse did not run from us. He just stood still, allowing Pablo to put a rope on him and lead him as we followed his tracks until we found David."

"We believe he stopped and built a fire to brew some coffee. The burned-out fire, filled coffee tin, and unrolled bedroll caused us to believe he died two days before," Jim told the people. "One thing we know for sure is that David was killed by a powerful gunshot, the kind buffalo hunters use. Pablo and me thought the buffalo hunters we saw in Viesca may have done this terrible act. One shot must have lodged in his heart. Then we saw where another bullet went through the left side of his head," Jim paused a moment, then added. "Molly, we believe he died right then without having to suffer any more."

"The strange thing is we found an arrow stuck into his chest," Cummuns said. "Pablo told us it is the kind the Waco Indians use."

"We searched for moccasin tracks but found none; neither did we find barefoot tracks," Jim added. "But we did find boot tracks. According to those, there were two men with him around the fire. Maybe David thought they were friendly settlers and insisted they drink a cup of coffee with him."

"Señora Molly, the Indians don't shoe their ponies," Pablo said. "All the tracks we found had shoes. My brother and me, we know the Wacos many years. Si, sometimes they rob and kill. But, Señora, we do not see them kill like thees."

"Like Pablo, I don't believe the Indians killed David," Cummuns said. "His jacket pockets were turned out and emptied, if they held anything. We could tell his boots were taken off after he died because he lay flat on his back."

Emaline Pharis heard little John crying as the noise and confusion aroused him from his nap, and he did not understand what happened. She kindly picked him up and carried him to her house as she knew he loved to go there.

Not explaining why, Herman Cummuns, Ramon Gonzales, and Oscar Mays, carrying shovels, walked up the hill. They went to the place Empressario Robertson had designated as a burying ground. A wooden cross marked the only grave, that of the husband of Annie Moffett. Now the men began to dig the second one for David.

Molly knew David must be buried soon. She did not hesitate, but painfully went to the wagon and brought back two quilts she had made and handed them to Jim to wrap around David. Then Pablo led Traveler as he carried the inanimate body of his master and friend to the freshly dug grave. Molly, Jacob, and Willy followed close behind. Then, slowly, the people of Veisca walked up the hill. Roy Pharis and Jess Wheeler gently laid David in the grave lined with canvas torn from the wagon cover.

A respectful quietness seemed to hover over the people. The only sound to be heard was the distant cooing of a turtledove as the people gathered around the grave. Every man stood upright and removed his hat. Jim Mason, standing closer to the grave, began to quote from the 23rd Psalm in the Holy Bible. Although written long ago, he knew it would provide comfort to the troubled hearts in this strange land.

> The Lord Is My Shepherd; I Shall Not Want
> He Maketh Me to Lie Down in Green Pastures
> He Leadeth Me beside Still Waters
> Yea, Though I Walk through the Valley
> Of the Shadow of Death I Will Not Fear
> For Thou Art with Me

Molly watched as Pablo and Ramon covered David over with newly dug sod. Overcome with grief for David and the fact her sons had lost their father, she found it difficult to realize they buried him in this country so far from his native home.

When the people returned to the village, they built a fire. They sat around it discussing the tragic event.

"Yes, I think the buffalo hunters who came through Viesca killed David," Jess Wheeler said. "They probably tried to take Traveler and leave their horse with the lame hoof. I'm sure Traveler ran off. We knew the Andersons in Tennessee, and we know a stranger could never catch Traveler. So, I think the killers took the saddle and rifle instead. That must have surprised David. But I'm sure he put up a good fight trying to protect his property. I think that's when they shot him."

After hearing Jess Wheeler talk, the men agreed the buffalo hunters should be tracked down and hung on the big tree by the Land Office.

"I see you all agree the hunters murdered David. If the men are found with the saddle, boots, and rifle, they will be dealt with. You know we have no written laws in the Nashville Colony, and no jail." That was when Jim saw the people wanted revenge without finding proof the hunters were guilty, so he continued to talk. "I hear murmurs among us of hanging the men even before a trial. If that is our only recourse, so be it. But we must be absolutely sure they're guilty of this terrible crime."

The fire where the people gathered slowly burned down. One by one they went to their sleeping quarters. Only Jacob and Willy remained with Molly. Emaline Pharis lay little John's head on her shoulder and carried him to her house as he was exhausted from crying. There, she quietly sat by him in case he awoke and became frightened.

"Maw, you're tired. Willy and me think you should go inside the wagon. Please do! You are cold and the fire has almost burned out," Jacob begged Molly.

"You are such good boys. Don't worry, I'll be fine. I just want to sit here a little while," she said. "You and Willy are tired, too. Climb into the wagon. I'll be there soon."

They did not want to leave her, but they knew they should obey. So they put another log on the fire and climbed into the wagon where they found Jim Mason waiting for them.

With a quilt around her shoulders to keep out the cold wind, Molly sat alone with her back against the wagon that contained the cotton and corn seeds—seeds that should have been their future and promise of a good life. She could not imagine what life without David would be. Desperately, she tried to control the grief she felt for this man she so passionately loved.

Slowly, methodically, she moved the smoldering embers farther into the flames as the wood began to burn. The eerie sound of a screech owl, perched in a bodark tree, caused her to cringe. Cassie, her dear friend, once told her to believe she was holding the owl by the neck and squeeze real hard and the screeching would stop. For one brief instant, a faint smile appeared as she recalled the many times she did that, but the screeching never stopped.

The lone, lonesome cry of a timber wolf echoed through the night. Then as if in response to the mournful howl, short, sharp yelps of coyotes joined in. Molly listened to the pack of gaunt, shaggy animals all barking in unison. The ghostly sounds of the night seemed to portray the sorrow she felt, and her body shook with sobs.

Looking up at the clear blue sky studded with millions of tiny twinkling stars, she wondered if they sensed her pain and loneliness. Suddenly, her thoughts turned to memories of her childhood and the first time she saw David.

Her mind wandered back to when her father, Captain Haynes, left with General Jackson to fight in the War of 1812. How, at ten years of age, she often became frightened of being alone at night and sneaked into Cassie's bed. She recalled how Cassie held her against those warm full-bosom breasts and softly sang a lullaby until she fell asleep. She recalled how her father told her he bought Cassie and Rube, her husband, at a slave auction so they could stay together. Although slaves and property by law, they were never treated as such in Molly's home.

She only knew her father said Cassie cared for her after her own mother died giving birth to her. So Cassie was the only mother she ever knew.

Suddenly her thoughts turned to the year her father ran a boardinghouse in Nashville where she helped Cassie cook and clean the rooms. One night she and Cassie were taking care of the supper table when the entrance door opened. A tall, young man with blonde curly hair and steel-blue eyes entered.

"Begging your pardon, young lady," he said, "I'm in need of a place to stay. Some kind gentleman directed me here. I would be much obliged if you could accommodate me."

Molly often saw strangers come into the boardinghouse looking for lodging. Nevertheless, this person seemed different. With a slight nod of her head in recognition, she offered to get her father. She acted calm but her heart pounded, and she felt tingly all over. "Miz Molly," Cassie said, "I done said yous wuz goin' fall in love. Now, I saw yore face so I think yous done it tonight."

Her father, also, liked this young man who said he was on the way to see the country west of the Mississippi River. Yes, it appeared this man was a sincere romantic and a dreamer. Yet, somehow one was led to believe he was not a fly-by-night adventurer.

David stayed on, always making excuses for not going west. Then late one evening he asked Molly to marry him. Two weeks later a Methodist preacher married them in the dining hall of the boardinghouse. They raced up the stairs among the cheers and well-wishes of the boarders.

David carried her into his room. Her entire body trembled at that memory, and she said, "Tonight I still remember, nor will I ever forget, the enchanting thrill of that night."

Soon her memories faded. At last she fell asleep with her head against the wagon wheel. A short time later the sound of barking dogs and men hurrying to eat breakfast at Annie Moffett's tavern woke her.

For a few brief moments she felt stunned, the trauma of the day before seeming more like a terrifying dream. Still, she saw the sun rising as bright as yesterday.

Right then she knew she had to accept the reality of the day and the days to come. She looked in the wagon. Jacob and Willy were yet sleeping, and a feeling of thankfulness came over her. She knew, they too, were experiencing untold sorrow.

Molly rushed to get little John, but Emaline had already fed him. She was roasting pecan and hickory nuts and insisted Molly take some to Jacob and Willy. The generosity of this gracious lady touched Molly. However, any attempt to thank her was futile.

"Now, Molly, you know I have no sons of my own. I've become very fond of your three. You see, one wants no thanks for things that please," Emaline said.

Two days went by before Marion Wheeler and Oscar Mays returned from looking for the buffalo hunters they believed killed David.

"Rains have covered the tracks the hunters may have made," Marion told Molly. "We rode all over the country, but we didn't even see any signs of a burned-out campfire. Anyway, we looked a couple of days longer and finally decided to come back to Viesca. Jim and Pablo went on west."

"Pablo wanted to find some Waco Indians. He believes they will tell him the truth—if they killed David," Oscar Mays said. "He says they will run the hunters out because they kill the buffalo. We're sorry we did not find the buffalo hunters. We still believe they killed David."

"Thank you for trying," Molly said. "Maybe it's best the two men got away. I want revenge for David, but I think hangings are terrible things. That wouldn't bring David back to us. You are all good men, so I don't want you to do a wrong for me. Besides, those men could be innocent. We will never know. On the other hand, I can't hold the Indians responsible for David's death even though their arrow may have killed him. Perhaps, we are all to blame. The Indians are being driven from their land. Maybe we should just let it be. I don't want my sons to be vengeful or bitter. Neither would David."

The following days were trying ones. Molly knew she must make a decision as to how she would care for the family. Jacob and Willy rarely spoke. Were they stifling their grief to protect her? Too, little John never left her side. What could be going on in his sensitive young mind? Oh, if she only knew their thoughts, she could plan better.

"I think we should go back to Nashville. I could run a boardinghouse like my father once did," she said one afternoon.

"But, Maw, Willy and me, we'll help you clear the land and farm," Jacob finally answered. "That's what Papa would want us to do. Jim'll help us when he's not with the surveyor. We talked a long time that night before he left to look for the buffalo hunters. Besides, Maw, I don't think I can drive the wagon all the way to Nashville."

Jacob did not wait for Molly to answer. He and Willy jumped out of the wagon and ran to take Traveler to drink from the river. The stallion whinnied and reared his front feet when he saw the boys.

"Jacob, do you think Traveler misses Papa like we do?" Willy asked.

"I don't know for sure," Jacob answered, "but I think he does. We need to take good care of him, ride him and let him kick up his hooves. Of course, we don't have a saddle. Not even a saddle blanket. We'll just have to ride bareback."

Willy untied the halter. He ran a few steps then leaped onto Traveler's back. "Look, Jacob, we don't need a saddle!" Off they went! Willy leaning forward, holding on to Traveler's mane. Faster and faster they went until they were out of sight. Molly looked out and saw Willy on Traveler at a steady gait. What a beautiful sight! David's son riding as if he were winning a race.

Willy slowly slipped to the ground when Traveler stopped by Jacob, who easily mounted the horse. Once more Traveler lunged forward. After going about a mile they came back. Jacob skillfully dismounted, and they led the stallion to drink from the river. Yes, David had trained his sons well.

"You two handled Traveler like grown men," Molly said when they came to the wagon. "I saw you riding. I'm truly sorry you do not have a saddle. Maybe someday we can get you one."

Moments like those caused her to hate the ones who killed David. Yet, from an unknown source, she knew hate would only harm her and the boys.

"I need to decide what to do. I want you to help me," she quietly said to Jacob and Willy. "Today I'm going to write a letter to your Grandpa Anderson, who lives in Virginia. Jacob, did you know your papa named you after him? His name is Jacob; just like you." Molly, trying to be pleasant, said, "Do y'all remember your papa telling about the big plantation he lives on? It's not far from the Atlantic Ocean. He raises cattle, sheep, horses, and even ducks. Wouldn't you like that, John? We could go on a great big steamship and live with Grandpa Anderson."

Jacob made no response. Neither did Willy. By that time she knew she must not ask them to make a choice. However, she knew it imperative they leave Texas. She did not want her unborn baby to come into this strange, foreign country that she could not accept as her home.

That afternoon she sat down and began to write to David's father, a person whom she had never seen. Yet, in a strange way she loved him because he was David's father. David had told her many times how he cared for his family after his mother died. It took a long time to collect her thoughts enough to write the letter, knowing it would bring sorrow and sadness to this man who also lost a loved one. Finally, she began:

> To Jacob Anderson—It is with pain in my heart that I am writing this letter to tell you David is dead. Some men believe that he was killed by buffalo hunters on the way to see his land. This is a strange country but David liked it. I do not want to stay here now. Jacob is fourteen years old and Willy is ten. They want to stay here and farm but they do not know how hard it would be. John is the prettiest little boy one ever saw, just like David. He is four years old. Another baby will be born in six months. I wish you could tell me what to do. Your loving daughter, Molly Anderson—Viesca in Nashville Colony—State of Texas— country of Mexico.

She neatly folded the letter and wrote on the back: To Jacob Anderson—County of Washington—State of Virginia in the United States.

"Jacob, I want you and Willy to give this letter to the captain of the first boat that comes up the river," Molly said. "That way your grandpa will get it sooner."

Each day the boys anxiously waited for a boat as Gonzales had asked them to load the supplies he had ordered onto his burros. On the third day they finally saw a small craft slowly come into view. This was the first steam-operated boat to come up the river since the Andersons had arrived at Viesca. So all the men and boys rushed down to see it and ask about things down south.

One sailor said, "We dropped anchor down the way. There wuz so many settlers that we emptied all the cargo, 'cept what Gonzales sent for."

Captain Jean Marquette and two men of Cajun descent manned the small vessel. In the center of the craft was a crude cabin with an odd-shaped hole that represented the "porthole." Sometimes the captain slept in the cabin as the sailors laboriously brought the boat upstream. Often they encountered huge boulders jutting out from the banks. When this happened the men were forced to use oars to prevent the craft from becoming stranded. Now they had reached the foot of the falls, but could not go farther. So they anchored the boat in a shallow cove on the west bank of the Brazos River.

"Ho! Gonzales, I've got something you'll like," Captain Marquette yelled as he came ashore holding up a gunnysack containing two pairs of red-top boots. "These, my friend, are the best boots in Texas. They wuz made by the Mexican bootmaker in San Antonio. Gonzales, he wants you to have them fur jest forty pesos—that's good, eh?"

Perhaps Marquette should not have insisted on the sale so quickly. On the other hand he knew Gonzales wanted the boots.

"He, ho, Marquette, but the price? Forty pesos?" Gonzales turned and whispered to Jacob and Willy, "I can sell them for two dollars in United States money, si? But, where can I find a man with United States money, or even Mexican pesos?"

Gonzales shook his head, reached into his baggy pants pocket, and handed Marquette the pesos for the coffee, sugar, and whiskey. He started to walk away, then suddenly turned and handed Marquette forty pesos for the two pairs of red-top boots.

After loading the supplies, Jacob and Willy led the burro up the hill. Celita was waiting for them, as settlers had bought all of her merchandise. As they unloaded the supplies, she wiped the dust from the top of the barrels. To be sure, Celita always made an effort to have everything tidy in her store.

Right there she saw the red-top boots. Realizing Ramon might not get his pesos back, she screamed out in loud, harsh words, "Gonzales, por que compraste los bots can mucho pesos? Hijo un cabrito gordo!" (Why did you buy the boots for so much money? You big fat goat!)

Instantly, she grabbed her rawhide whip and whirled it around

Gonzales's head. That was when Jacob and Willy saw Gonzales open a keg of whiskey, all the time pretending to ignore Celita. Jacob and Willy laughed as they walked out the door for they knew Gonzales and Celita would never come to blows.

Molly, the next morning, gave Jacob and Willy the letter she wrote to David's father and two United States coins to give to Captain Marquette.

"Emaline, do you think Marquette will give the coins to the captain of the ship sailing to Virginia?" Molly asked.

"Don't worry," Emaline replied, "Marquette is an honest man. He will give them to the captain of a large freighter. It is setting idle in the bay that empties into the Gulf of Mexico. Then it will sail east around the shores of the Gulf and enter the Atlantic Ocean." Not wanting Molly to be disappointed, Emaline added, "It might be a month or more before you get an answer, but I'm sure one will come."

On the way to the boat the following day, Jacob and Willy loaded the empty barrels and keg on the burros. They started down the hill to the boat. Gonzales looked back and waved to Celita, who waved back to him. Their silly quarrel the day before was forgotten.

"Wake Marquette. Tell him Gonzales is here with his empty barrels and keg," Gonzales called out.

When Jacob handed the letter and the coins to Marquette he asked, "Do you know Jules Ripperdeaux, the man who owns a ferry on the Sabine River?'

"Do I know Jules Ripperdeaux?" Letting out a gruff roar of laughter, Marquette answered, "Ah, me and that swabby run a boat up and down the old Mississippi. That is 'til he lost his left hand. If you see him, tell him to leave that dinghy ferry and come work for me."

He waved as Jacob and Willy watched him wade the shallow water and get on the boat. The wood-burning boiler had now generated enough steam to carry the makeshift craft south to the bay.

Late March brought gloomy, cloudy weather. Those days

Molly became restless, for as yet she did not know how she would care for the family. It frightened her to think of rearing them in this unfamiliar way of life in Texas.

Emaline sensed Molly's anxiety and frequently said, "You must be patient. It is very hard to get a letter from as far away as Virginia. Just keep believing it will come."

After thinking over Emaline's advice, one day Molly decided she must take control of her life. She thought, always strong, able-bodied men have protected me. Now, I alone must be responsible in caring for my family. Above all I must stay busy and not let my sons become aware of my sadness.

"Maw, Willy and me think we should put our things in the empty house where the Wheelers lived before they moved to their land," Jacob said one day. "You could cook on the fireplace and it would be warmer at night."

"You know, I think you're right. Let's get started," Molly said. But this became a difficult task. It seemed that everywhere she looked were memories of David. She recalled how he placed each object so the load in the wagon would be balanced. As tears fell down her cheeks she realized those memories must be put behind, at least for the present.

"Jacob, you and Willy harness the oxen and pull the wagon closer to the cabin," Molly told her sons. Shortly, the work began.

Jess Wheeler came by on his way to buy sugar at Celita's store. "I thought I should stop by to see if I could help you with anything," he said. "Now by golly, I see I can. Come boys, let's get to work."

All day they worked at cutting down a tree. They made a bed for Jacob and Willy from the trunk and chairs from limbs. Before long a pile of wood, to be used in the fireplace, lay near the door to the cabin. Things looked much better for Molly and her sons when Jess rode back to his home.

Molly almost felt content in the cabin. Living in a house instead of a wagon helped her to dismiss the idea they were nomads.

She took the books her father gave her from the trunk and

placed them beside the Holy Bible on the closed trunk lid that served as a table.

"I plan to lend these to Emaline, Annie Moffett, and that nice young Tillie Mays," she told her sons. "I would like to lend them to Celita Gonzales. But maybe she can't read, especially the English language. Jacob, do you know if Celita can read? If she can't, I'll teach her; that is, if she wants to learn."

Now, most days Molly felt confident she would find a way to leave Texas. Yet, often at night she tossed and turned, always thinking about food for her family.

One day she said to Emaline, "We will be fine until we leave Texas. I believe the money in the metal case will pay our way when we decide to go. You see, I have made up my mind. I do not want my baby I am carrying in my womb to be born in the country of Mexico."

Emaline did not reply. She only wanted what was best for Molly, her dear friend.

One day a stranger knocked on Molly's cabin door. "Mrs. Anderson, will you mend a shirt and a pair of pants for me?" he kindly asked. "Mrs. Moffett told me you sew very well. My name is Hootan. I'm on my way north to begin a trading post. I would appreciate you helping me."

That afternoon Molly took some of the treasured thread she brought from Tennessee. She carefully mended the torn places of the clothes and smiled when she saw the tiny stitches were barely visible. Mr. Hootan, too, felt pleased. He handed her two United States coins that she immediately put into the metal case.

Other times she helped Annie Moffett in her tavern if an unusual number of boarders wished to be fed. Actually, she looked forward to those days. They reminded her of her childhood days in Nashville.

Now and then she held little John's hand as they walked to the river where she washed the men's clothes, mainly officials who only stayed a short time in Viesca. They gave her one United States fifty-cent coin or a few pesos if they were Mexican officials.

Most days she felt a sense of pride in her work, but there were days when she felt extremely tired. She was now in the sixth month of her pregnancy and steadily gaining weight, but she did not complain. All the while she kept believing David's father would send for them and they would sail to Virginia.

In mid-May she sat by the door to her cabin. The whole country was ablaze with color. Bluebonnet lupines with silky foliage and sky-blue blooms emerged all over the hillside. Scattered here and there, tall paintbrush plants came to life, dressed in crimson array. Not far from the cabin she saw blackberry bushes so thick that the grazing cattle went around them. Even wild hogs avoided the prickly plants. A week later Molly noticed the white blooms that completely disguised the thorns had fallen. She knew then the berries, under the blossoms, would burst out in a greenish-orange color. Each day she watched the blossoms and, to her surprise, a week later she looked and they had become a shiny, purplish dark blue and ready to be picked.

She put on her bonnet and rushed to gather some of the delicious berries. Unwilling to let any of them shrivel, she used some of the valuable sugar to make blackberry jam. Feeling very proud of her accomplishment, she and little John took Emaline a sample.

"Molly," Emaline said, "I know you are not happy here. Oh, I understand why. We know you want to go to Virginia or maybe Nashville. If that's your wish, Roy will help you get passage on a boat. We don't believe it would be wise to travel by wagon to Tennessee. Jacob and Willy like it here, and I'm sure in time you will, too. Think about this and let us know what you decide."

"Thank you, Emaline. You are a good friend," Molly replied, "but I know I must leave Texas."

One sunny afternoon, Molly and her sons walked up the hill where they buried David. Jacob and Willy searched for the brightest colored rocks, some so heavy it took both boys to carry them. Carefully, they placed them around David's grave to mark the spot and keep coyotes away. Meanwhile, Molly and little John picked armloads of the choicest bluebonnet and Indian paintbrush blossoms and completely covered the silent grave. Molly planned one day before they left Texas to engrave David's name on the biggest stone Jacob and Willy found.

June came and Molly continued to help Annie Moffett at the tavern and mend the shirts and pants of the traveling men. Once, she opened the metal case and counted her savings. To her astonishment she found they had increased a sizable amount. Realizing that, she began to figure all the possibilities of leaving Texas. She thought, in the event David's father did not answer her letter, they would go to Nashville. They could take the wagon to the Mississippi River and sell it and the oxen. Again she reached into the metal case and picked up the coins and pesos. She tossed them back and forth. This money could buy their way on a riverboat to Nashville. They could live there in a boardinghouse until the baby was born.

Still all those plans did not seem right because she had not found a way to solve the problem of Traveler. She knew neither Jacob nor Willy would ever consent to selling him.

Night after night her well-planned ideas and wishes raced through her mind. Often she felt defeated, helpless, and deserted. Late one afternoon Jim and Pablo returned from surveying a league of land.

"Where are Jacob and Willy?" Jim called to Molly.

"The boys are fishing down by the falls," Molly answered. "I know they'll be here soon. I hope they caught enough fish so you two can eat with us. They miss David so much. I know they will be glad to see their good friends."

"Take this so the boys won't have to fish tomorrow," Pablo said as he handed Molly a big wild turkey, plucked and ready to be roasted. "Señora, not far from here we saw many wild turkeys. They eat the winter grass and insects so they get fat and tender."

About that time, Jacob and Willy came walking up the path from the river carrying a string of catfish. When they saw Jim and Pablo's horses, they gave the fish to Molly and ran to greet their friends, where a surprise awaited them.

"Hello, boys," Jim said, "we thought you could use a saddle so we got Alfredo, Pablo's brother, to make one for you."

Molly smiled when she saw a look of wonder in her son's eyes. Since David's death Jacob had tried to hide his emotions, to act like a grown man. However, this time he could not hold back his feelings. He did not only shake his friend's hand but gave each one a big hug.

"A saddle? You and Pablo brought us a saddle!" Willy screamed with delight. Quickly he drew his hand up in his sleeve. He held the cuff and rubbed the horn of the saddle to polish it. Right away they put the saddle on Traveler, and taking turns, they rode over the hills.

Molly, excited about having visitors, fried the catfish and made corn pone, Jim's favorite. Jacob and Willy brought in fresh wild onions and watercress greens they found. She cooked the onions and whirled the greens around to remove all the water, making them crisp and tasty.

"What a pleasure. This is a real good meal," she all but whispered. Suddenly, it came to her, she forgot the blackberry jam she had saved for a special day. Indeed, to Molly and her sons, it was a special day.

"I want to leave Texas before my baby is born," Molly said the following morning. "Maybe we'll go by boat to David's father in Virginia. Or, maybe we'll go back to Nashville and run a boarding-house. I'm waiting to get a letter from Papa Anderson. If it doesn't come soon, we'll leave Texas anyway."

She looked at Jim and Pablo. They did not appear surprised. Right then she knew Jacob and Willy had told them about her plans.

"I'll help you any way I can. It is up to you. Do what you think best," Jim, wiser than his years, said. "Jacob and Willy like it here. So does John. The land is cheap and it is good land." He hesitated a moment then added, "Still, like you, I'm afraid clearin' the land would be hard for the boys. But, I'm sure they could. Another thing that bothers me is that the Indians are raiding farms again. Molly, I am not trying to influence you to leave Texas. I have become very fond of your sons and would hate to see them leave. They are like my own brothers whom I have not seen in a long time."

"Señora, if you stay in Texas, me and Jim, we'll help you," Pablo said. "I don't want the Anglos and my people to fight, but all the time they quarrel. Maybe someday they stop. No? I'll show Jacob and Willy, and even the little one, how to drive the mules my brother raises."

Overwhelmed by their kindness, Molly could not fully express her thanks. She slowly turned and walked into the cabin.

The days that followed Jim and Pablo's visit seemed long and the nights too warm to be comfortable. She continued to help Annie Moffett at the tavern, but she tired more easily each day. At times she gave up hope that a letter from Virginia would come.

Each day she insisted Jacob and Willy go to the falls to see if Marquette's boat came up the river. She began to fear her child would be born in what she now considered "this horrible country."

Then one day Captain Marquette, in his makeshift steamship, came up the river. He dropped anchor in the shallow cove at the foot of the falls. Jacob and Willy ran to get Gonzales's burros to bring Celita's supplies to her.

"Yo, ho. You still work for Gonzales," Marquette yelled. "Where is the Señor? Here, take this mail to the people before you load the freight," he said as he handed them two letters, tied together. One read: To Mrs. Emaline Pharis. Written on the other: To Molly Anderson—State of Texas—Country of Mexico.

"Maw, look. Captain Marquette said to give you this and take the other one to Emaline," Jacob said, almost out of breath from running up the hill.

"Willy, run take the letter to Emaline, and when you come back, I'll read Grandpa Anderson's letter out loud," Molly said.

Willy left, but returned shortly—he ran all the way. Molly sat on the big bed with little John beside her. The well-written letter required two sheets of paper. Indeed, this man truly grieved for his son. Molly read:

> It would make me happy if you brought my grandsons and came to live with me. My house seems so empty. A black man, named Alex, will meet you. He will have money to pay your fare from Texas and will bring you in a buckboard to my home. Here, we can all be together.

Silence filled the room when Molly finished reading the letter. Jacob and Willy walked out the door and went toward the boat to help Gonzales load the supplies and take them to Celita.

"Jacob, I don't want to go to Virginia. I want to stay here close to Papa's grave," Willy said, then began to cry.

"Papa liked this country," Jacob said with tears in his eyes. "He wanted to farm and raise us here. I wish we could stay and do what Papa wanted. Willy, you know Papa always told us to do what Maw wanted us to. So we need to obey her even if we don't want to leave Texas."

At last, Molly, after knowing Grandpa Anderson asked the family to go to Virginia, felt more cheerful than at any time since David's death. She quickly began to plan the journey to Virginia, anxiously inspecting each item to determine if she could take them on board the ship. Perhaps this caused her not to notice her sons' quiet manner or the sad look in their eyes.

To be sure, Marquette's small boat could not carry them. Nor would he be back for another month, and she could not wait that long to leave. Only one alternative remained—take the wagon to Washington-on-the-Brazos. There she would be forced to sell the wagon and oxen, the big bed, and her spinning wheel and loom. Certainly, the corn and cotton seed would have to go, for they should already have been planted by this time.

She peered aimlessly at the letter of recommendation Roy Pharis instructed her to give to the official at Washington-on-the-Brazos. There a man would arrange for them to go to Buffalo Bay where they would book passage on a steamboat to the shores of Virginia.

One problem remained. That of leaving Traveler in the Mexican state of Texas. Until this time she had not told her sons they could not take the horse aboard the steamboat. Perhaps, she reasoned, it may be best to wait until Jim and Pablo come. She would ask them to take care of Traveler. But when they rode up, she immediately knew that they had already promised the boys they would take care of the horse.

"Traveler is out of a good sire and mare. We could sell him at a high price," Jim said, "but we'll not sell him. We promise we will always take care of him."

A heavy load fell from Molly's shoulders. Nevertheless, a feeling of guilt haunted her. She had not confided in her sons. All the decisions and intentions to leave Texas created a turmoil in her mind. Because of that, she did not feel overjoyed by the plan to sail on a steamship. She dreaded confronting strange people. To be truthful, she only wanted to hold her sons tight and to run with them and hide.

Finally, way into the night she admitted that she was only very tired. Tomorrow would be better. At last she fell asleep and slept soundly.

CHAPTER 3

"Jacob, will you and Willy take these clothes to the river?" Molly asked. "I need to wash them before we start on our long journey to Virginia."

Holding little John's hand she walked slowly down the hill behind Jacob and Willy. Not a cloud could be seen in the sky as she rubbed the wet clothes on a big rock. Neither did a strong breeze blow to dry the garments she spread on the bushes. Waiting for the clothes to dry, she and John sat on a rocky ledge.

She noticed that John seemed very quiet. But perhaps the warm sun made him drowsy and he fell asleep. When she gently reached over and touched him, she realized his face felt flushed. Quickly, she felt his body and knew immediately that the clammy feeling was not the warm sunshine.

"Jacob. Willy. Come quick," Molly yelled. "We must get little John to the cabin. He is sick with a fever."

Carrying little John, Jacob ran as fast as he could. Willy, holding Molly's hand, followed close behind.

"Put him on the big bed, Jacob," Molly said. "Willy, quickly, get me some cool fresh water."

Immediately, Molly began to bathe John's feverish body with the cool water. As she held him in her arms she felt a strange, hard lump in his throat. Suddenly, an uncontrollable fear raced through her. She knew the cool water would not lessen the fever.

For two weary days and nights she held him and softly sang, "Sleep, baby, sleep," the way she did each night of his life when she put him to bed. Repeatedly, she attempted to give him water to soothe his parched tongue. It fell drip by drip into his tiny mouth. Still, he did not open his eyes.

No doctor existed in or near Viesca, causing a hopeless feeling to come over Molly. This unknown sickness, to her, became a monstrous demon attacking her innocent, young son.

Then along about sundown on the third day, Molly felt a tremor in the body of her baby boy. She sensed one last movement, then utter stillness. She knew, without a doubt, it was the end.

Showing no emotion, she lovingly placed her lifeless baby son on the big bed. She held Jacob and Willy when they came to her crying out in anguish from their grief. Annie Moffett, Tillie Mays, and Celita Gonzales came into the room. Yet, Molly did not notice. Nor did she know when Emaline, understanding the turbulence in Molly's mind, took Jacob and Willy to her house.

Molly ran from the cabin down toward the big Brazos River. She did not weep. The pain had become too intense to cry. She only felt anger toward her God because of the loss of her little precious child.

On and on she ran until, from some unidentified source, the fury she felt for her creator vanished. Still, she kept running. At last from sheer exhaustion, she fell to the ground. Instantly, a desire for revenge against Texas flowed through her mind like a flaming arrow.

"Confound this country! Because of this country I lost my David, my love. Now, my little boy, my pride and joy," she hysterically cried out as she clinched her hands until they became blue. "But I swear with the help of my God that I will fight as long as I have breath. I will protect Jacob and Willy, and the child I am carrying inside my body."

Slowly, the tears did begin to fall down her cheeks. She sat there a long time. Then, wiping her eyes with her apron, she stood up and walked up the hill to her cabin.

The sun was almost above the eastern horizon when she returned to the cabin. She thanked the dear ladies who dressed little John in his best clothes. She shook hands with the men who made the tiny coffin where they lay her little child. With her two remaining sons, once more she walked to the lonely burying ground as the people of Viesca followed behind. There they buried little John beside David. Jim Mason stood sadly by the grave and quoted from the Holy Bible:

Suffer the Little Children to Come Unto Me
For Such Is the Kingdom of Heaven

As before, the people returned to their homes, many with tears in their eyes. Perhaps this terrible sickness could strike their children.

Several days went by and Molly did not mention leaving Texas. But a few days later she calmly said, "We're going to the Land Office. Put on your best clothes, and be sure your hair doesn't look tousled. This is an important day. I've decided to carry out your papa's wish. I'm going to farm and raise my family in Texas." By this time she knew she could never leave Texas, as a part of her would always be in this land she both loved and hated.

Hurriedly, she brushed her black, curly hair and untied her apron strings and placed it on the bed. Walking between Jacob and Willy, they started to the Land Office. She had no idea how she would communicate with the Mexican officials. Nevertheless, trying to look haughty, she entered the crude-looking building. Swallowing to clear her throat, she looked directly at the two Mexican men and one Anglo man and said, "Gentlemen, I'm Molly Anderson, the widow of David Anderson, who was killed a short distance from here. I've come to claim the land he paid to receive." Almost breathless, she added, "These are my sons. This is Jacob. He'll be fifteen years old next month." With her arms around Willy she continued, "This is William David, named for his father, but we just call him Willy. He just turned eleven."

It surprised her when the three men smiled and the Anglo man said, "Howdy" to the boys. He stood up and respectfully removed his big black hat when he spoke, "I'm William Shields, the commissioner. These gentlemen are Señor Valdez and Señor Romorio. They are the government officials who write the Spanish land grants."

"Señora, we know of the death of your husband and the death of your little child," Valdez sincerely said in fluent English. "Please accept our sympathy. However, there are some things we need to discuss with you. We know you are not familiar with our language, but Señor Shields consented to speak for us."

"Señora, would you like to be seated on this bench?" Romorio graciously asked as he carefully dusted the one rickety bench scarred by carvings from pocketknives the men carried.

"Empressorio Robertson told me David was well thought of in Nashville. I'm sure he would have been in Texas, too. We found him to be a good and honest man," Shields said as he sat on the edge of the aged desk with his right foot dangling.

Molly felt at ease for the first time since she walked into the office. She listened carefully to Shields telling about David signing for the land grant. But her eyes all but frowned when he said, "One thing puzzles us. We know David took the signed papers when he left this office. But the papers were not on him when he was found. Mrs. Anderson, that gives us reason to believe the murderers may have taken the papers."

"Oh, no," Molly interrupted as she opened the little metal case she clutched tightly in her hand, "David asked me to keep them in a safe place. Here they are."

"Bueno, bueno," Romorio said as he nodded in approval. After that he spoke in English so Molly would understand clearly.

"That is good. Your sons said you were going to leave Texas. We knew we must tell you this," Valdez said.

"Empressorio Austin was the first to bring settlers to this country. Later Empressorio Robertson opened the Nashville Colony. Now problems remain between them about the land grants they issue," Shields explained to Molly. "Even last week Austin's secretary sent me a record. It stated that Señor Maximo Morena received a grant for one league of land on Little River. It is dated October 8, 1833. That was almost two years before David applied. Mrs. Anderson, this is the same grant that your husband should have received. I checked into all these records. They are correct. This document legally cancels any claim you might have to this particular league of land."

"How can the Mexican government do that?" Molly asked.

"It is not the government. It is the empressorios, the men who issue the grants, not the government," Shields said. "I think they want more power and more land."

Her heart began to pound ever so fast, but she did not want to show anger so she pretended to smile and said, "I beg your pardon. But I have a signed and sealed document. Now, I want to move on the land."

Her outburst of high-spirited temper astonished her. Yet, she felt proud to have the courage to speak out. Shields, too, grinned, knowing Molly would do well in Texas.

"Mrs. Anderson, even though you cannot get this grant, there are others close by," Shields said. "I think you should know that only last week Indians raided the farms on Little River. They burned two houses. Now some of the settlers are taking their families to San Antonio to escape the Indian raids."

Definitely, this did disturb Molly. What could she do? However, one thing remained the same. She could not leave Texas. Not now!

"The Comanche Indians, more than the other tribes, are on the warpath," Shields said. "Of course, we are pushing the buffalo west and taking lands claimed by the Comanches. To my way of thinking, the Indians ought to live among the Anglo people. But it seems there is no way either side will try to make peace."

After saying that, he changed the subject. He pointed his marking stick to another location on the worn and soiled map on the wall. "This," he said, "is good farming land. But I'll tell you right at the front, these grants are surveys of one labor, that being 171.1 acres of land. Jess Wheeler, from Tennessee, got one of these grants and he seems satisfied. There are no more grants for leagues of land in this part of the Nashville Colony. That is, except the widow Banes, who has slaves to do her work."

The next morning Molly began to write another letter to

David's father. In the letter he wrote them, he appeared so very eager to see his grandsons, making it difficult to send an answer to him. When she came to the place where she must write about little John's death, she could not continue. She put the pen down, put on her bonnet, and walked outside.

"I've never seen a prettier sky," she said as she heard a whip-poor-will calling from the branch of a post oak tree. It echoed in every direction. "David always answered that call and taught little John how to answer the whip-poor-will. I swear to treasure memories like those, but today I must think about Jacob and Willy, and especially my unborn baby."

Oddly, her body did not feel as heavy as before. She stopped to pick some of the pretty bluebonnet blossoms growing near. Unconsciously, she turned to where David and little John were buried. There, under the dogwood tree, she placed the flowers over the graves. Brushing the tears from her cheeks, she quickly turned and walked down the hill. As she passed Emaline's house she called out, "Hello, Emaline."

Surprised to see Molly so early, Emaline called back, " Hello, Molly, isn't this a nice day?"

Without stopping to chat, Molly walked on to the cabin. She opened the door and went in. With trembling hands she picked up the pen and completed the letter to David's father. At last she began to accept her loss and look to the winding path that lay ahead.

"Maw, every day we hear men passing through Viesca talk of trouble with Mexico," Jacob told Molly. "Some men say the Land Office will be closed. And even the Mexicans have threatened to stop the land grants. Willy and me think all the people are planning to leave Viesca."

"Yes," Molly answered, "Annie Moffett said her tavern is idle most of the time. Yesterday, Oscar and Tillie Mays left for Washington-on-the-Brazos where they hope to run another boardinghouse."

War did seem inevitable. Believing that, Molly knew she must, at once, sign for a labor of land. Too, the birth of her child was drawing near. In many ways she considered the time spent in Viesca to be a continual nightmare.

Among all the excitement of obtaining a labor of land, Molly suddenly remembered that Jacob would be fifteen years old the following week. Since the death of David, he had assumed a great portion of caring for the family. Perhaps if he could claim Traveler as his very own it would make him feel important. Still, she thought, if I ignore Willy it would be unfair. Then the thought came to her, why not ask Jim and Pablo to find a pony for Willy. Two days later Jim and Pablo rode into Viesca with a yearling colt gracefully pacing behind Pablo.

"Pablo's brother who lives in the hills north of San Antonio catches wild mares," Jim said. "He breeds them with his burros and sells the mules that come from them. People buy them to pull wagons and plow the soil."

"Señora Molly," Pablo said, "the colt, she come with the mares when my brother catch them. He say he's goin' to take hem back to the hills. So, we take the colt we call Peppy, and teach hem to let us ride hem."

"Now, Willy, your duty is to take care of the pony," Jim firmly admonished Willy. "There's one thing I want you to remember. Never let him get out of control, but always be gentle. If an animal is never mistreated or beaten, he will be a good friend for life." As Molly walked back to the Land Office the next day, she heard loud voices coming from the men squatted under the big live oak tree.

"Jim told me Mexicans accused some Anglos of not obeying the law. They even tried to arrest one man. Of course, the Anglos wouldn't stand for that and the Mexicans opened fire. We jest ain't going to put up with that."

"Well, the Mexicans had better be careful. Acts like that will stir up the rebellion already in some of us."

"In the *Texas Republican* newspaper it says we need to form a convention and elect our own officials. I'm for that."

"But, that plan has been squashed," Jim replied. "Maybe the worst news of all is that Empressorio Austin is still under house arrest in Mexico City."

Regardless of all this disturbing news, Molly did not allow it to upset her. She hung onto the private mission she vowed to complete. She, with Jim and Pablo behind her, walked into the Land Office. But, unfortunately, Commissioner Shields was away working on some of the existing problems with the government. However, the officials greeted Molly with courtesy, as all true Mexican officials do. Then, they politely asked her to give them the original deed to the land on Little River—the one David signed. After that Señor Romorio wrote, in Castalian Spanish: Grant of one labor of land (171.1 acres) west of the Brazos River joining the Banes league of land on the south with a stream called Cow Creek running through the labor.

"I agree, within one year, to build a cabin, or shed, and to place a marker on each corner to declare my property," Molly truthfully said as she lifted her right arm.

She signed all required papers and handed them to Valdez. He in turn stamped the seal of Tejas (Texas) on the document and promptly gave it back to Molly, who immediately put it into the ever-present metal case.

On August 26, 1835, Molly and her two sons loaded their possessions into the wagon yet covered with canvas sheeting. They yoked the oxen and hitched them to the wagon in preparation to leave the village of Viesca to live on land they had never seen, probably thirty miles away.

"Willy, you and Jacob go say goodbye to Señor and Señora Gonzales," Molly said. She mounted Traveler carefully to prevent injuring the child she carried in her womb and slowly rode west to where her beloved David and precious John were buried.

Crimson-bottomed leaves covered the dogwood tree as the blooms were fading and dropping to the ground. The bluebonnets were withered as well as the Indian paintbrush that David admired.

Now wild rye grass spread over the graves, emitting a clean, quaint smell that could hardly be detected.

The rays of the sun felt hot that early morning and not a single breeze blew to fan the air. She sat quietly in the saddle staring far away at no particular spot. Tears fell down her cheeks when she read the markers placed at the head of each grave. She knew Jim and Pablo made them. Finally, she silently said goodbye, but she shed no more tears. She claimed this time to renew her courage and strength to continue onward.

Slowly, she turned Traveler and painfully started back down the hill. When she passed Emaline's house with its puncheon floors, she felt a brief moment of grief. The house now stood vacant. Roy Pharis had taken Emaline to be with her parents during this period of uncertainty in Texas.

"I won't be gone long. I want to say farewell to my good friend, Celita Gonzales," she called to Jacob and Willy.

"Señora Anderson," Celita said when Molly walked in, "I'm sad my people and the Anglos think they have to fight. I will ask the blessed Mother Maria to be with you and your sons, and the little one to be born. Maybe we go, me and Ramon, I do not know. Everybody, they go. That is good. No? You, I like and Ramon, he like the boys. Adios amigos, viya con dios," Celita said as tears fell down her face. She waved as Molly climbed into the wagon, took the reins, and yelled "gee" to the oxen. Molly waved back. But Señora Gonzales seemed very far away as tears, too, clouded Molly's eyes.

Molly and her sons headed south and west of Viesca and the Brazos River. There was no particular route to follow among the pines, oak, hickory, or other trees. This caused them to go in a zigzag manner. About noon they stopped to rest and to eat the food Molly prepared that morning.

"Maw, I'll drive the oxen," Willy said when they began another lap on their journey. "You can rest on the big bed in the back of the wagon."

"No, Willy, I'll set right here beside you. I want to see every inch of the way to our land," Molly answered.

Often they saw seldom-used trails leading in separate directions. They were on one such road when, all of a sudden, they saw cleared land. Before them lay a cotton field. The bolls on the stalks appeared as if they would soon open, and the fluffy, white cotton would be ready to be picked.

A patch of corn was already harvested, the plants cut down and neatly piled to be used as fodder for the animals. Farther down in the Gideon Creek Valley, they saw a log house. To Molly's delight it proved to be the home of Jess Wheeler and his wife. Jess recognized the family when he saw their oxen-pulled covered wagon and Jacob riding Traveler, with Peppy following behind.

"Look! I believe for sure I see Molly Anderson and her boys," he called to Mrs. Wheeler.

"Me and Ertha with our two young'ns live here with Pa and Ma. We left Little River because Indians raided our farm. Why, Molly, they even burned our house," Marion said.

"The commissioner told me it'd be best not to settle on that land. Now I believe him," Molly answered.

"You'll jest have to eat supper with us," Mrs. Wheeler said in her casual manner. They considered all people their friends, especially the Andersons.

"We've got plenty of food, more than most folks. We're able to raise a lot on this rich Texas soil," Jess proudly boasted.

Mrs. Wheeler and Ertha served a bountiful meal on a long, cedar-wood table brought from Tennessee. Jess raised his eyes toward heaven and earnestly spoke to his God.

"Oh, Lord, God Almighty," he began in a loud voice, "we thank you for our food, our comforts, and our home. And, Lord, we thank you for our friends. Amen."

Ertha ladled milk, yellow with thick oily cream, into tin cups. Each person crumbled warm corn pone into the milk and ate the delicious concoction. When Ertha offered Willy another serving of milk he pushed back from the table and said, "Thank you, ma'am, but I'm full to the brim."

That remark brought back memories of Tennessee. Back there,

in the mountain country, that saying was heard many times among the hill people. At that, everyone began to tell who first said the quote, and how it was said. Such an occasion created much talk and laughter of days gone by in a different land.

Afterward, they all sat under a big pecan tree by the cabin.

"Well, Molly, we never found the buffalo hunters," Jess said. "I still believe they are the ones who killed David." He looked directly at Molly and asked, "What do you think?"

Mrs. Wheeler knew talk like that should be put to rest. So, about that time she saw two hens and an old rooster scratching and pecking in the ground for bugs and she changed the subject. "Well, I swan. I think that old hen over there is trying to set. I predict she'll be hatchin' some chicks 'fore long."

"I decided to stay in Texas and farm," Molly said turning the conversation to another topic. "The other day I signed for a labor of land about ten miles from here. The boys and me'll build us a house before my baby is born."

"That woman's so stubborn," Mrs. Wheeler said when Molly went to her wagon. "Course, I like a woman with fire. But Molly needs help. Marion, you know she ain't use to this kind of living. Can you go help build her house?"

"Maw, you're right. As soon as we finish building the rail fence, I'll go help build a house," Marion answered.

"Mother Wheeler," Ertha said, "I'd like to go be with Molly when her baby is born. You know she's my best friend."

After a good night's sleep Molly and her sons started on another trek to their home. They traveled most of the day where they did not see a trail through the cottonwood, elm, and willow trees along the little Brazos Creek.

Unable to ford the creek, they went through country covered with acres of squatty mesquite and blackjack trees. Those were scattered enough to provide sunlight for the wild rye and wheat grasses to grow. Hundreds of longhorn cattle, like endless swarms of crickets, contentedly grazed on the tall grass.

Two black men riding horses, Jacob later described as good as

Traveler, came toward the wagon. Immediately, Molly grabbed the shotgun, pointed it at them, and said, "My sons and me are just passing through. We're on our way to settle on a labor of land. We hope it's not far from here."

"We didn't mean to skeer yous. We jest wanted to talk a spell. 'Cause we don't see many folks, 'cept maybe a lone rider or a few Injuns on a hunt. I'm Moses and this here's Jake. Mr. Banes died, but the missus stayed on. Jake and me, we take care of her cattle. Long 'bout fall Miz Banes gets some Mexican men to drive some of the cattle to New Orleans. I think a man there buys them, fer they shore send Miz Banes a lot of money," Jake said.

On hearing that, Molly put down her gun.

"Follow me and I'll show yous the big house. Miz Banes, she don't mind," Jake said, giving Molly reason to accept the men as friends. He rode beside the wagon until they could see the big house. Jake tipped his hat, turned, and rode back to help Moses with the cattle.

"You may spend the night here by my house," a voice from inside the house politely welcomed the family. Jacob and Willy were taking the harness off the oxen when a black woman came from the house carrying a pitcher of cool milk. "I'm Lizzy. Miz Banes, she say, everybody needs a sip or two of milk after a hard day traveling. I'll jest set it right here," Lizzy said.

"Why, what a kind thing to do! I am sure my sons would like a cup of the milk," Molly said to Lizzy.

"Miz Banes, she don't talk to folks much. Mostly she jest sets in her rocking chair," Lizzy said. "She's a good woman, but she ain't happy since our master died. Don't make no difference what we do, she don't smile. I think a body ought to smile and laugh once in a while even when hit ain't so good. Don't yous?"

"Lizzy, I think you're right," Molly answered.

"Oh, Miz Banes, she's good to us so we don't fret. Like jest now she said, 'Lizzy, you tell the lady to come rest in the house.' So come 'long with me," Lizzy said, motioning for Molly to come with her.

The house was in perfect order. Molly noticed right away that the furnishings were tastefully arranged and dusted until they were shiny. LaNora Banes, neatly dressed, came to the door and said, "Come in and rest. I am LaNora Banes. It is a pleasure to have you here."

"Thank you, Mrs. Banes. I'm Molly Anderson. My sons and I are on our way to a labor of land where we'll farm," Molly responded.

"My husband traveled to many countries," LaNora told Molly, "but he liked Texas more than any other place. So he returned to England, our home, and brought the slaves and me to live here. I learned to ride like a Texas woman, and we enjoyed days of hunting. Mr. Banes loved to follow buffalo to learn more about the behavior of those beautiful animals." She paused for a moment then continued, "One day he failed to notice a band of Indians chasing a herd of buffalo. The buffalo stampeded, but Mr. Banes could not ride fast enough to avoid the oncoming buffalo. He and his horse were trampled as the powerful animals raced over them."

About that time a strange look came over the face of LaNora Banes. She nervously said, "Thank you for coming. But I must rest now."

"Thank you for asking me," Molly said, "I enjoyed the visit." Mrs. Banes's abrupt manner confused Molly. She quietly walked out the door.

The following morning even before sunup, Moses and Jake helped Jacob and Willy harness the oxen. They inspected each wagon wheel and filled the barrel, attached to the side, with fresh water. "Now y'all come see us again. Take this fresh venison. Hit'll taste good tonight," Moses said.

LaNora did not come out to see the family off, but Lizzy did. "Thank you, Miz Anderson, fur talking to my mistress," Lizzy said. "She says y'all come again. Right now she's jest setting in her rocking chair and won't say a word to me. I don't know what to do. Maybe she's lonesome for England."

As the wagon pulled away from the house, Molly said, "Boys,

at first I did not like Mrs. Banes. But now I pity her because I know how sad she must feel. You know, when my baby is born I'm going to come back to see her."

That morning the weary family started on the last lap of a search to find a peaceful life in a country that at the beginning seemed so promising. Now, it was a means to survive—not from desire, but necessity.

They went south to a huge oak tree that marked the line of the Banes's league of land. They entered the once unclaimed and vacant labor of land where the crystal-clear water of Cow Creek flowed south across the entire grant. Molly, standing up in the wagon with her hands shading her eyes, claimed this to be her land—a place to build a house, to farm, and to rear her children. "I wonder if Abraham felt the way I do when God told him to look as far as he could see for that land would be his," Molly almost whispered.

They wandered among great oak, swaying pecan, and hickory trees loaded with nuts. Regardless of where they went, they always turned to follow Cow Creek. After some time Molly stopped the wagon. "Willy, ride Peppy ahead and tell Jacob to turn Traveler and come back. I believe we've found a perfect place to build our house."

She climbed out of the wagon slowly to be sure she would not fall. She walked to the edge of the water and looked down at her reflection in the clear stream of Cow Creek. There, Jacob and Willy saw signs that deer and other animals used that as a watering hole.

"Maw, Moses told us that bear, wolves, and sometimes mountain lions stay in land where people don't live," Jacob told Molly. "Now, I believe that to be true." So, they watched closely as they walked here and there searching for more animal signs.

"The sun is almost down so I think we should not go farther," Molly said. "Jacob, you and Willy cannot sleep on the ground. Tonight you sleep in the wagon."

"I think you're right, Maw," Jacob said, "and I'll tie Traveler to the wagon. Willy, do you think we can hobble Ole Blu and Bill?"

"I watched Papa so I think we can. I don't know what we would do if they ran off," Willy said.

Molly lay awake after she went to bed, trying to envision what David would do if he were here. However, she knew now this was her responsibility to provide for her children in this strange, foreign country that she could not yet fully accept. When her thoughts quieted, she fell asleep and slept soundly the rest of the night.

The morning sun was already beginning to feel hot when the sound of her sons talking awakened her. They were frying the venison Mrs. Banes gave them. Molly brushed her hair, braided it, and let it fall to the back of her head.

"I'm ashamed I slept so late. That venison smells real good. Are you ready to find a place to build our house?" Molly asked. "I think I'd like to build close to this pretty stream. But I think it best to build above the water. You know down close to the water, floods could wash a house away, especially in the spring."

"Maw, before you got up," Willy said, "Jacob and me found a real good place. Come on, we'll show you."

True, the trees growing there showed no signs of ever being flooded. And the aged, sturdy oak trees were perfect to use in building a cabin.

Walking through the oak trees, Molly and her sons turned north. Before them lay level farming land. Molly, sensing a thrill of anticipation, said, "Your papa would have liked this land. I think we can plant the cotton and corn seed we brought from Tennessee. First, we'll have to clear the land of brush and blackjack trees."

Quickly, they walked back to the wagon, filled the barrel on the side with fresh water from Cow Creek, hooked the oxen to the wagon, and went the short distance to the big oak trees.

"The first thing we need to do," Molly said, "is to mark off the house." She approximately stepped off twelve feet. "I think, at first, we'll just have a twelve-by-twelve-foot cabin. And a fireplace at one end. I'm tired of cooking on a campfire. We won't worry about windows. We'll make them later. Oh, to be sure, we need a door, but can we make a door with the broadax?" Molly asked.

"Maw, we can use the canvas on the back of the wagon for a door," Willy suggested.

"Willy, you solved that problem. Now we need to choose which trees to cut. Jacob, do you think that tall one would make two logs on both sides of the house?" Molly said pointing to a beautiful oak swaying in the breeze.

Felling the first tree was a difficult task for Jacob and Willy. The weight of the big ax proved to be almost more than they could handle. Hour after hour the boys pulled and tugged, yet they never gave up. Finally, they ran to where Molly stood and watched as the tree fell to the ground. Next came the job of cutting off the branches with the chopping ax.

Molly stepped off twelve feet of the tree and Jacob began to cut the first twelve-foot log. Near sundown Jacob said, "Maw, how can we get the log to where we want to build the house? It is too heavy for Willy and me to pull it."

"Oh, I know," Willy said, "I'll tie Ole Blu to the log and Maw can make him pull it."

Day after day they worked at cutting the trees, clearing the ground of all rocks and brush as there would be no flooring, at least not for some time. After they ate all the venison Mrs. Banes gave them, Molly decided to go hunting. She walked a long way into the forest land in search of game. Farther back in the trees she saw a herd of deer inching their way to drink from Cow Creek. She waited patiently until a big buck deer came in sight. Carefully aiming the gun, she pulled the trigger, and the buck ran a few steps then fell to the ground.

She walked toward the wagon and called out, "Jacob, I shot a deer. Bring Traveler. We will tie him to the buck and let him drag it to the wagon."

It took quite some time to gut and skin the deer. At last the job was finished, so Molly stretched the hide out to tan. Jacob and

Willy hung the carcass high in a tree so varmints could not reach it. The deer would supply them with meat for several days.

That night, around midnight, a loud vexing sound awoke Molly. It sounded like a dozen dogs were howling mournfully together. At once she sat up in the bed and thought, could that be a tribe of Indians on the warpath?

She reached for the shotgun and looked through the canvas rigging on the wagon. Two coyotes were fighting over the venison they had pulled from the tree branch. She knew they must ration the gunpowder so she did not shoot at them, as the venison now lay torn to bits on the ground.

Even though the venison was ruined she knew other game was plentiful. Untold numbers of wild turkey, squirrel, and rabbit inhabited the forest land as well as quail that nested nearby. Too, Cow Creek teemed with scores of little fish, tastier than the big ones Jacob and Willy caught in the Brazos River.

The process of building the house fell far behind what Molly hoped for, and lately she felt so very tired. Often she thought of giving up her dream to live in Texas, or perhaps, to sail to Virginia and live with David's father.

The middle of September came. The days remained hot and humid, yet the family continued to try to build the house. Nevertheless, the nights were pleasantly cool, so they all slept on the ground. Still, there were nights when Molly could not rest.

After one such sleepless night, she decided she needed to wait until her baby was born to finish building the house. She felt discouraged, but she tried not to let her sons notice her depression.

"I wish you boys would ride Traveler and Peppy to find the survey line of our labor of land," Molly said after an especially restless night. "On the way back, stop at Cow Creek and maybe you can catch some fish for our supper."

All morning she made no attempt to start the day's work. She sat idly trying to determine how she could carry on her struggle in Texas. The bright September sun stood directly overhead, causing the shade from the wagon to vanish. By that she realized it was noontime. Still, she made no effort to prepare a meal for her sons. At first she believed she was imagining strange things when she looked toward Cow Creek. She looked again. Surely, she saw a rider coming up the hill. At once she reached into the wagon for the gun. Right then she recognized their good friend, Jim Mason. But Pablo Estrado, his constant companion, was not with him.

Soon Jacob and Willy returned, carrying some fish they caught in Cow Creek. Molly, now feeling much better, fried the fish. As they ate, Jim said, "Pablo went to his brother's. The Mexicans are threatening to declare war against the Texas settlers. He is torn between his country and the Anglos, his newfound friends. I think he rode to the hill country to catch wild mares for his brother."

That afternoon Jim began work on the cabin. First he made the adjoining corners in a right angle as Molly and Jacob did not know exactly how it was done.

"Now, don't you worry about the work. Marion Wheeler said he would be here to help," Jim said.

Early the following morning, Marion did ride up as he promised. Shortly, he began to cut a tree down to make the walls of the house. He cut a notch in the trunk to prevent the tree from falling toward the spot where the house would be built. As the tree fell, a creaking sound echoed through Cow Creek valley.

For five long days the work never ceased. Molly guided Ole Blu and Bill as they pulled the logs to the building where Jacob and Willy held them steady to keep the logs from rolling. Then, Jim and Marion gradually raised each log, inch by inch. At last the twelve-by-twelve-foot cabin stood, at least six feet high. Afterward, they heaped the smaller limbs on the top to form a roof.

"Jacob, Willy, now we must make a fireplace," Marion said. "You two go down to the creek bottom and gather big stones to use in making the flue. And we'll need sand and gravel to mix with water to hold the stones together. When the sand and gravel dry and harden, a fire can be built and smoke will rise from the chimney."

"Yea, then Maw can cook our food and it will be warmer in the winter," Willy commented.

Jobs still needed to be done, but Marion was expected to be home that day. So, promising to return in a short time, he left to work on his own farm.

"Molly," Jim said the next morning as he prepared to leave, "I did not try to settle on my land. I spent most of the time with people whose families were killed by Indians, or in some instances, captured and carried away. Of course, I knew I had to make a living, so Pablo and me worked with the surveyor. Although, sometimes, we helped people bury their loved ones. You see, many Texans as well as Mexicans died of cholera and other sickness."

"Jim, my sons and me will never forget you and Pablo, how you helped when David was killed and when our little John died from that terrible illness," Molly said. "I believe you've escaped the Grim Reaper because you and Pablo never refused to help."

"I'm free to help," Jim answered. "My main concern is to help the Indians. The sad thing is the problem between the Mexicans and Anglos. That defeats all the power I once had with the Indians. Now, many don't trust me."

"Where will you go from here?" Jacob asked.

"I'll go to San Antonio. I want to meet with Colonel William Travis," Jim answered. He said goodbye to Molly and her sons then mounted his horse and rode off. Molly knew, as she watched him leave she could not repay him nor Marion. They spent long days of hard work. However, most of all they renewed her trust in this land that she once rejected.

In the days that followed Jim and Marion's leaving, Molly spent hours arranging the spinning wheel, trunks, and the big bed in the newly built cabin not much larger than the wagon. She gathered fresh moss to replenish the cornshuck-filled mat where Jacob and Willy slept. When she tested the deerskin she had stretched out to tan, it felt too raw to put under the mat. But by winter, she knew it would be soft and warm for her sons. Once more she took the two books and the Holy Bible from the wooden trunk and placed them on the closed lid.

"Maw, if you will show me how, Willy and me will take down the pine cupboard nailed to the back of the wagon," Jacob said. Fortunately, they did save the iron nails that held it. Now the hard work began, nailing the cupboard into the logs by the fireplace to hold it steady. When the job was finished, Willy yelled, "Hurrah, for Jacob. We have a place to put things."

From the branches of the felled trees they fashioned a sled and tied the barrel to it. So, each morning they hitched one of the oxen to the sled and went down the hill to Cow Creek where they filled the barrel with fresh water.

Many times they desperately struggled to make a table and chairs from tree limbs. Perhaps the chairs were the most difficult. They really never mastered the art of cutting the top and bottom so it would not turn over.

The month of October passed. Then cool days set in. At times Molly almost felt content. Yet, she stayed near the cabin as the time to give birth to her baby drew near. While she waited, she made a little blanket and long warm gowns from white material she brought from Tennessee.

Once she told her sons, "I remember Cassie saying that all newborn babies, boy or girl, should wear white."

Sometimes she walked down the hill just to listen to the limpid water of Cow Creek. It sounded as if it were laughing as it tumbled southward to the big Brazos River.

One day she saw two riders, and with them were two hound dogs. She recognized Moses and Jake, the slaves from the Banes place. Quickly, she turned and walked toward the cabin to welcome them. She immediately sensed they brought sad news. She was correct. LaNora Banes, who to Molly appeared to be a royal princess, could no longer speak nor walk.

"Miz Molly, Lizzy, she spoon feeds our mistress and Jake carries her to the bed at night. We didn't know what to do. Then one day Mr. Jim Mason, he come by. He says we must take her to England to be with her family," Moses explained to Molly.

"Miz Molly," Jake said, "Mister Jim, he sent all the cattle to New Orleans. But when we wuz coming here we found two heifers, and one looked like she was goin' to have a calf. And following behind was a young bull. Miz Molly, his horns was fixing to curl jest like the old bulls."

"Miz Molly, the heifers and bull strayed from the herd. Me and Jake, we drove them to your land," Moses said. "You'ns claim them. 'Cause if yous don't, they will foller a wild herd and maybe starve."

"Jacob, look over there. Do you see cattle grazing on our land?" Willy asked as he and Jacob were digging big stumps.

"Let's run tell Maw. Maybe they belong to Mrs. Banes. If they do, we can drive them back to her land," Jacob answered as they ran toward the cabin. They were surprised to see Jake and Moses, but the sight of the two dogs interested them most.

"'Cause we're going to England on a boat, we can't take the dogs with us," Moses told the boys.

"Me and Jacob can keep them. We need some hound dogs," Willy gladly offered. "Rover can be my hound and Jacob can have Ring." Before the men left, they built a pole corral to hold the cattle until they became accustomed to a new pasture. The last task became the hardest—that of tying the hounds to a wheel of the wagon to prevent them from following Moses and Jake.

Jacob and Willy softly petted the hounds. Nevertheless, the dogs began to howl when the men galloped off on their horses. Quickly, changing to a fast run through the trees, they were soon out of sight. A sad feeling came over the family. They knew that was the last time they would ever see their black friends, friends who had greatly enriched their lives.

Those were busy days after Moses and Jake rode off. Jacob and Willy drove the newly acquired animals out to graze each morning. Always, the hounds, Ring and Rover, went with them. They had an uncanny instinct when it came to herding cattle.

After a few days Molly decided it would be safe to allow the
cattle to wander off and graze alone. Later Jacob and Willy went
to look for them. The tracks, contrary to the usual direction, went
through the thicket toward Cow Creek. Ring and Rover ran ahead.
Suddenly, they began to howl, giving the boys a signal that they
were near a strange animal. They ran until they found the hounds
standing over a dead deer. The buck had been ripped open and the
liver, lungs, and heart were gone.

"Willy, I remember Moses and Jake telling us mountain lions
come down from the north hills and usually follow a stream," Jacob
said. "They kill deer, calves, and sometimes colts. Mainly they eat
the tender entrails. See, this buck is split open just like Moses said."

Immediately, they ran to tell Molly about the dead deer.
"Jacob, I believe you're right. A mountain lion surely killed the
buck deer. You take the gun, and we will all go look for signs of
another mountain lion roaming the country."

After that episode, Molly demanded that Jacob take the gun
with him everywhere he and Willy went. Could it be her labor of
land was no longer safe? Lone riders, passing through, told of
Indian raids and, without a doubt, war with Mexico became
obvious.

Molly, one day, picked up the newspaper Jim left her. She read
the words of the Empressorio Austin when he spoke in San Felipe:
"War is our only recourse. There is no remedy. We must defend
our rights, ourselves and our country by force."

She put down the paper and said, "Trouble is everywhere. Our
future is uncertain. If it comes to war, I fear we'll have to depend
on the untrained farmers to fight the military forces of Mexico."
Yes, she thought, it seems that even the animals were restless.
Neither the bark of the coyote nor the baying of the timber wolf
ever ceased at night. Now, mountain lions may be lurking close by.
How did I ever think I could survive in this land? Anger and fear,
mingled with unrest, penetrated her mind. Still, always the desire
to fight, to win, prevailed and she would fall asleep and sleep
soundly.

After one such night, she sat on a log by the cabin. She looked around her. The leaves on the trees were turning to beautiful colors: burgundy red, black purple, glittering orange and yellows all complimented by shades of brown and green. Leaving the log where she sat, she walked along the peaceful thicket, unmindful of danger. Hidden by the fallen radiant leaves she found a patch of persimmon trees. The once acrid repugnant fruit now was a pleasing orange hue and ready to be eaten. She formed a basket with her apron and picked enough to make a pudding for their dinner. Slowly the tumult in her thoughts subsided and she began to hum a tune Cassie taught her years ago.

In the first days of October, Molly sensed a slight tinge of frost in the air. She noticed also that the animals knew summer had ended as she watched them deposit their winter rations under fallen logs. Knowing this, she gathered hard-shell pecan and hickory nuts that lay under the trees. She knew those would be fully matured, causing them to taste better than those yet hanging on the trees. She stored the nuts in the cabin to be cracked open and the delicious kernels picked out, as David always said they contained much food substance.

One afternoon as Molly and Willy were gathering nuts, they heard the blast of a shotgun.

"Willy, that sound came from where Jacob is plowing the new ground to be planted in the spring. Run fast—he may be hurt. I'll follow behind as I can not run very well."

When they reached the plowed ground, Molly suddenly stopped, overcome with fear. There was Jacob standing over a full-grown bear with the gun still pointed at the dead animal.

"I heard Ring baying. I turned to see what was wrong. There was this big old bear," Jacob said. "He had his front paws wrapped 'round Ring, squashing my hound to death. I was afraid to shoot 'cause I might hit Ring. So I hit the bear on the head with the gun barrel. That scared the old bear and he let go of Ring. Right then I had a chance to shoot him."

They spent the remainder of the day skinning the bear so Molly could tan the hide. She took bark from an oak tree, then bruised and broke it into small pieces. After that she mixed it with fat from the bear meat and rubbed the mixture on the animal hide and left it to become tanned. As she worked she thought, this will make a real warm, soft rug for our bare sod floor.

The middle of October passed so Molly knew she would soon give birth to her fourth child. She felt so alone without David and little John that many nights she tossed and turned in her bed, often times regretting she had not left Texas.

However, to her surprise Marion and Ertha arrived.

"Oh! Ertha, I am so glad to see you. And, Marion, do tell me if you have heard anything about war with Mexico," Molly wanted to know.

"Well, Molly, I guess the war with Mexico actually started the second day of October, about two weeks ago," Marion answered. "A Mexican commander came into the town of Gonzales. He demanded a town official to surrender a small cannon supposed to be used in Indian uprisings. Well, to be sure the official refused. This caused the Mexican commander to bring in one hundred soldiers. But about that time, over a hundred Texas landowners got together. We just stayed there waiting for the Mexican soldiers."

"I wish I could have been there," Jacob said. "Did the soldiers really come?"

"Yes, but while we waited, we mounted the little cannon on a wagon and hung a white flag above it," Marion answered. "Then Mr. Carter wrote 'Come and get it' on the flag. I believe this surprised the Mexicans; anyway, the fighting didn't last long. Pretty soon they were all running west. After that we all went back home. But, I'll be going back in a few days."

"Molly," Ertha said, "Marion will be away and Mother Wheeler will take care of our children. You see, I'm going to stay right here until your baby comes."

CHAPTER 4

That night Marion, Jacob, and Willy made their beds in the wagon still covered with canvas. Ertha and Molly slept in the cabin. Even though news of war with Mexico alarmed Molly, she immediately fell asleep as the presence of her friends gave her a sense of security.

However, around midnight Molly awoke with a terrific pain in her back. She tried not to arouse Ertha, but perhaps by a motherly instinct, her friend knew that the time had come for Molly to have her baby.

"Molly, let's walk around the room a few times," Ertha said. "Mother Wheeler always said that helps between the pains."

"You are right, the pain is not as bad now," Molly said as they rested on the edge of the bed.

"Marion planned to help Jacob and Willy before he goes to Gonzales. I will cook their breakfast and let them be on their way to work," Ertha said as both women kindled the fire and began to prepare breakfast.

Around sunrise Marion and the two boys came in. They all sat around the table to eat. Still neither Ertha or Molly mentioned that Molly would soon give birth to her baby.

But later Ertha called Marion aside and whispered, "Don't go too far from the cabin. I might need you. Molly is going to have her baby. Be sure before you leave that the barrel is filled with fresh water from Cow Creek."

The day was almost ended when Marion, Jacob, and Willy drove the cattle into the corral for the night. They were taking the saddles off the horses when they heard Molly cry out.

"Now, don't worry!" Marion said. "The cries you hear are part of bringing a child into the world. I think your mama'll forget all about it when she sees the new baby. Finish with the animals, and I'll go see how things are going."

One glance at Molly's ashen face, streaked with perspiration, and Marion knew the child was almost here. He leaned against the bed with his back toward Molly and said, "You push real hard against my back when you feel another pain. I believe the baby will be here then."

After about three more excruciating pains the baby emerged and began to cry. Ertha handed Marion a pair of scissors, and he cut the umbilical cord. He smiled and handed the baby boy to Ertha, who stood by. She was ready to wrap the new baby in a warm soft blanket.

"Hey! Jacob, Willy. Your mama just had a new baby boy," Marion yelled when he returned to the cow pen.

They sneaked quietly into the cabin to see the long-awaited child. There they saw Molly asleep with the baby beside her. Willy reached over and tenderly touched the tiny baby.

"Molly needs to rest now. But when she wakes up, you can hold your little brother," Ertha whispered.

Jacob and Willy rushed back to finish their chores. Marion stretched logs across the gate to prevent the cows and bull from wandering off. Leaving Ring and Rover to guard the animals, they all went back to the cabin, anxious to hold the new baby boy.

"Maw, what's his name?" Willy wanted to know.

"George Washington Anderson," Molly answered.

"But, Maw, we don't even have any kin named that," Jacob said. "I know you and Papa named me for Grandpa Haynes. You told me you named Willy for Papa, and little John was named John Newton for Papa's brother, who died in the War of 1812."

"Maw, he's such a little baby for that big name," Willy said. "Besides, I don't think I can even learn to spell that."

"That's all right, we'll just call him George." Molly did not tell them David chose George Washington if the baby happened to be a boy baby.

"Molly, I want to stay a couple more days with you. But Marion promised to join the fight against the Mexican army so he is leaving today," Ertha said.

Molly felt sad when Marion left. She knew Ertha must be wondering if the war would continue, or if Marion would come home safely.

"Molly, what is bothering you?" Ertha asked when she noticed Molly appeared troubled. "Tell me, maybe I can help."

"I'm almost ashamed to mention my problem. I know you must be thinking that Marion might not return from fighting," Molly said. "I know you will keep asking, so I'll tell you. You know I love my baby, but I have this strange feeling I might try to pretend he is little John. Or, I could let this baby boy take the place of little John in my heart and mind. I'm really bothered about this."

"Don't think that way," Ertha said. "Sit down and listen. You're just feeling the way I did when my second baby was born. Did you know my first one died at birth? As time goes on, you will understand that each child is different. You love each one the same, maybe not always in the same manner."

"I'm sure you are right," Molly said. "I thank you for being my friend. Now I believe I'll be more content."

After three days Ertha told Molly goodbye. She mounted Traveler behind the saddle with Jacob. They rode off to her home with the elder Wheelers.

From there Jacob planned to go farther south to Goliad where he hoped to purchase a rifle and ammunition. Molly knew he would be gone over a week, but Marion believed there were no Mexican soldiers in Goliad, so she did not worry. She also knew Traveler to be a fast runner, and he would carry Jacob to safety if they ran into trouble.

Although Molly enjoyed driving the cattle into the corral in the evening, after Jacob left she asked Willy to take over the job. She thought it best not to leave George alone in the cabin except to get firewood.

One day Willy rode Peppy down by Cow Creek looking for a

duck Molly could roast for their dinner. Abruptly, he tightened the reins and stopped Peppy. About twenty feet away he saw a young boy about his age and height walking through a clump of willow trees. He was dressed in buckskin clothes carrying a bow and arrow with a flint-rock head. Willy did not know what he should do. But about that time, the boy waved and called to him in a language he did not understand. Willy realized then that he was merely a friendly Indian lad who wanted to play.

As the boy came closer, they looked at each other and smiled. The boy shot an arrow into the air, and Willy rapidly ran to retrieve it. Then an idea came to Willy—*maybe he can get a duck for me!* Motioning to the boy to come with him, they ran to the creek where a flock of ducks was swimming. They were catching minnows to eat. Willy stood very still as he watched the boy select an arrow, take aim, and shoot one of the ducks. Picking up the duck, Willy ran to tell Molly about his newfound friend.

Two weeks later, in early November, Jacob came home. He had a rifle strapped to the saddle and inside the saddlebag were ammunition and a bag of salt.

"Maw, in order to get the rifle and bullets, I promised to work as a courier," Jacob told her. "You know, carry messages to settlers scattered over the country and to volunteer soldiers."

Those remarks horrified Molly. Yet at the same time, she felt proud of him. He left home a young boy. Now he seemed to be a fifteen-year-old mature man whose blond curly beard had begun to grow on his upper lip.

"The war with Mexico is beginning," he said feeling very grown up. "Jess Wheeler told me a convention was held at San Felipe. They voted to go after Santa Anna if he didn't leave Texas. And they elected Sam Houston, from Tennessee, to be commander-in-chief over the Texas volunteers."

"Well, I'm happy to know Sam Houston will be training our soldiers," Molly remarked. "I remember how your Grandpa Haynes liked Sam Houston."

The fact that Sam Houston came to Texas brought hope to Molly as well as to all Texans. So, many of the farmers returned to their homes and began to prepare for the spring planting.

Molly, too, almost felt secure in her home and went about her daily chores. She noticed young George had grown too tall for his baby clothes. So she got out the spinning wheel and loom to use the last few balls of thread she brought from Tennessee.

Once, as she worked at the spinning wheel, a keen, loud whistle startled her. She turned around. Six black, bright eyes were peering at her through the hole in the wall. Her first impulse was to stand in front of George, who was lying in his cradle. She reached for the gun. Then she remembered Willy's Indian friend. She, also, recalled Marion saying some Cherokee Indians left Chief Bowl's tribe when they intermarried into the Caddo tribe. Now they lived in the unclaimed lands and raised a paltry patch of corn, hunted and fished, and never molested anyone.

She smiled at the men and motioned them to come into the cabin. Instead, they continued to look through the holes. She decided that they only wanted to see the white baby who did not have a great growth of black, bushy hair like Indian babies.

She gave them some coffee beans. Then she took some and they watched every move as she pounded the beans on a round stone. She boiled some in water to show them how to make the strong aromatic beverage, and then she took a sip and offered each one a taste. Perhaps the grins on their faces, as they accepted the gift, were those of thanks. They quickly turned in unison and ran toward their conical tents made from buffalo skin.

After that visit they came periodically, bringing pecan and hickory nut kernels they had laboriously picked out. Strangely, they did not enter the house, nor try to speak to Molly.

Yet, the young boy, Willy's friend, came frequently. He loved to feel George's little hands and blond hair. Each time he came, Willy tried to teach him to speak in English. Surprisingly, he soon learned several words, especially the names of animals.

One day he rushed into the room, tapped his chest, and yelled, "Running Wolf!"

Willy responded by pointing to his chest and saying, "Willy."

A friendship was quickly formed. They spent days hunting, fishing, or child-like, simply roaming the woods. Other times Running Wolf stayed more than one day and helped Willy herd the cattle. Often they worked at clearing the new land of big rocks and young sprouts as the roots of the trees were yet embedded in the soil.

Molly's life seemed to take on a new sense of pride and contentment as she went about her daily chores. Much work needed to be done before the spring planting. All the time, thoughts of war with Mexico remained with her. She told her sons,

"We live so far from most of the settlers that we never know how things are going. But, in another way, I am grateful I do not hear about all the fighting."

As the days passed, occasionally a lone rider or perhaps a small group from the United States stopped by the Anderson place. They were mainly from Tennessee, Alabama, or Kentucky on their way to join the Texas army.

Those were enjoyable times until one day Jacob said, as he tied his bedroll behind the saddle on Traveler, "Maw, I am leaving for a week or two. You see, I've offered to lead these men to General Houston's camp, probably one hundred miles away."

"My son, I am proud of you and I know your papa would have been. I wish you God's care and come back soon," she said as an agonizing fear for his safety almost overwhelmed her.

Anxious days followed Jacob's leaving. Still, Molly kept busy. Willy helped her harness Ole Blu and Bill and hitch them to the bull-tongue plow.

"Willy, stay here with baby George. I'm going to finish breaking the new ground. Your papa always said it is very important before we plant the cotton or corn," Molly said when she put the yoke on Ole Blu and Bill and harnessed them to the plow. With the reins around her head, she guided them from one end of the patch to the other.

Soon the other cow gave birth to a heifer calf. Fearing wild animals might kill it, Molly asked Willy to herd the cattle and look for signs of wolves. Sometimes she became so restless that she carried George and went with him.

They hunted Peyote cactus to make a tea to help prevent winter sickness. Or they looked for Jimson weed that she boiled and made a poultice to rub on wounds found on the animals.

Wild hogs became a nuisance. After they ate their fill of acorns, they habitually used their long, slender snout to root among the fallen leaves, even near the cabin, and bed down there until they became hungry again.

Once Molly walked out the door and there under the oak tree was a big hog grunting and wallowing in the fallen leaves. She simply turned, went into the cabin, picked up the shotgun, and walked outside. She aimed directly between the eyes of the fat hog. She fired the gun only once and the hog lay dead.

With great efforts she and Willy skinned the hog and removed the entrails. Some of those she washed and boiled in the iron pot. However, she saved all the fat to melt into lard to use in frying the meat. Next, she dusted salt, which Jacob had brought from Gonzales, on the remaining carcass. Then they attempted to hang it in a tree. This became a problem.

"Willy, I don't believe I can reach high enough so coyotes can't get to the meat. Besides, it is too heavy to lift. What will we do?" Molly asked as she sat down to rest.

"Oh, I know. Peppy will help," Willy said as he led Peppy to the tree, put a rope around his head, slung it over a limb, and tied it around the hog. Step by step Willy guided Peppy until the butchered hog securely hung on the tree.

In January, north winds swept through depositing occasional gusts of sleet and freezing rain. One night Molly lit a candle, her only source of light, made from tallow of the bear Jacob killed. The cold wind made a moaning sound as it came between the logs. Frequently, it almost extinguished the flickering candle. About that time, Jacob and Jim Mason opened the canvas door and came in.

"Willy, put more wood on the fire. I'll warm the coffee. I know you two must be chilled to the bone," Molly said.

Already things seemed better since Jacob and their good friend Jim were with them. Molly gave both men a hot cup of coffee, and they all hovered around the fire as Molly held George asleep in her arms.

"I was on my way home when I met Jim," Jacob said, "and he decided to come with me."

"I sure am glad you did," Willy, excited about seeing the two, said. "Now, Jim, you can see our baby brother. He's three months old, and growing every day."

"Yes, Jacob told me," Jim replied, "and that's one reason I came. Oh, I wanted to see you and Molly, too. I've been with Ben Milam and his volunteers. We went to fight the Mexicans in San Antonio."

"They run the Mexican general Cos and his soldiers right out of San Antonio. Clear 'cross the Rio Grande River," Jacob said, eager to express his knowledge.

"I'll be leaving in a couple of days," Jim said, "to join my friend General Travis at San Felipe. From there I'll go to be with Milam again. News reached him that Santa Anna is marching north into Texas."

"Jim, do you believe the settlers can beat Santa Anna?" Molly asked. "Although men still come by here on their way to fight, I worry that the army is too small. I believe Santa Anna has many well-trained soldiers."

"One thing that bothers me is the fact that many of our Texas officials argue among themselves, even having name-calling arguments. I'm like Sam Houston," Jim said, "all these foolish acts cause the war-crazed Santa Anna to plan more ways to control the Texas settlers."

"We saw Houston on our way here," Jacob said. "He was headed north to talk to Chief Bowls of the Cherokee Indians."

"He believes he may be able to persuade the Cherokees to stay neutral in the war," Jim told Molly. "Houston is trying to protect Texans and achieve honor and land for the Indians."

"I'll be leaving again with Jim," Jacob said. "General Houston asked me to deliver a message to the town of Refugio."

Hearing Jacob talk of the fighting and anger toward Santa Anna filled Molly's heart with fear. She did not sleep even though Jacob was there with her, at least that night. She wished again that she had taken her family to Virginia. Now it was too late.

She did not want Jacob to go so far away. Yet she knew David would have been proud his son was serving Texas. Once more she vowed to make a good life for her sons in the land that now threatened them, and by the same government that first welcomed them. Long after those thoughts, she went to sleep just before the dawn.

"Today we must finish repairing the cow pen. I believe the other heifer will have her calf in a couple of days," Jim said to the boys. "After that, we need to make some mud to chink the holes between the logs to make the cabin warmer."

As they worked, Molly washed and mended Jim's and Jacob's badly worn clothes. She opened the trunk and painfully took out David's shirt and made it smaller for Jacob. Tears came to her eyes when she held up the buckskin jacket David always wore. Now, her oldest son would wear it.

She did not cry the day Jim and Jacob left, but extreme apprehension and fear raced through her mind.

Jacob had been gone over a week when one night a pounding on the wall of the cabin awoke Molly.

"Wake up! Wake up!" a voice called out.

At first she thought Jacob had come back home. But immediately, she realized it was not the voice of Jacob. She reached over and got the shotgun. She peeped through the canvas door. There stood a young man, about the age of Jacob, knocking on the wall.

"Come in," Molly said as she pulled back the door, "and warm your hands. It is very cold tonight. I can tell by the breathing of your horse that you rode fast. Tell me where you are going and why you are here."

"Mrs. Anderson, take your family and go as fast as you can to Fort Milam," the young man said. "The Comanches are coming our way."

By the time the boy left, Willy held baby George in his arms snugly wrapped in a blanket.

"Maw, hurry, get ready to leave," he begged Molly. "I'll go harness the oxen and hitch them to the wagon."

"Willy, I don't believe we ought to go in the wagon. Indians would be sure to see us," she said. "Maybe it would be better to go through the forest. You run and let the cattle out of the pen. Be sure to make Ring and Rover stay with them."

A short time later they waded across Cow Creek and entered the many acres of tall trees, brush, and briars. They found it difficult and confusing to run in the darkness. Sometimes they were not sure they were running in the right direction toward Fort Milam, near Viesca, once their home. Nor could they see the moon, but the stars were shining.

"Willy, see that bunch of stars in the north? That is the Big Dipper. If we keep that in sight I believe it will guide us to the fort," Molly said as she pointed out the Big Dipper. Unexpectedly, George began to cry. The blanket was wrapped so tightly around him that he became frightened. Quickly, as she ran, she uncovered George's face so he would know he was not alone.

Eventually, the sun appeared as a reddish luminous flame in the eastern horizon, a welcome sight. Now the ever-present briars could be seen and avoided.

They became hungry and thirsty, but still they ran until they came to a little brook. At once they lay flat to drink from the trickling stream. Willy picked up some pecan nuts and cracked them with a rock, and they ate them as they ran. Another time they crouched behind a fallen tree to let Molly feed the baby from her breast. Then they started to run again as the sun slowly dropped from sight beyond the western hills.

Darkness had begun to hover over the countryside when, at last, they detected the outline of Fort Milam. There were no windows, only holes in the walls where soldiers aimed their guns at the approaching enemy. Jess Wheeler, staring through one of the holes, saw them. He pushed open the door and helped Molly into the fort. In one corner Willy saw a wooden bucket filled with water with a gourd dipper nearby. He filled the dipper with water and gave it to Molly, knowing she surely must be thirsty.

In the twelve-by-twelve-foot fort, there were three older men, including Jess Wheeler, and thirteen women and their children. Some of these women Molly knew since the fort stood about one-quarter of a mile on a hill above Viesca.

The arrival of Molly and her sons turned the attention of the people to young George, giving them, for a short time, an opportunity to ignore the scent of drifting smoke. The log houses of Viesca were burning, and the smoke filtered through the holes in the walls of the fort.

"Commissioner Shields left two days ago," one man said. "He took the land records to Washington-on-the-Brazos. Even Ramon and Celita Gonzales left. They had no reason to stay in Viesca. They had nothing to sell. I think they went to San Antonio where Celita's father lives."

All through the night the Comanches danced around the fires, shouting their war chants and cries of victory over Texans. Along about sunrise, the fires burned down and the celebration ceased. The Indian warriors mounted their horses and rode bareback toward the north country.

The lives of the frightened Texas settlers were spared. Still, they all wondered if their homes would be standing when they returned to them.

"Folks, I believe our homes are safe," Jess Wheeler said, attempting to calm their fears, "but, I think we should stay here a little longer in case the marauders come back."

The weary, alarmed settlers experienced a sleepless, terrifying night. Yet through it all, the fear of Indian raids brought them closer together. Those who came in wagons brought food that they shared with the others.

Jess said, "Nobody will have to walk home. The ones in wagons have offered to take the others, no matter how far away."

Molly and Willy climbed into the Wheeler wagon as Ertha held little George. Molly said as she slumped down on the wagon floor, "Ertha, I don't believe I could have walked further. The soles of my feet are covered with blisters. Besides that, my arms and even my clothes are torn from the briars that clung to us."

Late that afternoon, Jess pulled up on the reins of his mules and stopped at the Anderson home. A wonderful surprise awaited them. The cabin stood just as they left it. But now Jacob stood in the doorway and smoke rose from the chimney.

"I heard the men talking about the Indian raids," he told them. "I knew I must come see about my family. So, I asked permission to leave my duty of caring for the soldiers' horses."

"Jacob, have you seen Marion? What about the fighting? Is it better or worse?" Jess Wheeler asked.

"Yes," Jacob answered. "I saw Marion a few days back. He's safe right now. I don't think conditions in Texas are better. Santa Anna is pushing his men further into Texas all the time. I hear men talking. I don't believe they know how to deal with Santa Anna, the commander of the Mexican army, the one we call a 'madman.' Anyway, one good thing has come from this. The Indians now know Santa Anna tricked them. He did not give them the weapons he promised if they raided the farms."

Molly, listening to Jacob talk, could hardly believe her son spoke of government affairs as a mature man, and her heart beat with motherly pride.

After two days Jacob said, "Maw, I will be leaving in the morning. I know you understand. I made a promise and I must keep it. I know you are safe, at least for now."

"You are right, my son. I will miss you, but I'm also very proud of you. I know your papa would have been," Molly said and turned toward the cabin in order to hide the tears.

The month of March came and with it a rush of turbulent west winds Molly believed to be a forerunner of spring. This should have been the month to renew the hope of planting the crops. And the season for the return of the glorious masses of wildflowers with their lavish colors that seemed to come from unknown places. Often flocks of geese, banded together, flew in an ever-perfect formation and headed toward the north country.

Many days, Willy and Running Wolf wandered through the forest. They looked for tender wild rye grass emerging from the cold winter soil. There they drove the bull and two cows, with their calves, to graze.

Molly, carrying George, made frequent walks to Cow Creek, searching for early watercress greens among the marshy banks of the creek. Sometimes she gathered wild onions or poke greens peeping out of the ground on the hillside. Maybe Jacob and Willy fared well on meat and corn pone in the winter, but she still nursed baby George. She knew she should eat vegetables to enrich her milk and cause the baby to have strong bones.

Indeed, spring was in the air and Mother Nature's beauty covered the lands of southeast Texas. However, regardless of the splendor, sadness lingered over the country, and death loomed near the undernourished and poorly trained Texas soldiers. The horrors of war overshadowed the thoughts of spring planting. Molly desperately tried to believe Jacob was safe. Yet, she did not think only of Jacob. She acknowledged that the whole country suffered from a devastating commotion.

Resting one day by the trunk, she reached over and picked up the Holy Bible. She read how the wise man, Solomon, wrote: *There is an appointed time for everything, and a time for every matter under Heaven.* Then at the end she read: *A time for peace and a time for war.* She closed the book. Truly, this is a time of war. She did not comprehend her feelings nor did she attempt to. She knew her resentment of Texas had vanished. Neither did she feel a desire for revenge that had once controlled her. Now, her resentment fell only on Santa Anna. She knew that she, at last, felt an abiding kinship with the Mexican people.

"Willy, we have cleared most of the brush on the new ground. I think it is time to plant the corn. If you will stay here with your little brother, I'll start planting today," Molly said as she put on her bonnet and left.

Using strict precaution, she resolutely dropped the seed one by one. They were the seed David so scrupulously chose to bring to Texas. Finally, she stomped soil, free of little stones, over the seed to cover them.

"Willy, I think we will wait a while to plant the cotton," Molly said when she returned to the cabin. "Jim said the soil needs to be moist and warm in order for the seed to germinate and break open the ground. Besides, I expect any day to see Jacob, riding Traveler, come up the road."

However, she did not know the plight of the Texas army. Neither did she know Santa Anna continued to bring soldiers into San Antonio.

The middle of March came. Still Jacob had not come home. Then one day Jess Wheeler rode up. Instantly, Molly's first thought was of Jacob. Was he wounded? Could he have been captured by Santa Anna?

"Molly, Jacob is fine," Jess told her. "I saw him a couple of days back riding Traveler. He was on his way to deliver a message to General Houston's camp. He asked about you. I told him I would come by and tell you he is well. Another thing I believe you ought to know—we declared independence from Mexico."

"Jess, when did this happen? Maybe I'm glad. But, on the other hand, I am afraid the fighting will get worse. Tell me and Willy how this came to be!" Molly urged Jess.

"A convention met at Washington-on-the-Brazos. A constitution was agreed on, and men were chosen to put into action the newly formed government," Jess said. "But, even before we finished writing all the rules and regulations, Santa Anna brought in more men and camped on the outer edge of San Antonio."

"Jess, please tell me what you know about this. Were the Texans able to withstand Santa Anna?" Molly asked.

"Well, General William Travis stationed his soldiers in an old Spanish Mission building, called the Alamo, which was not in use. The walls of the building are three feet thick and twelve feet high. Travis had less than two hundred men in the Alamo. Most of them were from Kentucky, Tennessee, and Alabama. Some of them joined the fight just as an adventure, others because they believed Texas to be right. Then there were those who offered to fight for land promised to each soldier."

"Didn't other men come to help General Travis?" Molly asked. "Two hundred couldn't beat Santa Anna."

"Yes, Travis did send out riders to carry urgent demands to send reinforcements. Molly, Santa Anna told the Texans to surrender or the little garrison in the Alamo would be slaughtered," Jess answered.

"Do you know if Jim was there?" Willy asked. "He said he was going to see Travis, and I know he would help."

"No, Jim was not there then. That happened when Travis answered Santa Anna with a blast of a little cannon. Then he raised the new Lone Star Flag of Texas above the Alamo walls."

"Maybe Jim did not get there. Maybe he did not have to fight that awful time," Willy hopefully said.

"Willy, Jim did come. He and thirty-two other men climbed over the walls into the old mission. I have been told they were the last men to come, even though two more riders risked their lives by running to ask for more recruits."

"I wonder if the men who came by here were there. This is so sad. They all told me they had families. Of course, I will never know," Molly said.

Jess did not tell Molly and Willy, nor did he know that Santa Anna bombarded the courageous troops for over a week.

Nevertheless, the determined soldiers answered with a cannon and gunshots. They killed or wounded all Mexican soldiers who came in range of their weapons.

This tormented Santa Anna, so he sent for more troops to come to his aid. He announced, "*War without mercy would be declared on the soldiers trapped in the old mission by morning.*"

"Around five o'clock in the morning of March the sixth, Santa Anna began the final blow," Jess cleared his throat, wiped the perspiration from his face, and continued. "The Mexican soldiers climbed over the walls. Hand-to-hand fighting commenced. They used knives, gun barrels, or any available object they could find."

Molly saw Willy clench his hands and wipe tears from his eyes. She knew he was thinking of Jim. She wanted to ask Jess to stop talking, yet she realized Willy could not be sheltered from the horrors of war.

"That brutal battle was over in two hours," Jess said. "I've been told lifeless bodies of the heroic Texas soldiers lay everywhere. A few men did survive, but they were ruthlessly shot standing there."

Jess brushed tears from his eyes when he finished telling about the devastation and fall of the Alamo. Molly and Willy, horrified, huddled side by side. Even young George sensed sadness in the room and began to cry. Yet, Molly did not seem to hear him for she made no effort to quiet him. She held Willy close as he began to sob. He knew his good friend Jim Mason had died in the Alamo.

Silence filled the room even though there were many questions unanswered. Perhaps that seemed best, as Jacob was out there somewhere and he, too, could be wounded or dead.

Jess said little as he mounted his horse and rode away.

Now baby George lay asleep in Molly's arms. Willy began to talk about Jim. "Maw, do you remember the time Jim took Papa, Jacob, and me to see the big herd of buffalo? When Papa died, he was good to Jacob and me. Do you remember how he stayed when little John died?"

Then Molly was surprised when he said, "Jacob took Papa's

place. Maw, can I take Jim's place? I want to be like Jim. I want to help people like he did."

"My dear son," Molly finally answered, "I hope some day your wish will come true. But now, until you're older, I want you and Jacob to be happy here with me and your baby brother. I'm sure Jacob will be home soon and the war will be over."

After Willy went to sleep, and before Molly snuffed out the candle, she gently stroked his curly black hair. She kissed baby George, but she did not sleep until almost daybreak. Anger pierced her mind because of Santa Anna's treatment of the Texans, and the grief she felt for the families of the slain, gallant men in the Alamo. She felt an overpowering desire to know Jacob, so brave like David, to be safe. She wanted to shape situations and decisions. But she also knew no day should be wasted with idle wishes that could not cause wars to end. Nor would they allow her to see Jacob riding up the path. Too, endless chores remained, and soon she must plant the cotton.

Molly had not seen the wild hogs in a while. But she knew they often bedded down by Cow Creek where they could wallow in the mud. One day she saw an old sow with six suckling pigs lying under an oak tree. Why not catch the sow and let her raise her brood close by? We can fatten them to butcher in the fall, Molly thought.

"Willy, let's catch the old sow," Molly called to him.

Willy threw a rope around the hind leg of the sow and tied her to a stump by the cow pen. Next, they dug a shallow ditch and each day they filled it with fresh water and threw straw around to make a bed. But the sow and pigs rooted around in the straw, and it became wet and cold.

They fed acorns to the sow, and Molly saved bits of crumbs from the dinner table. She loved to watch the old sow eagerly devour them. Before long the newly acquired animals felt at home and did not wander off. Still, one problem remained. Ring and Rover barked and ran after them. Each day, Willy sat by the old sow and waited for Ring and Rover so he could demand they stay away.

Day after day, with George strapped to her back in the deer-skin pack that Running Wolf had made, Molly worked at the never-ending chores. Still, she never stopped believing that soon she would hear the sound of a galloping horse, with Jacob in the saddle, coming up the path.

One day, returning from picking wild strawberries, she saw an unusual sight. A covered wagon pulled by mules was coming toward her cabin. A young man, a pretty lady, and two small children were in the wagon with two cows tied to the back.

Ring and Rover also saw them and began to bark. Molly assumed the people meant no harm so she called out, "Ring, Rover, quiet. Hello, come on in. I'll soon be cooking supper and you're welcome to eat with my sons and me. We'd be pleased to have you stay."

"Thank you, Ma'am, but we must be on our way," the man said. "I'm Leonard Wagner. That's my wife, Bertha, and these're our three-year-old twin daughters. We named them Winnie and Minnie. We only stopped to fill our barrel with water from the creek. But just now I noticed I need to oil a wagon wheel."

"Where are you going?" Molly asked.

"I'm taking my family across the Sabine River into Louisiana where they'll be safe from Santa Anna's army. Then I'll come back and join Houston's command in the war."

Hearing those remarks gave Molly a chance to insist they stay and eat with them. Perhaps they may have seen or heard of Jacob, so she casually said, "My son, Willy, is good at fixing things. I know he will be glad to help you."

Willy did help Wagner, but it took a while so Molly said, "It's too late to travel. You folks can camp right here tonight. Supper's almost ready. Bring the family in and eat with us."

"My oldest son went to Houston's camp," Molly said as she cleared the table. "I wonder if you saw him on your way here. He's been gone a while so I keep thinking he'll be home soon."

"No, Mrs. Anderson," Bertha Wagner answered, "we didn't see anyone. You see, Leonard thought we might run into some Mexican soldiers so we did not travel the main road. Leonard, do you remember seeing the young man?"

"Well, come to think of it, maybe I did," Leonard Wagner said. "Once, at Houston's camp, two young lads took care of our horses. One could have been your son. I didn't talk to them. I do remember one rode a big bay horse with a prancing gait. Do you think he could have been your son?"

"Oh, I'm sure that was my son," Molly quickly said.

"I was with Houston when he went to Gonzales," Wagner said. "The men stationed there only had two days' rations and a scant supply of arms and ammunition. That was where we learned about the battle at the Alamo Mission and that a part of Santa Anna's troops were headed east. Houston knew we couldn't stand another attack, so he ordered us to move north. We were on the banks of the Colorado River when I left to take my family to safety."

Later Leonard and Bertha, with their twin daughters, went to their wagon. At daybreak they resumed their travel toward Louisiana and away from the threat of Santa Anna. Watching them leave, Molly knew she would never see them again, but she felt thankful they gave her hope of Jacob's safety.

The first of April arrived. The bluebonnet blossoms were in full bloom. Even the redbud trees scattered among the tall trees glistened with bright crimson color. Molly knew that shortly the dogwood trees would begin to bud out. Believing that, she smiled and remembered that the pure white flowers, with a slight stain of yellow resembling a ripe lemon, were her favorites.

Days like those, she grew restless. She took George down by Cow Creek and gathered wild herbs. Often she said to Willy, "They will whet our appetites and cleanse our digestive system."

One such day as she rinsed the greens in the creek, she saw two riders come through the brush. One man, with an arm in a sling, led the other horse. The rider was slumped over in the saddle, almost unconscious. Molly led them to the cabin. She helped the wounded man into the room and lay him on the big bed. When she took the soiled bandage off, she saw where a bullet had almost penetrated his right eye. After giving the man some brandy, she cleansed the wound and put on a clean bandage.

Then she carefully removed his torn shirt. A bullet had pierced his right side, but thankfully it did not lodge in his body. However, blood oozed from the wound. So she washed it as best she could. Finally, she pressed a strip of raw venison over the wound to stop the bleeding and wrapped a cloth around the man's waist.

The other man had a broken arm. However, she believed it was beginning to heal.

"Now, both of you drink this broth. Just rest for awhile. Afterward, I want to know how you were wounded and why you were traveling on this road," Molly said and walked out the door.

"I'm Molly Anderson," she said when the men awoke sometime in the midafternoon. She offered them a cup of coffee as she pointed toward Willy. "This is my son, Willy. The little one is George, my youngest son." But she did not mention Jacob until she learned more about the strange men. "I'm glad to see you're rested. I made some fresh venison stew. I think you ought to eat some now. Where are you going, and where did you get wounded?"

"Thank you, Mrs. Anderson. We have not eaten in a day so we will be happy to get the food," the man called Hank said. "Of course, my friend was wounded bad and could not eat. But we did find water. We're on our way to my uncle's across the Sabine River. We escaped from Goliad a week ago and hid in the marsh reeds a day."

"Please tell me what happened," Molly said after she determined them to be honest men. "My oldest son is somewhere with General Houston. I want to know if he is safe."

"Yes, ma'am, I believe your son is safe at this time. General Houston marched his men north; they're camped at the Groce plantation," Hank answered. "That Mexican general Urrea is slaughtering the men like Santa Anna did at the Alamo. He killed, or captured, twenty-six men at Aqua Dulce Creek. From there he went on to Refugio and tore up the town."

Molly, trembling with anger, could not speak. She could not understand why stalwart young men should suffer such pain.

"We were with that good captain, Fannin, when Houston sent orders for us to go to Goliad to help hold the town," Hank continued. "On March the seventeenth we began our move. We traveled slow because we had a little cannon with us. We'd just entered an open field a short distance from Goliad, by the Caleto Creek. That was when Urrea and maybe six hundred men surrounded us. For a while we drove the Mexicans back, but too many men died and Fannin was wounded."

"We spent that night in the prairie without water, all the time hoping help would come by daybreak," Pete, for the first time, began to speak. "Then sometime about dawn, Urrea fired a cannon at us. We fired back, but it was useless."

"Fannin, even though hit by a bullet, rode to Urrea waving a white flag and surrendered. Right then Urrea's men marched us to Goliad and locked us up in an old fort," Hank said.

"Was that when you got away?" Willy asked.

"No, we believed we would be treated fair as prisoners of war," Hank answered. "Instead, on Palm Sunday they took us to the open country, lined us up, and started shooting. I don't know how, but I missed the bullets. I crawled inch by inch through the dead bodies of my companions. I accidentally touched Pete and could see he was still alive."

"How did you mange to get away with Pete shot?" Molly asked. "You are brave men. Do you know if other men got away?"

"Mrs. Anderson, I do not know, but I hope others crawled away," Hank said. "I lay down beside Pete and pretended to be dead. After the Mexicans walked away, I pulled Pete into a thicket where we stayed all of the next day."

"These are not our horses. We did not steal them." Pete eager to explain said, "We just needed to get away. Hank will bring them back when we get to his uncle's house. Maybe they belong to one of the dead men, we do not know."

Regardless of Molly's offer for them to stay until Pete became stronger, after three days the men went east and crossed over the Sabine River.

"Maw, I like Hank and Pete. I'm glad they didn't get killed. Do you think we will see them again?" Willy wanted to know.

"I don't know, but I am glad Hank has family to help them," Molly said as a longing for Jacob raced through her mind.

April showers set in after Hank and Pete left, quickly becoming a torrential rain. Cotton planting time came. Still, the sod remained too wet to plant the seed. Molly could not take George out in the rain, so she had to stay inside. She had time to spend with Willy and to teach little George to crawl on the bearskin rug.

One day when Running Wolf and Willy were hunting near the Banes place, they saw wagon after wagon going east toward the Sabine River. "Mister, where are you going?" Willy asked.

"General Houston moved his army farther north. Now our families are not safe. Maybe Houston is afraid of Santa Anna. If that is true, Santa Anna will follow behind and all Texans will be overrun," the man told Willy.

Willy saw women walking, carrying bundles behind their backs or a child in their arms. Then there were those riding horses with two or more children perched on one horse.

Those riding in wagons loaded much of their possessions and families and started east to safety across the Sabine River into Louisiana. One wagon came near the Andersons. They offered to take Molly, Willy, and George with them.

"No, sir, I will not go. I have no fear of Santa Anna, only contempt, " Molly said. "Besides, my oldest son is still away. I would never leave without him. Thank you for your kindness."

When Jacob went back to Houston's camp, more men had come to the soldiers' aid, bringing the number to almost one thousand. The large number created a shortage of beef for food. Jacob, among others, volunteered to hunt deer to replace the beef. He saddled Traveler and headed north.

About that time Santa Anna divided his men into three divisions. He sent them in different directions. He ordered General Geona north toward Nachogdoches. However, they had not gone far when Santa Anna issued orders to turn back south.

Jacob did not know this. He thought only of proving his sportsmanship. There, before him, lay a wooded area of tall pine trees. Surely an ample supply of deer could be found among the underbrush.

Jacob cautiously urged Traveler farther into the brush. Suddenly, he saw a herd of deer grazing peacefully. Sensing the smell of Traveler, a big buck with an enormous rack of horns looked directly at Jacob, who aimed his gun and shot.

At once, blasts of gunpowder passed above Jacob's head. Seeking safety, he urged Traveler farther into the trees. Another blast of shots came closer, and Traveler was hit between the eyes. He ran a few steps, stumbled, and fell to the ground. Jacob fell with him, leaving one foot under Traveler.

Assuming Jacob to be dead, the Mexicans laughed and marched on south. Mercifully, Traveler died as he fell. Jacob lay unconscious as the rays of the bright sun beamed down on him.

Later in the day Jacob felt a drip of water on his face. Someone had lifted his head to give him a drink. At first Jacob did not recognize the person, but as his eyes became clearer he saw his good friend, Pablo Estrada.

Pablo had seen Geona's men going south. Not being sure what could happen, he hid behind some brush where he heard the first shots and then the soldiers talking. Even though he was a Mexican, he believed it best not to return to the main road, so he drove his mule into a dense thicket.

There he saw Jacob lying beside Traveler. He knew the shots he heard were those that killed Traveler and wounded Jacob. He tied the horse's body to the mule and drug it away, thus freeing

Jacob's leg. That was when Pablo saw Jacob's leg was broken between the ankle and knee for the bone bent inward.

"Compadre, be still. Do not move. I will help you," Pablo, almost whispering, said to Jacob.

Jacob did not answer. He felt intense pain in his leg, but the pain he felt at the loss of his treasured animal was greater.

Pablo knew no alternative. The fractured bones must be pulled together. He did not welcome the task, but he began to compassionately press the bones until the leg lay straight. Jacob screamed out in pain. Then he again became unconscious.

Pablo attempted to remove any dirt from the wound. Then he bound it with strips of cloth he tore from his shirt. Afterward, he revived Jacob by splashing water on his face. Finally, he cut a tree branch to make a splint for Jacob's leg. Next came the problem of getting him onto the hay-filled cart. Twice he fell. On the third try, Jacob held onto the cart and lay on the hay. Pablo tied him down with a rope and drove the mule northwest to his brother's house.

When Pablo came near his brother's house, out came a half dozen barking hounds, followed by Alfredo, Francisca, his wife, and six young children. At once Alfredo recognized Pablo and called the hounds back.

"This is my friend, Jacob Anderson. He needs help. See, he is wounded," Pablo said as he and Alfredo carried Jacob into the house and placed him on a straw-filled bed.

Without asking questions, Francisca began to make him comfortable when she saw the broken leg. She removed the soiled bandage Pablo applied, and cleansed the wound with warm soapy water. Afterward, she gave him a sip of brandy before she poured some on the wound. Assuring him all the time, in Spanish, he would heal. It truly saddened her that her people wounded a fine young man like Jacob.

The bone did start to knit together, and each day Francisca continued to keep the wound clean. She insisted Jacob drink boiled Peyote cactus water mixed with a bit of brandy to prevent infections. Before long he walked around with the aid of a tree branch as a cane.

Pablo and Alfredo did not join the Mexican army—nor did they fight with the Texans. But they did a great service for the Texans, their newfound friends. They captured and trained wild horses, the ones many Texans rode in the fight against the dreaded Santa Anna.

"Pablo and me, we will take more horses to General Houston at the Groce plantation," Alfredo said to Francisca.

They reached the plantation, but Houston and his soldiers were gone. "General Houston, two days ago, marched his men south toward Harrisburg. Don't ask me why, 'cause I don't know," one of the slaves told them.

So, in order to do what they agreed to, they left all the horses there; that is, except one light-colored sorrel with a white mane and tail. They started back to Alfredo's house to tell Jacob that Houston had left the plantation.

"With General Houston gone from the plantation, I think I will go home," Jacob said, and Francisca agreed. She knew his mother would be happy to see him. Too, his leg was healing. Although neither understood the other's language, a bond was formed that lasted many years. Francisca, with her black hair, dark skin, and intriguing pale-blue eyes, was a loving, kind person. She forever scrambled here and there, shouting at her six children or talking to herself.

Jacob felt happy to be able to go home. Yet he also felt sad to be leaving that peaceful, laughter-filled home. He said goodbye to Francisca, patted each Estrada child on the head, and walked out the door, supported by the use of a hickory limb.

Alfredo and Pablo were waiting. Tied behind the two-wheel cart stood the chestnut-colored horse, already trained to ride, that Pablo and Alfredo had brought back from the plantation.

Jacob, so overcome with emotions, could not speak. The Estradas had saved his life, and he could never repay them for all the kindness shown him.

Unknown to Jacob, Pablo had cut the girth and taken the saddle off Traveler. Now the saddle was mended and cinched on the horse they called Pancho. Tears fell down Jacob's cheeks regardless of the efforts to hide them. He hobbled onto the cart, turned, and waved as he and Pablo started to the labor of land on Cow Creek.

Three long weeks Molly waited for Jacob; still he had not come home. She constantly tried to believe him to be safe, but she often doubted her reasoning.

Unrest hovered over Texas. Wagons, two-wheel carts, and horseback riders continued to ford the rain-swollen streams and push through the boggy marshes on their way to safety.

As with most quirks of nature, the rains began to lessen. Soon the soil became dry enough to plant the cotton. One bright, sunny day, with George on her back, Molly walked through the cleared ground. She saw sprigs of corn breaking through the sod. This gave her hope for a good harvest.

Just then she heard Willy calling, "Maw, where are you? Come home! Come quick!" Trying to stifle the thoughts that sad news awaited her, she quickly started toward the cabin. There stood Jacob and Pablo. She saw that Jacob had been wounded and another horse now took the place of Traveler, yet she felt extremely grateful Jacob was alive and home.

"My leg will soon be good as new," Jacob told the family. "Maw, Francisca is so pretty and happy. She sings and laughs all the time, even when her children run from her. She put bandages on my leg every day. And, she made me drink goat milk in the mornings. At first I thought I would not like it. But it's real good."

"Señora, Traveler, he died because the bullet aimed at Jacob hit hem. My brother and me, we know the chestnut sorrel cannot be like Traveler, but he is a good horse," Pablo said.

Molly believed she could rest well that night since Jacob came home. Still, many unanswered questions raced through her mind. Why were the Mexicans and Texans fighting, when the Mexican people were kind and good? Why did men from Tennessee, Kentucky, or Alabama fight or die for a country not their own? There is something unexplainable about this country. I have a genuine desire to uphold and call this my home although I cursed it at the beginning.

Around midnight, her thoughts quieted, and she, like King Solomon, concluded there is a season for all things. She prayed this to be the season for peace in Texas.

Pablo said goodbye to the Andersons the following morning. He turned the two-wheel mule-drawn cart toward his brother's home, almost one hundred miles away.

Now that Jacob was home the sky seemed brighter. Even the west winds blew soft, gentle breezes when Molly went about her daily work.

"Willy, you can let the cattle graze free now that the calves are bigger. But, I think we should ride Pancho more often, especially until he gets familiar with his new home," Molly said. She bridled and cinched the saddle as Pancho stood still. She put one foot into the stirrup and easily slung the remaining foot to the other side.

"Maw, don't you know ladies ride with both legs on one side of the saddle?" Jacob said as he and Willy laughed.

At first Pancho did not like Molly on his back. He snorted and pitched from one side to the other. Molly sat firm, spurring at every move. After a few more quick jumps, he quieted down. Molly reached over and rubbed him on the head, and he trotted down the path.

Yes, life on her labor of land seemed safer. Nevertheless, dread and fear of Santa Anna with his army haunted her. People continued to run to Louisiana to escape the irate anger of Santa Anna and his many soldiers.

Then, around the first week in May, Marion rode up. He let out a loud whistle and yelled, "The war is over! Santa Anna surrendered!"

Everyone gathered around anxiously waiting to hear what happened. "Well, you know lots of people thought ole Sam Houston was afraid of Santa Anna and his big army because he kept pushing us east," Marion slowly began, "but I think Sam was smart like a fox. Instead of being afraid, he was bidin' his time to get the old rascal. On the seventeenth of March Sam turned us south to Harrisburg."

"So, that is why General Houston left the Groce plantation! The slave said he took his men toward Harrisburg," Jacob, shaking his head, said.

"The next day we wuz on Buffalo Bayou," Marion continued. "After that we moved to the west bank because Santa Anna, with his fancy dressed army, headed t'ward the San Jacinto River. Three days later Sam moved us to where the Buffalo Bayou joins the San Jacinto. Then, that same day, Santa Anna took his men to a prairie, 'bout three-quarters of a mile frum us."

"I would liked to have been with you then," Jacob said, "but on the other hand I'm just proud the fighting is over."

"The next day, on April the twenty-first—Willy, don't ever forget that day—" Marion said, then continued, "we saw the Mexican flag flutterin' from across the prairie. But it all seemed quiet in their camp."

Molly saw Marion begin to shift his legs from one side to the other. He tossed his hat to the floor and wiped the sweat from his face. Molly knew he, in a manner, was reliving that day. Still, she said nothing. She, too, sensed a strange feeling of relief mixed with sadness.

"About the middle of the day Sam Houston called a meetin' of his officials," Marion said, cleared his throat, and continued. "He asked them to decide if we should attack Santa Anna that day or wait. There was so much bickering among his men that he just walked away." Marion almost smiled, then said, "I think ole Sam wuz gettin' us riled up. He wanted us mad enough to go after the whole Mexican army."

"Didn't General Houston issue any orders to the men?" Jacob wanted to know.

"About three o'clock that evening he ordered us to assemble for attack." Marion did not answer Jacob, he simply continued talking. "Sam raised his sword that signaled us to come out of the woods and onto the prairie. There was even a band; of course, it was just three fife players and a young drummer boy. Molly, they wuz playing that pretty song I've heard you sing. That one about 'come with me to the bower.' That sure pepped us up."

"That is a pretty song, Marion," Molly answered, "but didn't the Mexican army hear you coming?"

"Well, you know the Mexicans like to take a nap, they call a siesta, around that time of the day. Some of the soldiers, along with Santa Anna, was taking their siesta, but some had gone down to the river to water the horses." Marion again shifted his legs, cleared his throat, strangely looked around the room, then continued, "We wuz right on them before they knew what was happening. Right then we started yelling, 'Remember the Alamo! Remember Goliad!'

"That was when we opened fire on the whole camp and grabbed all of their artillery we could," Marion paused long enough to clear his throat, wipe the saliva from his lips, and begin to speak again. "We started fighting hand to hand. About that time a lot of the Mexicans, including Santa Anna, ran way. After fifteen or a few minutes more, they didn't run anymore." For one brief moment Marion did not speak, then he said, "The killing kept on until sundown."

"Marion, I thought Santa Anna was captured. What did happen to him?" Willy asked.

"Santa Anna was found hunched down by the swamp. He had changed his flashy uniform to a common man's clothes he took off some peon," Marion answered. "One man asked as he saluted General Houston, 'Do you want to be the one to shoot Santa Anna?' Old Sam roared back, 'Nobody is going to shoot Santa Anna. He can help us more alive than dead.'"

"The battle was over. I ain't proud to say it, but all Mexicans, if we found them, was killed. I guess we couldn't forget what Santa Anna did, so we got revenge." At that Marion stood up, put his hat on, and walked out the door without saying goodbye.

"Yes, Willy, Marion is right. April 21, 1836, is a date to remember," Molly calmly said. "The day that Texas won independence from Mexico. And the day a powerful, self-ruled nation came into existence."

CHAPTER 5

The defeat of Santa Anna spread quickly throughout the land. People on their way to Louisiana, to escape from the Mexican army, were camped on the east bank of the Trinity River. Hearing the news of Santa Anna's surrender, they turned their teams around and started back home. But the river still at flood stage hindered their crossing. Still, many people forded the raging water that often swept furniture and supplies from the wagon as women held crying children in their arms.

"Maw, Running Wolf and me saw lots of wagons going west. Do you think they know Texas whipped Santa Anna and they are going back home? I wonder if they have anything to eat," Willy said.

"Willy, you are right. We need to take them some food," Molly answered. "You and Jacob hurry to harness the oxen, and we will take them something to eat."

Without hesitating, she began to roast venison and wild turkey. She said, "Some of the women with young children have lost their husband in the fighting, so we need to take them more food. I think I'll put in the pecan and hickory nuts Running Wolf's father gave us. And some of the dried cherries we have left."

Leaving Ring and Rover to guard the calves, the family went the ten miles to take the much-needed food to friends they did not know.

That year the spring rains came at the time necessary for a good harvest in the fall. Although things looked better, Molly somehow sensed things with Mexico remained unsettled, and that haunted her. True, Santa Anna signed a treaty promising to take his army and leave Texas without efforts of retaliation against the Texans. He agreed also that the Rio Grande River would be a permanent boundary between Mexico and the newly formed Republic of Texas.

"Houston ordered us farmers to go home, but it is too late now to plant the cotton," Marion Wheeler said when he came by the Anderson place. "I'm glad to be home. The soldiers left in the camps are stirring up trouble and it looks like the Mexicans are champing at the bits to satisfy them."

In early July the corn began to tassel. By that, Molly knew that unless a hailstorm occurred, they would have a good crop. Before long the ears of corn were large enough to pull. With George strapped to her back, she gathered some of the ears. She stripped off the shucks and gave them to the old sow and her pigs. She smiled when she removed the silks and saw the delicious, sweet tender kernels she boiled for their dinner.

"Jacob, I believe your leg is healed enough for you to ride Pancho. Will you and Willy ride to the Wheeler farm to see if Jess has heard anything about government affairs?" Molly asked. "Somehow, I just don't feel that Santa Anna is carrying out his promises he made in the treaty."

"Maw, lots of people from the United States and other countries are coming into Texas," Jacob told Molly when he and Willy returned. "Most of them come to buy cheap land. But Jess said some came to get away from paying debts they owe in their home state."

Not long after that Jess Wheeler came by and told Molly how he attended a convention at the capitol in Harrisburg. "The old settlers, and especially, Sam Houston, are getting tired of all the bickering going on. The title States of Coalhuila and Tejas (Texas) has been erased from the government papers. Now, our name is Republic of Texas. But that is only the beginning. We have lots of work left to do. I think when we hold another election in October, we will see some relief from our problems."

"I certainly agree," Molly replied, "but until a Congress is formed the laws cannot be written and passed. Most of all, our Republic must not be run only by a president."

As Jess rode away, Molly reasoned, I am a citizen of the Republic of Texas. I own one labor of land and have committed no crimes. Besides that, my sixteen-year-old son was wounded serving this country. She rose from her chair and walked to the door. She looked around at all the beauty. Acknowledging her work, she simply wanted to know, why she was not allowed to vote in the coming election? Laughing, she mused that maybe, just maybe, some day that will change.

The warm sunshine of September forced the cotton bolls to open. Soon the fluffy cotton was ready to be picked. However, they had no gunnysacks or baskets to put the cotton in when they picked it. But as usual Willy suggested a solution. "Maw, I will run get Running Wolf. He can show us how to make baskets."

Even before the day ended the family was making baskets from willow limbs. As a reward for helping, they handed Running Wolf a basket filled with the soft cotton to take with him.

"My people grow corn and pumpkins. We never grow cotton. We make our clothes from buffalo skin," he said.

Each time the family filled a basket with the picked cotton, they emptied it into the wagon. But Molly kept a small portion to separate the seed by hand. She saved those to plant the following spring. After she removed the seeds, she planned to make the airy cotton into threads on the spinning wheel and weave them into cloth on the loom.

When she bent over to pick the cotton, she felt grateful she could, once again, make clothes for her sons. Recently, she noticed their present ones were threadbare so she could not mend them again.

By the first of November, frost had turned the cotton stalks to a dark brown. By that, she knew they must take the picked cotton to the gin at the Groce plantation. She made corn pone and roasted venison to eat on the way and placed tanned deerskin on the cotton where they planned to sleep at night. She drove the oxen, with George beside her, while Jacob and Willy rode Pancho and Peppy ahead.

Along about midafternoon they came to the Brazos River and turned south. The sun was almost out of sight behind the western horizon when Molly stopped the oxen. They camped by the Brazos River for the night.

The next morning, Jacob rode ahead a short way, then turned and came back. "Maw, I found a shoals just a short distance downstream. We can cross over to the east bank there."

They had not gone far after they crossed to the east bank when Molly excitedly called out, "Boys, look. Look to the east. That pretty house reminds me of Nashville."

"Maw, that's the plantation of Mr. Jared Groce," Jacob said as he galloped back to the wagon. "That's where I stayed in a row of canvas tents with General Houston's army. See those black men— they are slaves that farm the land and run the cotton gin."

She hardly believed what she saw. To her, the well-kept surroundings, including the castle-like house and the flowers around it, appeared to be a paradise.

"Well, Mr. Jacob, we shore are glad to see you. We wuz 'fraid you'd been killed when yous didn't come back from the deer hunt," one man said as he shook Jacob's hand.

As Molly listened to Jacob tell about how Traveler died from the bullet intended for him, she realized her son was quickly becoming a young man.

"Miz Anderson, your son told me yous never raised cotton 'fore you'ns come to Texas. So, I'm goin' tell yous 'bout ginnin' the cotton," a black man called Rance said. "Now the seed will pay for the ginning and tying the cotton into bales. Then the cotton is shipped to New Orleans where some man sells the bales. Course, the man, he takes some of the money for his work. I don't know how all that goes, but he'll send you a paper to use like money."

All of this seemed unfair to Molly, as she did not fully understand how she would ever be able to care for her family. Yet, she realized this was the only means she had of purchasing things important to their livelihood.

She wanted shoes for one-year-old George, who now walked

everywhere. Jacob and Willy needed shoes. Only recently she made new soles for their present ones from tanned deerhide. She longed to buy wheat flour from New Orleans and brandy in case the winter sickness set in. The gunpowder used to hunt meat for the table, protection from wild animals, or to ward off hostile Indians, was almost depleted. Certainly, the gunpowder was a necessity. Even as these thoughts went through her mind, she knew those things could not be bought at this time.

On December the twenty-fifth the yearly Christmas holiday arrived, but there were no celebrations. This disturbed Molly. That night with Jacob, Willy, and young George sitting quietly on the floor beside the big bed, she opened the Holy Bible. And by the light of a flickering candle, she read the story of the Christ Child to her sons.

The following day Mother Nature dumped a heap of snow on southeast Texas. To Molly, the countryside resembled a wonderland. Yet, the beautiful sight escaped the eyes of the people. Problems with Mexico still remained. Hundreds of Texas settlers went hungry and shivered from the cold in their ill-constructed homes.

A sometime fatal disease, later diagnosed as diphtheria, struck the children of the land. Some did not survive. True, Molly did consider the deaths and suffering in the fight for Texas independence a tragedy. But she also knew the death of one's child supersedes all sorrows.

When Marion came one day to see if the Anderson family was well, he told Molly, "Another sickness, some people call pneumonia, is ravaging the entire country. It hits the young children as well as the old folks. Even Empresserio Austin, who brought the first settlers to Texas, died of this terrible disease."

However, around the first week in January, Jess Wheeler came by on his way home from the capitol. He told the family, "Two weeks ago on December 27, 1836, Sam Houston was inaugurated as the first president of our struggling Republic of Texas. Mirabeau Lamar, hero of the Battle of San Jacinto, was declared vice president. Molly, things will be better now. We even applied for annexation to the United States. They turned us down. But we'll just try again."

In spite of all the good news, problems yet remained. The matter of finances hovered over Houston.

"The war with Mexico all but emptied the Texas treasury of the small amount of revenue still existing," Jess told Molly one day. "Now all the people able to help are sending money to build up the treasury."

After Jess rode back to his home, Molly took the metal case from under her bed. She opened it and counted out four fifty-cent pieces. She said to Jacob, "I want you and Willy to take this to Sam Houston at the capitol in Columbus. It's a long way, but stop along the way if you see any farmers. You can camp by their place. You know we don't have much, but David always said we need to share whatever we have. So, here is four fifty-cent pieces to help do our share."

"Maw, some people who don't have money give cattle, horses, or even hogs to be sold in New Orleans and the money is put in the Texas treasury," Jacob told her.

"You know, we've got more pigs than we need," Molly said. "Let's catch four of the young pigs the old sow had in her last litter. We'll send them to the capitol."

Catching the young pigs turned out to be a tiresome job. Each time a pig was caught, the old sow started for Willy or Jacob in an attempt to rescue the pig. Finally, they did catch the four pigs and with Jacob or Willy holding them, Molly tied the two back legs together to prevent them from running away. Then they lifted the squealing pigs into the back of the wagon.

"Well, as Cassie always said, this ain't much, but ever little bit helps," Molly laughed and said as she wiped her hands on her apron and pushed her hair out of her eyes.

When Jacob and Willy left, Molly waved. She looked up at the sky and thought, I'm glad the wagon is still covered with canvas sheeting. It looks like a cold winter is settling in.

The weather did remain unusually cold. Molly seldom took

George with her. She feared he would come down with one of the winter sicknesses.

Ten days later Jacob and Willy came home. Immediately, Molly noticed Willy looked a little pale and had a persistent rasping cough.

"Willy, I believe you need to go see after George. I'll help Jacob finish the work," she said.

Willy did go to the house, but he did not even say hello to George. He slumped onto the big bed and closed his eyes. This frightened Molly when she came into the room. Her first thought was that he came down with one of the terrible diseases, the kind that almost wasted the entire country.

She covered him with quilts and bathed his face with cool water. Yet the high temperature never left his body. She sat by his side for seven long days and nights. Then one day she remembered how her father opened the windows when a boarder became ill. He once told her that fresh air is important when one is sick. She had no windows to open, but she took some chinking from the holes in the wall allowing fresh air to filter through.

She made clear broth from a beef they had butchered in the fall, and boiled wild onions and garlic to make a poultice from them to spread on Willy's chest. Slowly, the fever began to lessen. A few days later she heard Willy say, "Maw, I wish you wouldn't put that stuff on me. It stinks real bad." From that remark, she knew he would recover. That night she lay down beside him and slept peacefully until the dawn.

That bleak, cold winter of 1836–1837 proved to be one the Texans would never forget. It also affected the Indian tribes that had been driven north. They came in large numbers searching for buffalo or other game to prevent the starvation of their people. As they came, they raided farms of cattle and especially horses. They plundered homes looking for food and set fire to many dwellings. They killed ruthlessly, and even sometimes captured women and children, often carrying them away from their families.

Some men turned their homes into forts to fight the Indians. Perhaps that was the salvation of many of the people who rushed there to escape the murdering Indians seeking revenge on the white man who drove them from their lands.

"President Houston called in trusted volunteers of both Anglo-Americans and Texas-Mexicans to squash the Indian uprising," Jacob said when he returned from the Wheeler farm. "But he told them to stay away from Chief Bowl's Cherokee tribe in the Neches River valley."

"Well, I've always thought the Texan's desire for land unjustly forced the Indians from their homes. But I don't think they should be allowed to kill and torture people, especially the little children." Molly said no more.

She made no effort to run from her home. She reasoned that the mixed tribe of Cherokee and Caddo Indians were their friends and now Running Wolf was like her own son. Even so, she kept the shotgun near her and demanded that Jacob take the rifle wherever he and Willy went. Often the sound of howling wolves interrupted her sleep at night, and she trembled with fright as she wondered if the sound could be that of the Indian war whoop.

Finally, the winter subsided and slow gentle rains came. Soon wildflowers and green grass began to appear, bringing hope of a good fall harvest.

Molly and her sons planted the corn seed and cleared the cotton ground of weeds and brush in preparation for a crop. The corn seeds sprouted and were out of the ground. They began to show signs of tasselling when suddenly the rains ceased. Before long the stalks were bare of plump ears of corn, producing only short nubbins that contained little or no food substance for man or beast.

Only once or twice, a mass of billowy clouds dropped a few showers of rain, then quickly vanished.

"Maw, we won't have a good crop of cotton this year," Jacob said when they walked over the land. "Just look how the bolls are shriveling before they open. See, the small bolls that did open have only knotty burrs."

"I know, my son. Still, we will have some cotton to pick and take to the gin," Molly replied. "But first we must gather the puny nubbins of corn. Then you and Willy can cut the stalks; they'll make good fodder for the animals during the cold winter. Do that while I pound the best ears on the big stone so we'll have corn pone." She didn't say, but she knew there could be no wheat flour for bread.

They did pick the cotton. But when they took it to the gin, it did not make a standard bale after the seeds and hulls were separated from the cotton. Molly felt discouraged. She wished for windows and puncheon floors for the cabin. Again, she knew she would have to wait. Furthermore, those were merely selfish wishes compared to salt or brandy for the winter sickness.

"We must be patient, rains will come. Crops will be better next year," she continually told her sons.

Nevertheless, her Texas home seemed to be crumbling around her. She heard rumors that Santa Anna failed to comply with the Velasco treaty, or to honor the Rio Grande River as the Texas border.

"Maw, there's talk that Houston spent all the money in the treasury, and now he is trying to borrow money from rich people. Is that true?" Jacob asked.

"I don't believe that to be true," Molly answered. "Only last week Jess Wheeler told me that Congress passed a law that people have to pay a tariff on goods from other countries. Now we have to pay a tax on our property. Even men have to pay a tax to vote."

Talks like those caused her to doubt her wisdom of staying in Texas. One day she said, "First, the rains stop coming and now the government is in trouble, always short of money. Maybe we should just pack up and go to Virginia to live with Grandpa Anderson."

Neither Jacob nor Willy said anything. They looked at each other, turned, and walked out.

"Well, I guess that tells me they do not want to leave Texas. Come to think of it, I really don't want to leave either. I just get lonesome sometimes for David and little John."

In late December, Marion brought Molly a recent issue of the *Telegraph and Texas Register* newspaper. As she scanned the paper, one article attracted her attention. She read: *Any person owning one labor of land on March 2, 1836, when Texas became a republic is now eligible to receive 4,605 acres of land, known as a First Class Headright.*

"My father and me will be accepting this offer," Marion said. "I don't expect to go back to my land on Little River because of the Indian raids."

Hearing this, Molly's eyes sparkled with delight. Now she could satisfy her anger against the empresserio system that to her actually spelled "swindle." She could have land equal to that the Empresserio Robertson sold David that Empresserio Austin had sold earlier to another man. Her first impulse was to go to the Land Office and apply immediately. Thinking further, she decided that perhaps it would be prudent to wait until spring to deal with the land commissioner.

When Running Wolf came to see Willy he told Molly, "My father, he say acorns fall too soon from trees. No rain to grow nuts to feed animals. Bad winter ahead."

Molly, believing Running Wolf's father to be very wise, took George and gathered nuts to crack open in the cold winter months. Just as Running Wolf's father predicted, the winter of 1837 did equal that of the previous year. Even the grass that normally grew high was soon eaten to the ground by the thin, hungry deer that hovered together to keep warm. Coyotes lurked near the cabin at night as the dim, flickering light of the pale candle attracted them, and their mournful cries echoed in the wind.

That winter, Molly spent much of the cold days at the spinning wheel. She skillfully formed the cotton into balls. Then she placed them on the wheel that pulled them back and forth, finally twisting them into threads. At last, taking two or more threads she interlaced them at right angles forming the cloth from which she made winter underwear and shirts for her sons.

Once, she had enough cloth left to make a skirt for herself.

This sure is beautiful white cloth, she thought. However, when she ran her fingers over the soft, white material, she changed her mind. I can't wear this, it would show dirt when I pick cotton or slop the old sow and her pigs. She neatly folded the cloth and stored it in the trunk. When the wild blackberries ripened she would boil the bright red berries with the white cotton cloth and it would become a mingled crimson color that did not show any soil.

By the middle of March the disagreeable icy days were almost forgotten. The warm south winds from the Gulf of Mexico gave promise of spring. The persimmon, dogwood, and redbud trees showed signs of buds popping out everywhere.

That year, April showers came early, watering the dry thirsty land. Then the wild rye grass became a shiny, pale green creating a badly needed supply of tender grazing for cattle and wild animals.

Often Molly and George roamed over the land searching for Lamb's Quarter greens. Once they saw a mother bear lying under a tree. She was playfully slapping her two young cubs as they climbed atop her. At first Molly started to grab George and run; instead she whispered, "Shush! Shush! Let's not scare the mother bear and frighten the babies."

So, holding George's arm, they silently sneaked down the path, hoping the mother bear did not see them or smell their human scent.

The forest seemed to come alive with deer and young spotted fawns running back and forth to the does. Cottontail rabbits, squirrels, raccoons, and gray fox feasted on the bounties of the welcomed spring. Once again the bubbling flow of Cow Creek energetically ran south to join the Brazos River.

One morning just before dawn, a strange sound, like the cry of an injured child, awoke the family. Suddenly, the bull began to bellow and snort. Pancho and Peppy whinnied, reared their front feet, and repeatedly pawed at an unknown object. Molly and Jacob grabbed their guns. They opened the canvas door. In the light of a full moon Willy yelled, "Look! That's a panther! He's going to kill our baby calf!"

Willy proved to be right. A full-grown black mountain lion, commonly called a panther, was about to grab the young calf.

"Jacob, we must do something quick. I've heard a panther will kill a human if they smell blood," Molly called out.

That was when she pulled the trigger, hoping she would not hit a cow or a horse. Fortunately, she did miss the farm animals, but she only slightly wounded the panther, making him even more vicious.

At that, Jacob edged a little closer. He waited until the panther made another run around the cow pen. Holding the gun firmly, he carefully aimed and pulled the trigger. The beautiful, yet dangerous, animal took a few steps, roared, and fell to the ground.

"David said panthers mate in the spring. So, Willy, you stay with George. Jacob and me'll ride over the land and look for signs of another panther," Molly told Willy.

Having found no signs of a mate of the panther, the task of skinning the big cat began. Long into the late afternoon, they pulled the skin onto a level spot under a tree and weighted it down with large rocks.

"Boys, what a nice, warm rug this will be on our sod floor," Molly said.

Gentle, refreshing rains fell in the spring of 1838, as if they came to compensate for the drought and cold winter of 1837. Bright sunshine, yet not too hot, seemed to radiate over the whole of the Republic of Texas.

In the fall, Molly and her sons harvested a good crop of corn and cotton. She did not go to the Groce gin, but she sent Jacob and Willy with a wagon filled with soft, white cotton to be ginned, baled, and sent to New Orleans.

She watched until the boys in the wagon were out of sight. She smiled and went about her chores. She pounded enough corn on the big stone to make corn pone for the winter. Still, as she worked, the thought of owning more land never left her mind.

Jacob and Willy, to be sure, in the future, will find a wife and leave home, she thought. *Later, George will follow. I want to give them land of their own, a place to raise a family. There is no better time than now to claim the land offered me in that new law.*

Already it was the first week in November, so she began to prepare to go to the Land Office.

"I've been thinking about getting more land for a year," Molly said when Jacob and Willy returned from the cotton gin. "Well, while y'all were gone, I made up my mind to do just that. Tomorrow we're going to the new Land Office. I have everything ready. I even propped open the gate to the cow pen and scattered cornstalks so the animals will have fodder. Of course, the old sow and her pigs will be fine."

"Whoopee! Hooray!" Willy yelled and threw his hat in the air. "We're goin' to the Land Office."

"Willy, come on. Let's go check the wagon tongue and oil the axles. We want to be ready to go in the morning," Jacob said, laughing at Willy.

Early the following morning Jacob and Willy put the straw-filled mat and the deerskin rug in the wagon bed to use as sleeping pallets. Meanwhile, Molly securely placed the food she prepared for the journey in the back of the wagon, along with a gourd bucket of milk from the young heifer.

Finally, they dragged a huge oak log in front of the door to keep squirrels, skunks, and other varmints out of the house. After that the Andersons began their adventure to a new Land Office they had never seen.

Sitting on the spring-seat with George beside her, Molly drove the oxen. Riding ahead to open a trail were Jacob on Pancho and Willy on Peppy.

"Maw, Marion told me the Land Office is east of the Brazos River at a village called Bucksnort. We'll have to cross the river like we did when we first came to Viesca," Jacob said.

"We've got plenty of time. Let's go by the Wheeler place," Molly suggested.

But when they arrived at the Wheeler place, they could see that the house stood empty and the livestock were gone.

"Marion told me they were going to apply for more land, but he didn't say they were leaving the Gibbon Valley," Molly said. "I'm disappointed, because I wanted to visit with Ertha. And I thought maybe I could trade some cotton to Mrs. Wheeler for a couple of hens and a rooster."

That night they camped by the empty house and the next morning started north. Just before sundown they reached the west bank of the Brazos River and camped for the night.

Molly seemed tired, but she could not fall asleep. Her mind went back to the time the family camped at the same location, almost four years before, with hopes of a happy life. *Now I feel so old and haggard. But most of all, I am lonely for David and little John. Sure, I am grateful for my two older boys and one who will soon be four years of age, but he will never see his father. I must allow each one to live his own life, but I, also, must teach them to be honest and happy.* After a while she fell asleep.

The next morning Jacob and Willy rode slowly in front of the wagon as Molly urged the oxen across the clear water to the east. There they turned south on a well-traveled road following the bends of the river perhaps some twelve or more miles where the road went east. Sometime around midafternoon, they spotted a knoll, void of trees, and the recently elected township of Bucksnort.

In the center of the hill stood a trading post built with pine logs that yet emitted the smell of rosin as it oozed from the logs. This proved to be the home of Jericho Springer, owner of the trading post, and his young Mexican wife, Ramona.

"Maw, where do the people live?" Willy asked. "I don't see any houses."

"I don't see houses. But look around. See all those burned-out campfires and wagon tracks? I think the people just camped there until they received their grants to buy land."

A hitching post where riders tied their horses ran the full length of the trading post. Flies and gnats swarmed around the horse excretion that accumulated as riders stopped to talk or to buy whiskey or other liquors that Jericho sold.

Molly's first impulse was to enter the door of the trading post and to leisurely walk through the store and look at every item. However, she knew she came only to apply for land. So, holding George's hand, she walked to the foot of the hill, followed by Jacob and Willy.

Waving peacefully atop a log building she saw, for the first time, the new red, white, and blue Texas flag. The lone star in the center represented the Republic of Texas. She paused, looked up, and tears of joy and gratitude trickled down her cheek. She wiped her eyes, pretending to remove dust so her sons could not see her cry. She looked the other way, turned, and walked ahead. A few feet from the office they passed a small cabin.

"Oh! This may be the home of the land commissioner. Maybe I can meet his wife," Molly said.

She walked ahead and calmly opened the Land Office door. Unlike the office at Viesca she saw no Mexican officials—only one person, the commissioner. He introduced himself.

"Howdy! I'm Calvin Hill. Born in Kentucky. But, now a citizen of the great Republic of Texas."

"I'm Molly Anderson, a widow. These are my three sons, Jacob, Willy, and George," she said as he shook her hand. "I own a labor of land west of the Brazos River where we farm. Not long ago I read in a newspaper that a new law was passed. It said early settlers could get more land. Sir, is that true?"

"Yes, Ma'am, that article is correct. People west of the Brazos River are moving east to escape Indian raids."

Quickly, without answering, she opened the metal case. She handed him the document to inspect.

"Mrs. Anderson, this proves you lived in Texas on March 3, 1836, when Texas declared independence from Mexico. If you would like to be seated here on this bench, I will explain to you. Under the new law, instead of leagues, the land is surveyed in sections. That is 640 acres. According to the law and these papers, you are entitled to 4,605 acres of land. That is, if you give back the 171.1 acres where you now live. But, if you want to stay on the labor, those acres will be deducted from the new grant."

"I've never thought of moving to another place. You see, that is our home," Molly answered.

"You don't have to move and live on the new grant. Still, you might be interested to know there's talk of building a public school near these grants," Hill answered.

"Mr. Hill, I want my sons to go to school," Molly answered without further questions. "I've taught them reading, spelling, writing, even arithmetic. Still, I know I've neglected their learning. I want you to fill out the papers for us to move east of the Brazos River."

Hill made no comments. He filled out a certificate awarding Molly Anderson a First Class Headright grant of 4,605 acres of Texas land. He signed the document and gave Molly a copy. "When these papers are received at the General Land Office in Columbus, the capitol, a title, called a patent, will declare you owner of this land. Then, probably in two or three weeks, a surveyor will survey the land."

After that, he drew a map showing her the location of the grant. Hill handed it to Molly and said, "This land is about thirty miles east and south of here. There is a stream called Walnut Creek running all the way through the grant, dividing it in half. Perhaps by this, you will find your land."

"Mr. Hill, I want to thank you for your help. My husband was killed right after we got to Texas. Then my little baby died from one of those terrible sicknesses. Now, I feel like things will be better," she said as she detected a glimpse of deep sympathy in his emerald-green eyes.

"Did you know Jim Mason?" Willy asked.

"Yes," he replied, "I knew Jim even before the fighting. I'm sorry he was one of the brave men killed at the Alamo. He died a hero. I'll always remember him and the others who died that terrible day."

"Miss Molly," he said as he shook her hand, "I see you are a wise women. I wish you well. Perhaps we can meet again."

"Goodbye, Mr. Hill," she smiled and said. She walked out the door. At last, she admitted to herself, I am proud to be a woman— a Texas woman.

For reasons unknown to her, the steps now seemed lighter as she walked up the hill to the trading post. Four years had now passed since she had entered a mercantile store, except the place of Ramon and Celita Gonzales.

The door to the trading post was open. They went in. Barrels of sugar, coffee, salt, and wheat flour were neatly stacked along the wall. The name of each product had been handwritten on the barrel. The sight of wheat flour tempted Molly. It had been three years since she used the last morsel they brought from Tennessee. She thought, George probably does not even remember the taste of wheat flour.

Jacob, having transported supplies from Brazaria and Goliad during the fighting, wanted to show off his knowledge to Willy. He explained the cost of each thing as they went from item to item. George cared nothing about the cost, but he followed behind.

The thing that attracted the boys most were the four pairs of boots, tied together, hanging on the wall.

"Maw, come see these boots," Willy called out.

At first she did not answer. She wanted to buy them shoes. Since they had never worn boots, she did not believe it would be wise to buy them. However, as Jacob tried on a pair, he said, "Maw, see. They almost reach my knees. They'll protect my legs from briars and thorny brush."

Willy tried on a pair, and Molly noticed they were rather large on him. "Maw, you told me last week I'm growin' real fast," he said. "I think I need this pair. I'll just stuff cotton in the toes."

After that remark she could not refuse. She allowed them to wear the boots. Molly saw George laughing when both boys strutted around in their brand-new boots. She thought, he must be a bit resentful. His shoes are those I made from the deerskin I tanned.

"Mr. Springer does not have boots for little boys your size," she told George. "Maybe by the time we move to the new place, he will have some."

"Mrs. Anderson, I can get your young son a pair of high-top shoes," Springer told her. "I'm goin' to San Antonio soon. The bootmaker there also makes shoes."

"Thank you, my son really needs shoes," Molly said. About that time she remembered the twinkle in Calvin Hill's eyes and added, "Oh! Can you get me a pair of ladies' shoes?"

Instantly, she felt remorseful. *How do I dare to buy such a frivolous thing? I can make do with these shoes I am wearing until we harvest another crop.*

Later in the day she purchased a half-barrel of wheat flour, sugar, and coffee. Furthermore, she could not resist buying each one an apple from a barrel in the middle of the room that smelled of apples from Tennessee.

Near dusk, Jacob and Willy took the harness off the oxen and let them graze on the hillside. Later, Jericho Springer and pretty Ramona came to the wagon.

"Ramona and me are happy you came here. She doesn't see many ladies, mainly just cattle drovers that stop by. But lately, people wanting to settle east of the river come to the Land Office. Of course, some go on to other places." Jericho with his rough laughter and kind words impressed Molly. Although Ramona did not speak English, she smiled and nodded her head as she held George in her arms until he fell asleep.

The Andersons returned to their home on peaceful Cow Creek and prepared to move east of the Brazos River.

The early days of December were warm and sunny. However, the nights became cold and, often, morning frost was seen covering the ground. Those were busy days. They made wooden slatted crates to cage the old sow and her six pigs. Jacob and Willy carefully checked the wagon to be sure the wheels were steady. On and on, it seemed chores did not cease.

"I do not know if wild hogs roam the land east of the Brazos River," Molly said. "Maybe it would be wise if we took a boar along to breed the old sow."

They found a herd of swine down on Cow Creek valley. When Jacob attempted to catch one, the hogs all fled in different directions. That is, except one big old boar that stood his ground. Even Ring and Rover backed away. Jacob threw a rope to lasso the squealing boar. Right then the animal turned and started toward Molly, with the tusk of his snout protruding. Quickly, she ran to Jacob, who was astride Pancho. She grabbed his outstretched hand and with one big leap landed behind Jacob.

"On second thought—" Molly stopped to laugh, then she said, "I think I'll forget about taking a boar to our new land."

She hoped to be on the new grant before Christmas. But unfortunately, a norther blew in and powerful winds swept through. She knew that it would be difficult to drive the cattle, so she decided to wait another day to leave Cow Creek.

The following morning, on Christmas Eve, Running Wolf came to see Willy and George, his "pale-eyed" friend. At sundown he started to leave.

"Running Wolf, stay here with Willy tonight," Molly said. "We will tell you how white people celebrate the time we call Christmas."

That night they all sat side by side on the bearskin rug. By the light of a flickering candle, she opened the Holy Bible and read the story of the Christ Child. Afterward, with signs and simple words, Jacob and Willy attempted to tell Running Wolf the meaning of the story. Surprisingly, he seemed to grasp the story of Christmas.

When Molly opened the canvas door the next morning they saw the sun rising above the frosty ground and heard the mooing of penned-in cattle echoing down Cow Creek. At once Jacob, Willy, and Running Wolf ran to drive the cattle to drink from the creek.

"Now, don't wander in the forest too long. I have a surprise for everyone," Molly called to them.

To be sure, they wasted no time in doing their chores. Hurriedly, they raced back to the cabin. They stood in a semicircle watching Molly make Christmas candy. She measured the exact amount of sugar into a cast-iron pot and poured twice that amount of water into the pot. At the last she put in the most important ingredient of all, a tiny bit of dried mint she saved from the past summer. She constantly stirred the concoction until it thickened. Then she spread it out to harden. At the last, she showed the boys how to take a portion of the candy, pull it back and forth making it into a rope that almost reached the ceiling. Shrill, boyish laugher filled the room as they all rubbed sticky fingers on each other. To Molly, that was a happy Christmas Day.

She emptied some of the coffee into a small basket and filled a cotton cloth with the sugar candy. She handed them to Running Wolf and smiling said, "God bless you, my son."

"I go tell family white people laugh and play on day called Christmas," Running Wolf said.

Prior to this time he feared white people. Now he knew all white people are not the same. He quickly ran toward the teepee of the mixed tribe of Cherokee and Caddo Indians and soon vanished among the oak, hickory, and pecan trees.

"Maw, if we leave Cow Creek, I will miss Running Wolf. Do you think we could stay here?" Willy asked.

"Willy, we will all miss Running Wolf, even George. But before long, he can visit us in our new home," Molly said in an effort to console him.

Darkness still lingered over the land the next morning when the Andersons were awake and busy. They were anxious to begin the journey to a new land, leaving Cow Creek behind. Jacob and Willy prepared to go drive the cattle into the pen and yoke the oxen. They opened the canvas door. There stood Running Wolf holding a wooden bowl of freshly made pemmican his family sent as a gesture of goodwill to their white friends.

He watched as they loaded the big bed, trunks, and household items into the wagon. However, he asked to help when they anchored the wooden crate with the old sow in it onto the sled tied behind the wagon.

By the time the sow was safe in her cage, the sun was directly overhead. That led them to know it was time to eat the noon meal. They all squatted down in a circle and ate the delicious pemmican Running Wolf brought.

"My people say you like it?" Running Wolf proudly asked.

"Say to your people, we like it," Willy replied.

Saying goodbye again to Running Wolf, they began the almost fifty miles of travel to the land they had never seen. Molly drove the wagon and George sat by her holding his constant companion, a raccoon he called "Coony."

Willy, with Ring and Rover, followed behind to keep the little herd of cattle together. There were the bull, two older cows, one young heifer, one yearling bull, and two calves.

Jacob, blazing the trail, rode ahead. Sometime near sundown, he turned toward the Wheeler place where they prepared to spend the night. After allowing the cattle to drink from Gibbon Creek, with the help of Ring and Rover, Willy drove the cattle into the corral where they bedded down. As the oxen grazed, the family carried water to the caged swine.

The morning light was barely visible when the family was up and on the way to the one possible place where they could cross the big Brazos River. That was the shoal above the ten-foot waterfalls.

But when they arrived there, due to recent rains, the river now was a raging torrent. Nevertheless, Molly insisted, "We must cross before the water becomes more dangerous. Jacob, ride Pancho ahead. Do you remember how your papa did when we crossed the Trinity River? Do like he did so you can find a safe place to cross."

As he rode here and there in different directions, once Pancho had to swim through the water. Finally, he found a shallow place he believed to be safe. He rode Pancho close behind Old Blu, urging him on. At one point the water almost covered the squealing sow and her pigs, yet Molly managed to drive the oxen through the rampaging water.

When, at last, they reached the east bank of the river, Jacob rode back to help Willy get the cattle across. He was holding the youngest calf in his arms while Ring and Rover dog-paddled behind the cattle, driving them forward.

Molly knew, after safely reaching the east bank, that the oxen should rest. So she insisted they remain near the crossing a short time. But the roar of the river and the sound of floating logs lashing toward the bank disturbed the frightened cattle and especially, the caged swine. So they headed south again.

"I had hoped to get to Bucksnort before dark, but we wasted a lot of time crossing the river," Molly said.

Along about midafternoon only Ring and Rover seemed anxious to keep moving. They nipped at the bull's hind legs to force him on—still the animal made no effort to move faster. Suddenly, the sky became overcast, and a dark cloud covered the northern skyline.

"A norther is coming," Molly called to the boys. "We must find a place to stop."

She drove the oxen until she saw a high rock ledge of a butting hilltop and drove the wagon to the base of the rock to get protection from the icy cold windstorm.

"Willy, Jacob. Come over here," Molly yelled.

Jacob ran to help and they stripped the harness off the oxen and slapped them on the rump, and the animals shrewdly plodded to a clump of brush under the ledge. Jacob threw a leather lariat onto the old sow's head and led her into a cave-like indentation under the ledge. That was when Willy turned the pigs out and yelled, "Ring! Rover! Go run the pigs into the cave with the sow." Not waiting for a second command, the dogs nipped the butt of the pigs, and immediately, they ran squealing into the cave with the sow.

That night Jacob and Molly took turns staying with the cattle to calm them so they would not stampede. Even Pancho and Peppy turned their tails to the north.

By morning the wind appeared calm, but the sky remained

cloudy. The warm breath rose like smoke as it left the nostrils of the animals. Still, Molly believed they should go on. Sometime around noon, they reached the village of Bucksnort.

One family was already in the Trading Post and Jericho Springer welcomed the Andersons. The people all stood around with their backs to the roaring fire, talking about their new land. That is, except Ramona, who held little George in her lap.

"Molly, you stay by the fire. There is plenty of men to help Jacob and Willy bed down the animals. In fact, this man here will be your neighbor. Molly Anderson, meet Oran Taylor," Jericho said. At that, Jericho, Oran Taylor, Jacob, and Willy walked out the door. They drove the cattle into a round-like corral. Then they released the sow and pigs from the cages and herded them into a pen with other swine.

True to his word, Jericho brought two pairs of shoes from San Antonio. A pair of high-top shoes for George and a pair of ladies shoes, laced far above the ankles, for Molly. She reached inside the metal case and handed Jericho a certificate from the sale of the cotton.

"Molly, I can't accept this for only two pairs of shoes," he said as he handed it back to her. "Mostly, people just give me a calf or yearling, hogs, or animals skins they tan. Sometimes they bring in corn or other produce in exchange for what I sell. I'll make a trade with you. I'll give you the shoes and throw in three hens and a rooster for three suckling pigs, the ones you have out there with the sow."

"I'll make that trade," Molly chuckled and said, "I've been wanting some hens; now I'll have them. You can have the pigs."

The cold wind began to calm, so Molly left George with Ramona and walked down to the Land Office. However, only the surveyor was there.

"I'm Molly Anderson. I received a First Class Headright of land a while back. Do you know if the land was surveyed?" Molly asked.

"Yes, Mrs. Anderson, we surveyed the land and marked the

corner boundaries of your claim. Hill said to tell you he is sorry to not be here when you come. He went to the capitol for the inauguration of the new president, Mairabeau Lamar. We kinda hated to see Sam Houston go. But, our constitution says a president can only serve two years."

"Thank you, sir, goodbye," she said and walked out. Yet, she felt good all over. *Now I am sure a school will be built. Furthermore, this president may persuade the United States to make Texas a part of that great Union.*

Late in the evening Oran Taylor and his wife, Lacy, came to the wagon to visit with Molly.

"We can not get a Headright on our land. You see, we haven't been in Texas very long. But my sons and I have already built a house on our land. We are on our way now to live there," Oran said. Then he added, "By the way, Springer said your land will not be far from ours. Why don't we form a train and travel together the remaining miles?"

When they came to the Taylor land, Molly saw a new two-room log house with a side room on the back that formed a kitchen. But what surprised her most were two fireplaces. Although the Taylors asked the family to camp near their house, Molly said, "Thank you. But we are anxious to find our land. Maybe we will see each other again." Waving goodbye, the family started toward their First Class Headright land.

They entered a thicket of walnut, post oak, hickory, and live oak trees, causing Molly not to be sure which direction to drive the oxen, until Jacob said, "Maw, keep going south. We'll come to a creek—that way we can tell what direction to go."

Soon they were in the Walnut Creek valley. That night they camped by a stream that was bigger and deeper than Cow Creek. Still, the water looked very clear. Willy rounded up the cattle under some tall trees and left Ring and Rover to guard them. They tied the old sow to a tree, but they left the three remaining pigs to run free and root and wallow in the puddles of water. Even Ole Blu and Bill were not hobbled.

Jacob built a big fire and, twice during the night, Molly rekindled it as she could not sleep. At times she had felt safe and content at Cow Creek. Now she was not sure she had made the right decision to move to this place. Over and over, doubts came through her mind.

Can we build another house? Perhaps, one like the cabin in Cow Creek. But never one like the Taylor house. Can we clear the land before planting time? Maybe a small amount, but never enough for a good crop. On and on the questions went through her mind until finally she fell asleep. She only awoke when she heard George say, "Maw, wake up. I can't find Coony. Will you help me look for him?"

Dear young George is such a pleasure. Why do I fret over things like I do? Molly said to herself.

As usually occurs after Texas northers, that day remained clear and calm. It seemed like a perfect time to find the proper location for their new home. Jacob rode Pancho with George in front of him in the saddle. Willy rode Peppy.

"No, I will not ride with either of you," Molly said as she put the bridle on Ole Blu. She threw a deerskin rug on his back. Then she put one foot in Jacob's outstretched hand. He slightly boosted her as she slung the other foot over Ole Blu.

"Jacob, for a second I thought you were going to throw me over Ole Blu. But I'm fixed now. Let's go look over the land," she laughed and said as she spurred Ole Blu into motion.

No trails were visible among the low-lying brush and trees, so they decided to follow the stream.

"Maw! Jacob! Look back! Bill is following us," Willy yelled. Sure enough, not far behind, came Bill faithfully plodding behind his companion, Ole Blu.

"I don't believe we will find a location for our house this way. We can not even see our way ahead," Jacob said.

"You are right," Molly said, "maybe we should just go back to where we are camped."

Retracing their steps, they returned to the wagon on the crest of a hill above Walnut Creek. Molly looked down on the transparent flowing water. Turning around, she saw before her a wide expanse of prairie lands covered with wild grasses. Silently, she gazed at the beauty around her.

"Maw, I'm hungry," George called to her.

"Yes, I think it's time to eat," Molly, shaking her head to clear her thoughts, answered.

They spent that afternoon clearing a spot on which to build a cabin. Molly, once more, began to measure an approximate twelve-by-twelve-square-foot area for the house.

"Why can't we build our home like the Taylor house?" Willy asked. "Then Jacob and me won't have to sleep on the mat."

"Don't you remember how hard we worked to cut and raise the logs of our Cow Creek house, even with the help of Jim and Marion. No, for now we'll just build one room. Then maybe some day we can build on," Molly told the boys.

"Maw, which trees do you think we should cut for the house?" Jacob asked.

"I've been thinking I would like to have those pretty pine trees growing across the creek," Molly said. "They have such a sweet smell."

"Yes, they are pretty. But, it would be real hard to get them across the creek," Jacob said.

"You are right," Molly grinned and answered. "I don't believe it would be wise to try. We'll use some of those tall sturdy walnut trees growing close by."

By daybreak the next morning, Jacob built a fire to take the chill off the air as clouds began to drift in from the Gulf of Mexico.

"Look! I think I see a wagon comin' up the hill," Willy said. "Wait, I think I see another one not far behind."

"Run. Get the guns!" Molly called to Jacob. "Willy, go stay with George in the wagon. Now don't act as if you are afraid!"

"Maw, can't you see?" laughing, Jacob said, "that's the Wheeler wagon and mule team. The other one is our neighbors, the Taylors, who live in the new house we passed."

"Well, maybe I don't see too good," Molly calmly said.

Ertha and her two children were with Marion. Oran Taylor, his twin sons, Eli and Elias, and the young son, Matt, were following behind the Wheeler wagon.

Without further talk, work began on the Anderson house. Evidently Oran Taylor knew how to construct a house.

"I helped many people build houses in Alabama," he said. "Of course, that was before we came to Texas."

"Mr. Taylor, we can do with a twelve-by-twelve-foot cabin. Like the one we had at Cow Creek," Molly told Taylor.

"Oh! No, Molly," Marion protested, "we might as well put up a two-room house. We've got plenty of help. Besides, two more riders are coming up the hill."

Bob Brewer, whose land adjoined Molly on the east, and Benito Mendez, a brother to Brewer's wife, galloped up the hill. They had heard of the plan to build the Andersons a house at the Springer Trading Post, and they came to help.

The creak of falling trees and the steady forceful whir of the broadax continually sounded down Walnut Creek. Taylor brought a ripsaw to split the logs for a floor and to cut the ceiling joists. Finally, he split logs to make a door. But Benito Mandez made the hinges from rawhide so the door would swing open.

"See how the smoke is rising from the rock fireplace. Watch how it's settling to the ground," Marion said. "That's a sure sign another Texas norther is on its way. But I believe we can make it home before it hits," Marion said when the work was completed.

Well-wishes and handshakes were exchanged as the people prepared to leave. Then, tipping his hat, Benito shouted, "Adios, señora. Adios, amigos. We hope to see you again."

Molly turned as if she might be walking away. She did not want her sons to see the tears trickling down her cheeks. They were tears of gratitude, humility, and love for this strange breed of people. People that fought, fell to the ground, brushed off the dust, and started again. They were people who suffered and endured the pain. Molly truly knew these were unique people with an unwavering faith in their God, and a never-ending love for mankind, regardless of who they might be.

In 1839, the latter part of January proved to be one of those times when blasting, cold winds never ceased blowing. Still, Molly and her sons worked at clearing land for the spring planting. The work seemed endless. A shelter must be made for the old sow, since she would soon have another litter of pigs. Certainly, a rail fence needed to be built around the cow pen. On and on, the need never ceased. Yet, no day went by without Molly sweeping the prized split-log floor with willow boughs. Realizing it would be some time before she could buy window glass, she stretched canvas, used as a door at Cow Creek, over the windows to keep out the cold wind.

Those were busy days. Yet no person complained. They were seeing a dream fulfilled right before their eyes.

About the middle of February, the first signs of spring appeared. Cottontail rabbits hopped around everywhere. When Molly saw them she thought, *tomorrow I'll show George their burrow. I'm sure at least six little bunnies, without hair and unopened eyes, are lying in there.*

"Maw, George. Come here, look down at the creek," Willy called out one morning. Majestically wading in the water were two large, rather tall stork. They were dipping their long stout bills into the water attempting to catch unsuspecting minnows. Standing in awe, the family watched the maneuvers of the stork. They knew that tomorrow the birds would probably fly north, declaring spring to be on the way. Then busy days of farming would surely follow.

One morning Molly hastily began to prepare their noon meal before helping Jacob and Willy clear more land for the spring planting. However, she paused and turned her head to one side when she thought she heard a knock on the door. "Oh! Perhaps it's only one of the hounds scratching his belly," she said. Then when it sounded again she thought, maybe Ertha is bringing her children to play with George. At that she quickly opened the door. There stood Calvin Hill, tall and straight with his big, black hat in his hand.

"Good morning, Molly Anderson," he said in his slow, lengthy drawl, "I happened to be riding by. I stopped to see how you and your sons are doing. But from what I see, you are doing well. Could you spare me a cup of coffee?"

"Oh! Good morning, Mr. Hill," smoothing her hair and pushing it to the back, Molly said, "I am pleased to see you. Come in and I'll warm the coffee. My sons and I are real lucky. People came and built our house. Of course, we knew the Wheelers in Tennessee. But, I hardly knew the others. When Marion left he told me you are the one who told the people we needed help. Come on, sit over here and drink some coffee." Smiling, she moved the chair for him to sit on. "We sure do thank you for that. We could never have built a house like this without the help of friends."

Taking George with them, they walked toward Walnut Creek until they found the meager head of cattle.

"Molly, these are good cattle. But, you need another bull and more cows—ones not out of these cows," Hill said, walking among the cows and feeling their udders and hind legs. "In the fall when you finish harvesting, I'll be glad to help Jacob and Willy find some longhorn cattle. Of course, that is, if you would like me to."

"Thank you. I'll ask my sons about this," she answered.

"This has been a pleasant day. Can I come to see you again?" he asked, mounting his horse to ride off.

"Calvin, I would like you to come any time," Molly said without hesitation as she gently touched his hand.

She tried to look poised and graceful when she answered Calvin. Instead, she wanted to dance and sing and tell the whole world she was happy.

Lying awake that night she thought, *this man is like David. So kind, honest, and always thinking of others.* Suddenly, she sat straight up in the bed. She thought, *am I trying to replace David in my life with another man?*

She tossed and turned until she finally came to a conclusion. *These are two separate and different men. I must think of them as such! The memory of the fulfilling years I spent with David will remain and sustain me. Still, I believe I can learn to accept the love of another person and not feel guilty.* At last she fell asleep.

CHAPTER 6

Planting time in the spring of 1839 seemed to come early to Molly and her sons. They had managed to clear land for the corn crop, but much of the cotton land still remained covered with stumps, rocks, and even some tall trees. In order to plant a cotton crop, they knew they must finish that job. Otherwise, there would be no money with which to buy the longhorn cattle Molly wanted.

Each day, from the light of early morning to the setting of the sun, they labored at clearing the land. Jacob and Willy cut down the trees. They wrapped a chain around the tree trunk, then to the saddle horn on Pancho. That way, they could drag the felled trees into a heap and later cut them into fence posts for making a corral. The more crooked branches and the brush would be burned.

Many days Molly walked behind the yoked oxen, Bill and Ole Blu, with the reins around her shoulders, and her hands tightly clinched onto the plow handle. She drove the oxen from one end of the clearing to the other. Often the heavy plowshare hit big tree stumps that caused her to fall to the ground. However, some way she always managed to get up—to continue until the day ended.

By the middle of May the corn seeds they planted had germinated and pushed open the ground. Soon, a gentle spring rain fell. Now she knew the cotton would soon burst open with the tiny seeds yet visible.

One morning George saw Calvin Hill riding up and ran to meet him. "Hello, George," Calvin said. " I just came from the Wheeler farm. Look, Ertha sent your mama eight hen eggs."

Hearing Calvin's voice, Molly suddenly became aware of her appearance. She wished she had her new shoes and a clean apron on. "I must look like an old hag," she muttered to herself.

"Yesterday I heard an old hen clucking. I knew she was getting ready to set," Molly said as she accepted the eggs, "but I didn't know where I could get eggs for her to sit on. I simply must take George and ride Pancho over to thank Ertha for these."

Calvin ignored her rambling talk. He hoped she was only trying to hide her joy at seeing him. For the first time he believed she cared for him as much as he did her.

"Calvin, how are things with the government at the capitol? Has President Lamar opened any schools?" Molly asked.

"No schools have been built," he answered, "but Congress set aside lands to build primary schools and a smaller amount for at least two colleges."

"I'm real happy to hear that," she said, "but I believe we need schools now. There are too many children around here who can't read or write."

"I'm hoping that the schools will soon be built," Calvin said. "President Lamar is a writer and a poet. He understands that education is important. But the Congress is slow to pass new laws. It may be the people should open their own schools."

"Calvin, I believe you're right," shaking her head in approval Molly said. "We must begin soon."

"President Lamar is a good man," Calvin continued, "but he has no concern or compassion for the Indian tribes. I believe his greatest desire is to run them out of Texas. I can't agree with such actions. Sometimes I wish our beloved Republic would be annexed to the United States."

This unexpected outburst of anger surprised Molly. Still, she often felt the same way.

That afternoon they took George with them and, again, walked down the hill to Walnut Creek. They sat in the shade of an aged oak tree and watched George wading in the clear water. Molly's long black hair glistened in the sunlight, and she pushed it away from her tanned face with her callused hands.

"Molly, don't you see I love you?" Calvin asked as he reached for her hand. "I want you to marry me. I promise I will take care of you and your sons."

"Calvin, from the first time I saw you, I think I have loved you," she quietly said. "I would like to be near you all the time, but I can't give you an answer, not right now. Maybe we can talk about this when you come again."

Calvin said no more. He reached over and fondly kissed her on the cheek. She returned his passionate look, but only for one brief moment. She knew her heart would rule over the common sense in her mind. After Calvin went back to the Land Office, Molly kept busy. Yet, the feel of that one little kiss on her cheek never left her mind.

With little effort, that afternoon, Molly and George found an empty hen's nest in which to put the eggs Ertha had sent her.

"A baby chick will come from each egg, and by the time you start to school we will have lots of chicks," Molly explained to George. Then she asked, "Would you like to go to school with Willy? You can learn to read and write."

"Maw, Jacob and Willy can read and write now. They showed me how to write my name," he answered. "Besides, I don't want to leave Coony at home 'cause he would be lonesome."

She said no more. She realized school did not interest him at that time. She smiled and went about her work knowing he would attend school when classes began.

In July the weeds in the cotton and corn were pulled. Only then did Molly admit the crops were "laid by." On Sunday morning the house was filled with laughter and excitement since it would be the first time Molly dared to venture very far from the cabin on the hilltop. They were going to travel the ten miles to visit the Wheeler families.

"It's going to be good to see Ertha and the others," Molly told her sons. "Now Jacob, you and Willy be sure to put on those fresh-washed clothes and I'll see to George."

Jacob and Willy harnessed the oxen and hitched them to the

wagon. Molly rode on the spring-seat with Jacob driving. She let her bonnet fall to the back of her head as she thought bonnets always kept one from seeing all the beauty.

"You know, I've always thought that Sunday was created for us to enjoy things like friends," she said to no one especially, then added, "I wish President Lamar would build a schoolhouse close by. People could use it as a church. I believe Jess Wheeler would make a good preacher on Sunday mornings."

"Maw, don't forget, I told you I want to be a preacher," Willy said. "Maybe I could help Mr. Wheeler."

Hearing that remark, Molly felt remorseful. She had not encouraged Willy to fulfill his desire. Yet, she decided not to spoil the day, so they began singing songs her cherished friend, Cassie, taught her when she was a child. When Jacob joined in, she looked at him and smiled. She thought, *Jacob's voice is like David's since he has grown up. Why! He even looks and acts like David—so handsome and good.*

To be sure, the visit to the Wheelers was a joyful occasion. However, the news Marion told of the battle with the Cherokee Indians irritated Molly.

"On July the seventeenth, Texas soldiers surrounded the Cherokee Indians on the Neches River. During the fight Chief Bowls and his son were killed. Now President Lamar has ordered all Cherokees to leave Texas," Marion told them when he came home. "Houston always did right to the Indians. But Lamar feels different."

"The Indians were in Texas before the Anglos came. Why should they leave?" Molly vehemently stated. "Oh, some people say they are just savages, but I know better. I think our president is wrong."

Her angry outburst embarrassed her. "Perhaps I should not criticize the president," she quickly said, "for he is trying to do what he can."

Wisely, Mrs. Wheeler quickly changed the conversation to the subject of schools. "The settlers can get together and build a school.

We don't need to wait for the government to organize one. They have other things to do."

Not long after Mrs. Wheeler's suggestion, plans to form a school were made with great enthusiasm. By late fall, after the cotton harvest, they agreed to build a one-room school in the southwest corner of the Anderson land. This was a central location for the settlers in the new grants, and Marion Wheeler agreed to be the first schoolmaster.

When Calvin came to see Molly a few days later, he appeared as jovial and charming as usual. Yet somehow, Molly sensed something troubled him.

"You've not ridden all over your land. Would you like to do that?" he asked Molly. "I will show you the carvings on the big trees that mark the corners. I even brought along some dried beef for our dinner."

"Calvin, what a nice thing to do for me. But I don't think George would like to ride that far." Then she said, "Oh! Jacob, will you and Willy watch him while I'm gone?"

She did not wait for an answer from Jacob and Willy. She put on her new high-top shoes and untied the ever-present apron and threw it on the bed. She reached for her best bonnet. Then, on second thought, she tossed it beside the apron. She wanted to ride across the grassy prairie land with Calvin and let her hair blow in the wind!

George, excited to be alone with his brothers, chattered constantly. But Willy ignored him.

"Willy, what's wrong with you? Don't you see George just wants you to play with him? Are you mad at him?" Jacob asked.

"No, I'm not mad at George," Willy answered, "but I'm mad at Calvin Hill. He acts like he's our papa, always wanting to be with Maw. He talks like he belongs here. Well, he's not my papa. I don't want him to ever be. George is little. He can't remember Papa. So, I guess it's all right for him to like Calvin."

"We don't know Maw and Calvin Hill want to get married," trying to explain to Willy, Jacob said. "Maw just gets lonesome for

Papa and likes to talk to a man sometimes. She likes Calvin and I'm glad he likes her." Jacob paused, grinned, and then said, "When you're nearly eighteen, like I am, you'll understand why men want women to like them. It's like this. I want Era Taylor to like me and to go walking with me. But we don't want to get married."

However, after thinking about it, he was not fully convinced that the same feeling existed between Calvin and Maw.

Calvin and Molly went southwest, peacefully galloping side by side. They headed to the proposed school site. Pulling up on the reins, they stopped their horses and dismounted. As their horses grazed nearby, they sat quietly by the little stream, but Calvin did not renew the talk of marriage. Molly began to wonder why he acted so troubled.

"Calvin, is something bothering you?" she asked. "I would like to help if I can."

"Molly, I love you. That's why I want to tell you my story." He hesitated because he did not know how to begin. He pushed a twig back and forth in the dirt, then finally began to talk.

"I was a foolish young man when I came to Texas. I did not come to buy land. Nor, did I intend to stay here. I guess I just wanted adventure. Anyway, one day while following a herd of buffalo, I saw a tribe of Cherokee Indians north of here between the Neches and Angelina Rivers. Their way of living fascinated me."

Staring intently at the dried twig, he moved it from one spot to another as if he were an accomplished artist. He cleared his throat, kind of smiled, and continued. "They were friendly, so they welcomed me to the tribe. Molly, unless you live among the Cherokees you can't understand them. They have a straightforward, honest manner. Most of all, there is a great love of family." Again he sat silent, simply staring at no particular thing.

"Please, don't stop. I want to hear more," Molly said as she gently reached over and touched his shoulder.

"Well, I hadn't been with them long when I fell in love with a young girl," Calvin said. He now seemed to have regained his composure. "She was so like you with her coal-black hair and dark smiling eyes. Above all else, she possessed a feeling of warmth and love like you. We were husband and wife in the eyes of the Cherokees for about a year."

"You must have loved her very much. I see sadness in your eyes. What happened?" Molly asked.

Calvin did not answer. He rose to his feet and picked up a handful of rocks lying on the edge of the crystal-clear stream. Time after time, he threw one across the creek until they were gone. At that, he walked back and forth, saying nothing.

Then he looked at Molly, smiled, and sat down beside her. Clearing his throat he said, "Molly, I'm sorry. I didn't intend to make you sad." Then, once more, he began. "One day Laquana told me we were going to have a child. We were happy. Everything seemed to be all right until time for the child to be born. Laquana did not live through the birth. Neither did the child—a tiny son. I buried her, with our son, high on a pine-covered hilltop. That day I left the Cherokee village. I knew then I could never leave Texas."

Molly said nothing. She understood Calvin. She, also, could not leave Texas after the death of David and little John. Yet, she realized Calvin needed to talk to her to release the tension bottled inside his troubled mind.

"Calvin, you've never told me about your childhood. Tell me where your parents lived," she softly said.

"I grew up in Kentucky where my parents died when I was still a young lad. My uncle raised me and gave me an education. So I was able to get work with the Mexican officials when I left the Cherokees. Then when the war with Mexico began, I joined the Texas army. As you know, I still work for the government of our Republic."

Again, he rose to his feet. However, this time he picked up the very largest rock he could find. He threw it as far as he could. After a brief time, he casually turned and sat down by Molly.

"I supported Lamar in the election," he said, "but now he's stirred up trouble with the Cherokees, and the wise Chief Bowls and his son are dead."

He grasped Molly's hand, then reached over and kissed her.

"Forgive me, my dear, for telling you all this. I was a youth of twenty-one years. Now, I know I could never have endured the mental and physical strain of living with the Cherokees. But even now, memories of Laquana and our stillborn son are with me. Please believe the love I have for you is much stronger and more enduring."

Molly did not answer. She believed it was not the right time. She could see that Calvin had been hurt by the news of the defeat of the Cherokee tribe and the death of Chief Bowls. Instead, she tenderly held him in her arms as if he were her child. She, too, knew the anguish, the desire for revenge, and the terrible grief of losing loved ones. Only Calvin himself could conquer his grief and loss.

She smiled, as she now believed one could love the dead and the living. Yet, in a different way. She knew if Calvin sincerely loved her, in time he too could understand. Returning her smile, he reached over and kissed her again. They mounted their horses and simultaneously galloped to her home.

The hot days of the month of August came. The crops were "laid by," so they did most of the hard work early in the morning. Often in the late evening, they sat under a big live oak tree to enjoy the fresh breeze.

"George, do you hear that owl hootin' to his mate? I wonder where he's roosting," Jacob said.

When the hooting came nearer, Willy instantly ran into the brush and trees shouting, "Running Wolf!"

When he returned, Running Wolf walked beside him. Although the family was happy to see Running Wolf, they somehow sensed he brought sad news.

"Soldiers, they come. Say go. My father, he say we stay—gather corn, pumpkins. White soldiers say no. Cut down corn, pumpkin, burn teepees. We walk far away. Carry babies. I hide. Come see friends, say goodbye," Running Wolf told them in his broken English.

"Running Wolf, do not leave. Stay here with us. We will protect you," Molly begged him.

"I go help my people. Teach them white man talk and way. One day come see white friends." He waved. Holding Willy's hand, they ran into the woods.

Willy did not return for quite a while. Although Molly did not ask, she knew they renewed their vow to each other. When he did return, she said nothing. She stroked his curly hair and held him close as he sobbed for the loss of his dear friend.

In October the corn was ready to harvest. Even though they planted late, they made a good crop. After gathering all the matured corncobs, they cut and piled the stalks for fodder. Molly took some of the dried kernels and ground them on the big rock to make corn pone. As she worked she didn't see Calvin ride up, but George did.

"Maw, Uncle Calvin's here," he yelled.

"Who told you to call Mr. Hill 'uncle'?" Molly asked.

"Jacob did. 'Cause Willy won't let me call him Papa Calvin," George truthfully answered.

This embarrassed Molly, but Calvin roared with laugher.

"Molly, my love," he said, "I think young George is on my side. I hope now you will say 'yes' to being my wife."

Sitting under the big tree they talked about government affairs and the hope of the new school. Then the question came up about marriage.

"Calvin, I do love you with all my heart," she said, "and want to be your wife. But I believe we should wait a year. That will give me time to clear more land and get more cattle—the longhorn kind you spoke of. You see, I feel I must do this for my sons, on my own."

When Calvin rode off around dusk, Molly saw him happier than any time since the battle of the Cherokee Indians. She could tell he had put behind much of the anger and distrust inside his troubled mind. Not only Calvin, but she, too, felt a renewed closeness in the love of this appealing man who changed her life.

That fall, during the cotton harvest, even five-year-old George worked at picking the cotton. He followed Molly up and down the rows filling his short basket. At one time the wagon became so full the white fluffy cotton began to fall from the sideboards. Jacob and Willy climbed up and trampled it until they could put in more cotton.

This pleased Molly, yet she still wanted to clear more land. She continually told herself, *next year when I marry Calvin, my sons will have their own cotton crops.*

Jacob and Willy took the filled wagon to the gin. However, they did not go to Groces's gin. This time they went northwest to the new gin of Jericho Springer. When they arrived, already four cotton-filled wagons were waiting in line to have the cotton ginned.

Finally, after waiting two days, Jacob drove the oxen-pulled wagon under the long, sheet-iron spindle. They saw the cotton pushed into the spindle where the hulls and seed were separated. At last, they witnessed the white cotton mashed into a hard pulpy mass and formed into bales.

When they returned home Calvin was there. They could hear him talking as they walked in.

"Molly, there has been more Indian trouble. The Comanches promised to return their captives and hold a council. But, they only brought one captive with them," Calvin said. "Because of that, the soldiers attempted to capture the entire Comanche tribe and among all that fighting, many Indians were killed, including women and children. But those remaining went on a rampage. They burned everything they could not carry away."

Molly, listening to Calvin talk, saw anger in his usually compassionate eyes and heard it in his voice. She knew he believed Lamar to be responsible for the Indian uprising. Yet among all the problems with the Indians, plans to build a schoolhouse continued. Every one agreed that the best location would be in a southwest corner of the Anderson land, near a little stream later to be known as School Creek.

On the first Monday in December of 1840, people began to arrive at the school. Some rode horseback, others came in wagons or two-wheel carts. Indeed, this was a memorable time, the first day of school. Parents brought their children, some for the first time, to attend classes. They stood around waiting for the door to open. Jess Wheeler took out his watch attached to a long gold chain from his pocket. He opened it, looked intently at it, then closed it again. He looked at Jacob and nodded his head. At that, Jacob hurled a broken plowshare against a long iron chain three times. The sound equaled that of a hand-crafted bell as it drifted down the valley.

Marion Wheeler lined his eight students in a straight row with the youngest ones beside him at the front, and Willy and Matt Taylor, the two older boys, in the rear. He led them into the building and seated them on the log benches. He closed the door. The parents, laughing and talking, proudly returned to their home.

In January of 1841, less snow fell and fewer northers swept through the country. But torrential rains plagued the settlers. Often people kept their children at home because of the muddy trails. Twice, only Willy and Matt Taylor were present at the school. By the first of February, the clear sparkling water of Walnut Creek became a tumultuous, reddish stream. So Marion dismissed school until after the spring planting. The swollen streams were too hazardous for the children to cross.

Although Walnut Creek had not returned to its normal stream, Molly believed they should drive the cattle from the prairie land closer to water. However, as they reached the creek, the bull ventured too far into the water and walked into the bog. He bellowed and splashed in the mire, slowly sinking.

"Hurry, go get one of the horses and a long lariat. If we don't get the bull out he will soon sink and drown," Molly called to her sons.

Fortunately, about that time Calvin arrived at the house and heard the shouting. He spurred his horse into a run. He knew Molly and her sons must be having trouble. When he came closer, he saw the bull trapped in the bog so he threw a rope over the bull's long horns.

"Whoa, Chiefton, stand still. Don't let that rope slacken," he said as he patted his horse gently between the ears.

"Molly. Willy. Gather brush and limbs. Throw them as close to the bull as you can without frightening him," Calvin called out. "Jacob, wade out and scatter the brush as close as possible to the bull. Hold on to the heavy limbs so you won't begin to sink with the bull."

Step by step, Calvin slowly backed his horse until the bull was out of the water. When Calvin released the rope, the bull with his head lowered almost to the ground, let out a loud, continuing bellow and ran up the hill.

"Calvin, what would we do without you? It seems you are always near when we need help," Molly said.

"I've seen this happen many times, especially when we have big rains like this year. I'm glad I came when I did. Otherwise, you might have lost the bull," Calvin said.

The heavy rains gradually ceased and the sky, once more, became an azure blue. Yet, Walnut Creek bottomland remained an ugly sight. Uprooted trees, mesquite brush, and old rotten logs lodged along the creek bed. Too, the fallen trees, once used as a footbridge to cross the creek, had now become almost invisible. Logs from flooded homes, fence posts, and even bodies of dead animals that had not escaped the rapidly flowing stream collected on the old tree, creating a dam.

"We must do something about this rubble," Molly said. "I'm afraid water snakes will bed down in this useless waste."

So, Jacob and Willy tied a chain to Ole Blu. Little by little, they dragged the debris into a heap to be burned when it dried.

"I feel better now," Molly said when they had finished the task. I've always worried about snakes. Water moccasin bites are poisonous. If the venom gets into the bloodstream a person is sure to die. So, always watch for water moccasins."

To Molly, in the spring of 1841, the land of southeast Texas became a "Garden of Eden." The harsh winter rains had cleansed the earth. Seeds that once lay dormant broke through the ground. Often she and George wandered among the trees and along Walnut Creek. There she saw flowers and plants she had never seen before, ones for which she did not know the names.

"When Calvin comes," she said to George, "he can tell us their names and if they are good to eat." She did not tell George, but she always marveled at Calvin's knowledge and love for Texas. *Sometimes,* she unwillingly thought, *he is so much like David. No wonder I love him so.* At that, the question came to her, *am I being unfair to this man I say I love and want to marry?*

By July the corn and cotton seeds were planted and the crops laid by. Classes at the school began. This time George rode behind the saddle on Peppy, and he started his first class. Too, Marion and Ertha's daughter, Susan, and two of the young Bower boys enrolled. This brought the number of students to twelve.

Due to work at his farm, Marion did not teach. But eighteen-year-old Era Taylor agreed to hold the classes. The term, agreed to by the parents, began in July and ended the first of October. That way the children could help the parents pick the cotton.

Calvin did not visit Molly often that summer. Newcomers constantly came to the Land Office wanting to buy land in Texas. She watched each day, hoping he would come riding up the path. And she always felt disappointed when he did not come. Then one day, when she least expected him, she saw him coming up the hill.

"I can't stay long. I just wanted to give you these," he said as he handed her two young apple trees. They were no more than twelve inches tall and were wrapped in moist, hemp burlap. "A traveling salesman came to Jericho's Trading Post selling them."

Together they planted the trees. As Calvin dug the holes he looked at Molly, laughed, and said, "Molly, when the first apples are yet green, will you make me a green apple pie like my aunt always did?"

"Now, Calvin, by the time these trees bear apples, we will be married quite a while, and you will be tired of all my apple pies," she answered.

Later in the day, they walked down to the creek and sat under their favorite old oak tree. They planned their lives together.

"In a year we can marry. I will give some of my land to Jacob and Willy. Then I will take George and we can live with you."

In midsummer there was talk throughout the countryside of an upcoming election. President Lamar would not be eligible to run for a second term. But Burnet, the vice president, entered the race to become president of the Republic of Texas. After that, Sam Houston added his name to the ballet.

Calvin became so engrossed in his desire to reelect Sam Houston as president that he saw little of Molly. When he did come, she listened to him talk of the government through his own way of thinking. Twice he rode horseback from place to place "stumping" for the election of Houston, his favorite candidate.

"Calvin Hill," looking directly at him Molly once said, "how handsome you must have looked standing tall when you spoke. Surely all the people admired and respected you. I would have been pleased to have heard you speak."

However, by the latter part of September, Calvin came more often. Molly sensed the zeal for electing Houston was beginning to burn out in him.

"The conflict between Houston and Burnet for the presidency of the Republic of Texas is becoming intolerable," Calvin said when he came. "They accuse each other of drunkenness, theft of money, and cowardly deeds. I believe all this bickering is harming any efforts to be annexed to the United States. This may all be over after the election. But, right now, I think I'll just work at issuing grants to newcomers at Bucksnort."

"Now, Calvin, you have done what you could," Molly said.

"Just wait patiently until October. You know the best man will win in the election. No matter who he is."

In October Sam Houston did defeat Burnet in the election almost two to one in the counted votes.

"Now, maybe the country will get back to normal," Molly said. "I still don't understand how grown men can be so foolish. Anyway, I'm glad Houston will be president again. Now we must think about harvesting the corn. Then after all the cotton is picked and ginned, we should think about getting more cows."

That year seemed to pass quickly. Yet one thing would always be remembered—the Christmas of 1841.

On Christmas Eve, Molly and her three sons walked out onto the prairie land. They had not gone far when they heard rustling among tall grass and the gobble of a wild tom turkey. It ran in one direction and then another to escape Ring and Rover.

"Ring, Rover, come, sit right here. I might shoot you instead of the turkey," Jacob cautioned the hounds. Then he fired the gun.

"Maw, this is a big one," Willy yelled. "So big, I don't think George can eat all of a drumstick."

"Maw, say I can eat a drumstick, say I can," George yelled.

"Willy, don't tease George anymore. George, don't try to pick a fight with Willy," Molly warned them. "I declare, sometimes I don't know what to do with you two."

That night Molly lit a candle. She reached for the Holy Bible that always remained on the log table.

"Boys, each one sit down here on the bearskin rug," she said as she opened the Bible and began to read as the candle seemed to glow above the sparkling flames in the fireplace. She read the old, yet ever new, story of the Christ Child. She slowly closed the sacred book and looked at each son. Truly, she felt blessed.

Christmas morning, a mass of snowflakes like little crystal stars fell to the ground. But, they suddenly vanished. Then around noon the snow began to fall again and collect when Calvin rode up. At last, Molly felt her day became complete.

After they ate their fill of turkey, the boys begged Molly to make sugar Christmas candy. The fun began when George put some of the sticky candy on Jacob. At once, he chased George around the room pretending to be angry. Laughter filled the house as they pulled the candy into long ropes.

Even among all the laughter, Molly noticed Willy walk out of the room. She could see him leaning against the wall looking far away. She knew he was remembering the Christmas that Running Wolf spent with them. When he came in, she saw little teardrops on his cheeks. She knew he truly missed his Indian friend.

"I miss him, too," she whispered as she put her arm around Willy's shoulders.

"Sam Houston will be inaugurated December twenty-ninth for the second time as president of our Republic of Texas," Calvin said the following week when he came. "I'm goin' to the capitol for the inauguration. I'd be pleased if you and your sons went with me. It will be a big celebration."

She did not tell Calvin, but she felt that neither she nor her sons would be properly dressed for such an occasion. She looked at her briar-scratched hands covered with calluses and said, "Thank you, Calvin, but I believe I'm coming down with a winter cold. Perhaps I should stay home. You just don't dance too long at the ball with those pretty young ladies."

She laughed when she answered Calvin. But deep inside she wished for a long, flowing evening gown with elbow-length gloves. Yet, most of all, she wanted to dance the night away with Calvin.

When he returned, she did not question him about the ball. Nevertheless, he gladly told her, "My dear, no woman there could compare to you."

"Now, Calvin," she shrugged her shoulders and said, "I know better than that. But I love you for saying such a nice thing." Then she changed the subject. "The boys and I've been thinking we should get more cattle before spring. Do you know where we can find some good ones?"

A week later, Jacob and Willy each tied a bedroll behind the saddles on Pancho and Peppy. They rode toward Bucksnort where they knew Calvin would be waiting for them. They swam their horses across the Brazos River and went south and west, perhaps fifty miles, where Calvin knew they could get cattle. As they galloped over a hilly ridge, Calvin stopped his horse and said, "Boys, look over there. All those longhorn cattle in such tall grass resemble prairie dogs. See that adobe house? That's the home of Cliff Bradford. He knows we're coming."

"Well, come in, Calvin," Bradford said as he greeted them. "It's good to see you and these young men. It's been a while since we chased old Santa Anna out." Shortly, his Mexican wife came into the room. She did not speak, but she smiled and poured each a cup of steaming black coffee.

A disappointment awaited Jacob and Willy. Prior to the election, Lamar issued new paper money, referred to as "red-backs" by the people. "These bills," Bradford said as they walked among the cattle, "now are worth about fifteen cents less on the dollar."

Jacob called Willy aside and said, "Willy, I counted the certificates Maw sent with us. We can only get about, maybe forty or forty-five head. Maw wanted a hundred."

Bradford continued, "Because I have more cattle than what my grazing land can carry, I believe fifty head would be a fair price for your money. Some of the cows have calves. Of course, the calves go with the mothers. Tomorrow, if you agree on the price, you can cut out the ones you want and start back home."

"Let's tell the man we'll settle for fifty head because these are good stock," Jacob nudged Willy and said, as he really wanted the cattle.

Calvin mounted his horse and turned to ride away. This left only Jacob and Willy to drive the cattle to their land.

"You are now young men and good ones," Calvin said. "I know you'll be able to drive the herd by yourselves. You see, I must get back to Bucksnort to the Land Office."

"Willy, Maw planned this," Jacob said when he saw Willy was

angry with Calvin. "I heard her and Calvin talking. He said we must learn to do for ourselves."

After that, Willy seemed to respect Calvin.

The trail drive home began sometime in the afternoon of the following day. But it became a difficult, weary drive. Willy watched the herd in the early hours of the night. Then around midnight, Jacob took the most tiring watch. They killed and roasted quail or rabbit to eat. Once they even had duck for supper.

Bradford had told them where to find a shoal to get the cattle across the river. So, they had no trouble with the crossing as they made the cattle stay in a moving huddle until they stepped on dry land. At times Willy became impatient. He yelled and threw his lariat on the cattle to prod them on. But Jacob insisted they go at a slower pace to prevent a stampede. After almost two weeks, they entered the prairie grassland. They were now on their First Class Headright claim.

"Jacob, Calvin was right," Willy admitted. "We did learn, but I sure am tired."

A calm fell over the Republic in 1843 after the election of Houston. "Molly, Houston has renewed his method of dealing with the Indians. Even the Wacos and some of the little tribes signed a peace treaty. At last it seems we will have peace," Calvin told her.

In order to cut government expenses, Houston closed the Land Offices every other week. Even so, people from the United States and other countries flocked to Texas to buy cheap land, not only in the Brazos River valley, but even farther west.

That was the year Molly got her own horse, a young black and tan male, called Prince. Calvin came often and they rode side by side across her land and among the longhorn cattle. Those were delightful days. Yet, among all the hope of peace with the Indians and better government finances, there remained a fear. Santa Anna entered the Republic at San Antonio. However, the army drove him back into Mexico.

"Houston does not want war," Calvin said. "He's now working with Mexico on some kind of agreement. The good news is I believe other countries are beginning to recognize us as the free, independent nation we rightfully are."

In June, school opened for three months, but Era Taylor developed a rash and could not teach. This left only Molly to teach during that time. Although much work remained at home, she felt it important to keep the school open, as eighteen students now attended classes. Willy, soon to be eighteen years of age, did not attend. But George, eager to ride behind Molly, went each day. By August, Era's rash disappeared, and Molly went back to her chores at home.

In the fall of 1843, Molly and her sons harvested a good crop of corn and cotton. Even though the red-back dollar yet had little value, Molly purchased glass windows for the cabin at Jericho's Trading Post. And Calvin helped her set them in the open window. They made the house look more like a home; still Molly was not satisfied. She spun enough cloth from the new cotton to make curtains for the windowpanes. She stepped back, viewed her handiwork, and smiled, "Yes, they look real pretty."

True, life seemed to be getting better for the Texans. Many improvements surfaced in the Republic. Among them were the two men who brought in a mill at Jericho's Trading Post. No longer did women crush the corn with large stones to make corn pone.

That was when Molly decided that George, almost nine years of age, should help the family more. She showed him how to harness the oxen to the two-wheel cart and load the cart with corn. She handed him a paper to give to Jericho and food in a gunnysack for his dinner. Then she sent him off to Bucksnort.

Young George now considered himself a man—that is, until he got to Walnut Creek. About halfway across the stream the oxen stopped. They refused to go farther. George yelled, lashed out again and again. Yet the oxen would not move.

Out of desperation, he sat down on the bank of the creek. He tried to figure out a way to make Ole Blu and Bill move. Finally, it came to him! He filled his hat with corn and stood directly in front of the animals. But he held the corn far enough away so the oxen could not reach the corn. The oxen took one step forward and George took one step back. At last they were out of the creek.

George, lying in the hay barn at the mill that night, tried to understand why such docile animals acted as the oxen did. Finally, he simply said, "Well, at least they brought the corn to the mill." He turned over and went to sleep. He slept until the sun awoke him the next morning. He put the freshly ground cornmeal into the cart and started home. When he came to Walnut Creek, he whipped the oxen into a fast run and crossed the creek with no problem.

Molly saw him coming and rushed to help him unharness the oxen. She told him, "My son, I'm proud of you. You have done a man's job."

George smiled. But he did not tell her about the oxen balking in the creek.

In December, Molly worked by candlelight in the evenings. She made pillows for her sons and Calvin as gifts at Christmas from the feathers she had painstakingly plucked from the chickens, wild turkeys, or ducks they killed for food. The ones she did not use, she saved to make into a feather mattress.

That year they raised an extra good crop of corn. So they fed the hogs more, causing them to produce more fat. Molly rendered much of the fat into lard in the iron pot and took it to Jericho's Trading Post. There she traded it for wheat flour, sugar, and other necessary items.

Calvin came often those days and Molly's tasks became less boring. She never tired of him telling about his trail rides driving cattle far to the north in Kansas. Other times he told of his days in school in Kentucky. Perhaps what she enjoyed most were the poems he recited to her. He made her feel as if she were the one for whom the verse was written.

"Molly Anderson," he once said, "you never stop. I wonder how you find the time to do what you do. You can ride a horse, handle oxen, and plow as well as any man. But I promise if you will marry me, you'll never do that hard work again."

"Well, tell me, Calvin Hill," she laughingly said as she pushed back her curly hair, "who will cook you food, clean your house, and wash your clothes when I marry you?"

The winter of 1844 proved to be rather mild. Still, enough snow fell to retain moisture in the ground. The big rocks and tree stumps were all gathered and stacked in big piles. They were finishing the corn and cotton planting when Molly noticed Ole Blu walked as if his hooves were lame. She took him to the barn, removed the harness, and led him into the stall. He stood still as she lifted his front leg. Much of the hair was gone and the flesh above the hoof was swollen. Hurriedly, she went to the house and boiled peyote cactus from which she made a solution to apply to the swelling. Afterward, she put moist mud, free from filth, on the infection to keep flies away.

"Jacob, do you think a poisonous snake bit Ole Blu?" Molly asked.

"Maw, we know Ole Blu and Bill are getting old," Jacob said. "Willy and I've been thinking we should get mules to work. We can get some good ones from Pablo and Alfredo. Remember, I told you how Alfredo raises mules, and how they work real good."

"Jacob, I never drove a mule in my life. I'd be afraid to try now. Your papa brought Ole Blu and Bill all the way from Tennessee. And he always said they were good workers," Molly reminded him. "No, I won't get rid of them!"

"Maw, we don't have to get rid of them," Willy told her. "We have lots of grass and water. We can turn them out to pasture, and in the winter we can feed them."

Almost two weeks later Jacob and Willy came from the Estrada place, each leading a mule behind their horse. Perhaps what interested George most was the piebald pony pacing behind Peppy and Pancho. The black-and-white-spotted pony seemed to prance as his black mane and tail glistened in the sunlight. Molly knew Pablo had trained him to be ridden. Willy, without speaking, handed the reins to George, who jumped upon the pony. He hung onto the mane and off they started in a slow trot. Then, suddenly, they changed to a fast run and soon were out of sight.

"What will you name your pony?" Jacob asked.

"Pablito, of course," George answered, "Pablo gave him to me so now he's little Pablo."

"I'm not sure I can harness these mules," Molly said, "but I'll try in the morning. I heard your papa say one time that mules kick a lot. Well, if they do, you boys will plow the fields." They laughed as she walked to the house uttering something they did not fully understand.

Actually, she found it easier to harness the short-legged mules than the big, clumsy oxen. But she swore to never admit it to her sons. She, also, learned quickly that the mules did kick, especially at Ring and Rover, who tucked their tails between their legs and went off howling.

Molly and George hung the oxen yoke in the barn the next morning. Then they drove Ole Blu and Bill out to pasture. Molly took the rope from around their necks, patted them on the rump, and they slowly trudged toward the prairie grassland. She hated to see them go, but she knew she would see they were cared for.

It was in late summer when Calvin came. "Houston sent representatives to Washington to bring talks of annexing the Republic to the United States," he said. "Their president, Tyler, seems to be willing to listen. But I'm afraid they are demanding too high a price. They are asking we deed all public lands to them. If we do that, they'll pay our big national debt. But Texas will only be recognized as a territory. I'm against that. So are most of the people I talk to."

Molly, too, did not see this as a solution to their problems. But she did not reply, as she completely trusted Calvin's judgment in government affairs. So, why discuss it further?

However, Calvin did bring good news. Houston signed a treaty with the Comanche Indians. He believed it to be the right thing for both the Texans and the Indians. Yet, Molly felt the treaty unfair to the Comanches as they were pushed farther north and west.

Late one day as Molly prepared their evening meal, Jacob walked through the kitchen. That was not unusual so she went about her work. But something looked strange about him. She turned and looked again. To her dismay, he stood quietly looking at her with a gun in a holster hanging low on his belt.

"Jacob, where did you get that gun? Why did you get it?" she asked. "I've never seen one like that. I don't want you to carry it. You could even kill someone."

"Maw, I've joined the Texas Rangers. They sold me the gun," he answered candidly. "It's a powerful weapon. I can shoot it six times without reloading it. Marion showed me how to use it. We'll go together when we are needed." He remained silent for a moment. "Maw, I want a badge to wear on my shirt to show I'm a Ranger. Would you make me one like Ertha made Marion?" he asked.

She said nothing else. She turned and began to make a badge like the one Marion wore. Feelings of utter impending danger and dread swept through her mind. Still, at the same time, feelings of pride penetrated her thoughts.

"Ertha, I truly regretted David was not here to see his oldest son swear on the Holy Bible to enforce the law and protect the citizens of this unique Republic of Texas," Molly told Ertha when she came to visit.

"Did you know Jacob joined the Texas Rangers?" Molly calmly asked Calvin when he came the following morning. She suspected he knew all the time about Jacob's intentions.

"Yes, Molly," Calvin truthfully answered, "he talked to me, but I did not say yes or no. I believe this is his decision and that he should be the one to tell you. So many renegades have come to our country. They rob and, at times, even kill. Too, men fight over land boundaries, causing more trouble. They often steal cattle to prove their point."

Molly did not answer. She knew Calvin to be right.

"I don't think you should worry about your son," Calvin continued. "He will only do his duty. He has a level head on his shoulders. I think he is doing this to prevent murders. I know he still remembers how his father died."

By July of 1844, the corn and cotton showed signs of a "bumper" crop. Then one morning as Molly came from the cow pen carrying a bucket of milk, she heard a peculiar, buzzing sound. It became louder and louder. Then at once the sky was overcast. She looked upward, yet she saw no cloud. The eerie sound seemed closer and closer.

"Jacob, Willy. Come! Hurry! See that big swarm of odd insects!"

About that time Bob Brewer and Benito Mendez rode up.

"Molly! Hurry, call your sons," Brewer yelled. "There's a big swarm of giant grasshoppers coming your way. They've already stripped much of our crops bare."

"What can we do?" Molly asked.

"Send George to warn other farmers. Benito has seen this happen many times. He is setting fire now to the north edge of the field, hoping the flames will roast the wings of the hoppers."

However, this time they flew above the fire. They settled on the ground, and like a big scythe riddled the plants as they went. Soon other people came to help fight the grasshoppers. They fought with sticks, stones, rocks, or whatever they found.

Even the horrible buzzing sound disturbed the animals. They all ran toward the prairie land. At last, the buzzing stopped, and an uncanny feeling came over the people. It seemed the grasshoppers vanished.

Benito knew the grasshoppers would rest a while, then go farther south. The people also went south to help other farmers fight the unwanted insects that ravaged their cotton and corn. Although the grasshoppers destroyed a portion of the crops, the people never gave up.

Another election was to be held in October. But Sam Houston could not run for president. The law forbade a president to serve two consecutive terms. So Anson Jones joined the race. He did not fully agree with Houston's policies, but still the voters considered him to be on Houston's "camp." Vice President Burleson ran on the opposite side. Some of the people declared him to be a follower of the former president Lamar. But he declared that to be a false statement.

Calvin Hill proudly claimed to be a dyed-in-the-wool supporter of Jones. On the other hand, Oran Taylor believed Burleson to be the best man for the job.

"Oran and me, in the best interest of the people, will be holding a meeting at the schoolhouse," Calvin told Molly when he came to see her.

"Just what do you plan to talk about?" she asked.

"Well, our main subject will be the annexation of the Republic to the United States. Then we can argue over the problems with Mexico. Each man will have equal time."

With the help of Willy and Matt Taylor, the announcement of the proposed meeting spread like wildfire, giving the people a chance to put behind the unpleasant episode of the giant grasshoppers.

Molly sincerely looked forward to the meeting. She was anxious to hear Calvin speak, and most of all, to see him standing tall before the people. She knew he would turn the congregation to his point of view. Of course, she knew Oran to be a good and honest man, but she knew Calvin to be the best.

Finally, the day for the meeting arrived. Even by midmorning people came from all around the country. Everyone visited, and mostly the men discussed the election, as children played games.

At exactly twelve o'clock, each family put out food they brought to share with each other. The women especially enjoyed this. They tasted each pot, trying to decide which tasted better.

"This is impossible to decide. Maybe next time we will select two men to judge," one woman said, "but don't choose my husband, he won't stop eating."

Later, they put any leftover food they had in baskets, hoping it would be free from the millions of black and red ants they knew thrived on such sweet stuff.

When they all went into the schoolhouse there were so many people they could not all be seated. Most of the men stood along the wall or squatted down so others could see the speakers.

Calvin and Oran sat behind the teacher's desk, and Jericho Springer declared the meeting to be open. Instantly, the men removed their hats and bowed their heads as Jess Wheeler looked upward and said, "Oh, Lord God Almighty! We beseech thee to bless our Republic and these people here today. Amen."

Earlier, Jericho heard a rumor that some cattle drivers made a bet they could stop the meeting. Jericho considered this to be only the talk of drunken cowboys. Yet, to be on the safe side, he asked Jacob and Marion to stand watch.

Complete silence filled the room when Jericho started to announce the first speaker. Then, two unknown men staggered through the door. They shot a hole in the ceiling just above Jericho's head.

"All yous turn and walk out the door. If yous don't, we'll shoot agin. But this time we ain't goin' to shoot at the ceiling," one of the men yelled.

At once women grabbed their children and started to run out the door. That was when Marion and Jacob rushed through the front door. They took their guns from their holsters and shoved them against the men's backs.

"Drop your pistols! Now, turn around. Walk out the door. Get on your horses and ride off to wherever you came from!" Marion demanded.

They did throw their pistols down, and Marion and Jacob marched them out the door and watched them mount their horses and quickly vanish out of sight.

Jericho reached down, picked up the drovers' pistols, and put them on the teacher's desk. He simple ignored the incident, and the meeting began.

In October, Jones defeated Burleson by a small margin. Then in January of 1845, Jones replaced Houston as president of the growing Republic.

"Jones is leaning more toward annexation all the time," Calvin said. "Still there's no end to things to work out."

"Mexico promised to accept Texas as an independent nation. That is, if we drop efforts to be annexed to the United States. He signed a treaty then, but there's been trouble ever since," Calvin said. "Jacob, I think we all still remember the Alamo and the inhumane treatment the men suffered at Goliad."

"Calvin, Texans can never believe Santa Anna," Molly joined in the conversation. "I think he's up to his old tricks, trying to fool us. I keep hoping our new president can persuade the United States to let Texas join the Union. After all, most Texans were, at one time, citizens of that land. I believe most people still think of it as home. We'd be good for the Union and the Union would be good for us."

The wheels of justice did begin to turn swiftly in 1846. In February, the United States did accept Texas as a state. And Texas accepted the terms offered.

Jones called for a convention at Austin in July and the majority accepted the offer. A committee to write a new constitution was named to compile a new document, and all qualified voters were required to vote on the question of annexation.

"Molly, I've a lot to tell you about the convention," Calvin said when he returned from Austin. "But first, I want to know how you and the boys are doing. I see you've done a lot of plowing. And, shucks, Molly, can't you see I missed you?"

"Calvin, I missed you, too," Molly replied. "Sit down and I'll pour you a cup of coffee. You can't believe this. But I just knew you were coming, so I made a fresh pot just a while ago."

In October a public vote was held whereby annexation as a state to the United States and a new constitution were duly approved by the voters of the Republic of Texas. Patiently, all the people waited for a reply from the United States. Then, not long afterward, the *Republic-Herald* newspaper printed a special edition and without hesitating, Calvin rode to show Molly a copy of the paper. The headlines in big bold print read:

December 29, 1845 President Polk signed the final bill that made Texas a state in the United States of America

The article stated that Texas would, at once, be proclaimed a full-fledged state. It also stated, that all public lands would remain as the property of the new state of Texas.

On February 19, 1846, Molly, with Calvin by her side, walked the streets of Austin as her sons followed behind. Calvin had made sure they would witness this great moment.

The sun shone brightly that day as the Texans stood, almost in reverence, and quietly waited. The newly elected officials stood on a rostrum at the front of the statehouse and solemnly took the oath of their office.

At the last, Anson Jones, with trembling hands and voice, turned his final executive power over to Pickney Henderson, who became the first elected governor of the new state of Texas.

In his long speech, Jones related the good and the bad times of the Republic of Texas. At the end he took off his glasses and closed his book. He stood tall and spoke loud and clear, "The Republic of Texas is no more!"

Instantly, the Lone Star flag was lowered and the Stars and Stripes, the flag of the United States, waved above it. One brief moment of silence prevailed. Then, suddenly, shouts of joy echoed through the crowd and dancing was seen in the streets.

Texas had become the twenty-eighth state of the United States of America.

CHAPTER 7

Texas was no longer a self-ruled struggling nation. It was now an accepted state of the immense lands of the great Union of the United States of America.

Molly now believed she could put behind her the grief and unrest in that period of her life. Regardless of brief flashes of troubled memories, she experienced a genuine feeling of security after becoming a part of the country she cherished. Yet, in one way, nothing changed. The ground still must be plowed and seeds sowed. So, life went on as usual.

In 1846, the month of March arrived with steady gales of south winds from the Gulf of Mexico. They brought showers of refreshing rains with hope that spring would follow.

Molly first noticed a tinge of color in the wild plum bushes, then the dogwood and redbud trees. Soon they were covered with white, crimson, and almost pink blooms. Too, the winter grasses were slowly becoming a bright green. Bluebonnets, Indian paintbrush, and the prickly wild, rambling rose with its purplish red and snow-white blossoms came alive.

One day she put on her bonnet and started to go search for poke greens and wild onions for lunch as she knew they were at the best stage for eating. She walked out the door and saw Calvin coming up the hill. When she met him, he left his horse to graze and they walked along the creek bed looking for tender watercress greens.

"Molly, I have orders to close the Land Office at Bucksnort. It will not be needed," he said, "for the only grants remaining are those for the soldiers who fought in the war or their families."

"What will you do?" Molly asked.

"I've been asked to work as a clerk in the capitol at Austin. My only regret is that you will not be with me." He held her hand and said, "My dear, I'm begging you to come with me. At least promise me you will talk to your sons about this. I don't want to think of losing you."

"Calvin, this doesn't surprise me," she said. "Jacob told me last week the Land Offices were being closed. This is, indeed, a hard decision to make. I must think about it before I give you an answer."

Their goodbyes were not happy ones. Yet Calvin promised to be back in a month. Molly, with a lump in her throat, waved as he rode out of sight. She felt as if she were repeating another chapter in her life. David never felt content to stay in one place. He had a controlling desire to see what "lay on the other side of the mountain." From those memories she saw a bit of David in Calvin.

She thought, *I was always willing to go with David wherever he went. Now years have passed and my sons are yet with me. Perhaps it is best I just wait and see how things turn out before I decide what to do.* She sat quietly as those thoughts raced through her mind. *Yet I know one thing will remain the same—David and Calvin will always be entwined in my heart.*

The ink on the papers of annexation to the United States was hardly dry when Mexico began to harass the Texans again. But this time the problem fell on the shoulders of the United States.

"The fact of the matter is that Mexico feels betrayed," Calvin told Molly when he came. "Their complaint is the border. But to my way of thinking they are angry because the United States admitted us to the Union."

"Calvin, didn't Santa Anna sign a treaty at Velasco? Didn't he agree that the Rio Grande River would be the border?" Molly asked.

"That is true. But skirmishes have already begun," Calvin answered. "The good thing is the United States is bringing in men to fight the battles."

Seeing Calvin ride off to his job in Austin, Molly felt a sense of fear. She knew his job was important to him and to the country. Furthermore, she was happy he could do the job he liked and was qualified for. But she also was not convinced she would be happy in Austin without her two older sons.

Only two weeks after Calvin went back to Austin, news that Mexico declared war against the United States spread through the country. Then on May 13 the United States retaliated by officially pronouncing war with Mexico.

"Many men are ready to join the United States Army. Like them, I believe this is still our fight with Mexico," Jacob said. "Maw, I want to do my part. I hear reports that Texas Rangers are needed. Tomorrow I'm leaving to serve as a guide for the soldiers."

"My dear son, I've been expecting this. Calvin told me about the need for army guides when I saw him last," Molly said. "I know you will be in great danger. Still, I can not ask you not to go. I know this is what your papa would want you to do."

"Maw, I knew you would understand, you always do," Jacob said with tender emotion. "I may not have to go at once. On the other hand, I could be ordered to begin duty any time."

"I'll go cook hard-tack for you to eat on the way to your commander. Then I'll pack your bedroll," Molly said as she turned to hide the anguish in her tear-stained eyes.

The crops were planted, even before Jacob left. Yet, it seemed work never ceased. Molly often rode Prince to see if there were any newborn calves. Once George went with her. They found a cow trying to give birth to her calf. But, the little animal would not come out.

"George, ride back and tell Willy to come," Molly called out to George. "I don't think the heifer will live unless we can help the baby calf to come out."

"But, Maw," he said, "I'll show you what to do." He pulled on the head of the calf, but it seemed to be lodged in the birth canal of the heifer. "Maw, help me." Even though they worked together, they made no progress.

"I'll do like Jacob did," George said as he reached for his rope.

He tied it around a portion of the calf's head that he could see, then to the saddle horn. He led Pablito back one step then slowly another step. Out came the calf. George took the rope from around the calf's head. For one brief moment the calf almost lay lifeless, then quickly began to struggle to its feet.

"George, we'll let the mother cow do the rest. Animals are very wise when it comes to their babies, just like people. I believe we have another bull calf. Did you notice?" Molly asked.

"Yep, it's a bull," he answered.

Even though it was now July, classes had not begun at the school on School Creek. They had no teacher as Era Taylor married and moved father south. So, again, Molly offered to teach the first month and Lacy Taylor would teach in August. After that, the school would close in the fall until they picked the cotton.

Molly really enjoyed teaching the children. Still, she knew many chores at home were never done. Weeds growing among the okra, pumpkin, and sweet potato plants needed to be hoed. She even left a hen to set on one egg. Now, only one little chick followed the mother hen. Then in August, Lacy Taylor taught at the school and Molly resumed her work at home.

One day she prepared to make soap in the iron pot. She put in equal amounts of hog fat and water. Then she stirred in lye, leached from wood ashes, and built a fire around the pot. As she pushed a wooden paddle around in the mixture she sang:

"Row, row, row your boat gently down the stream!"

Then loud and clear sounded from behind: "Merrily, merrily, merrily, life is but a dream."

She turned around and there was Calvin on his horse laughing at her. At first she felt embarrassed but seeing his smile she began to laugh and said, "Calvin Hill, just for sneaking up on me, you can stir my soap pot."

"Let's go for a ride. I'll quench the fire and saddle Prince for you," he said.

She removed the paddle from the pot and ran into the house. She untied her apron and threw it on a chair. She put on her new high-top shoes. Then she started to braid her hair, but on second thought, she brushed it until it glistened and let it fall to the back of her head.

Calvin had saddled Prince and off they went. Their horses pranced in a slow gait until they crossed Walnut Creek. Suddenly they changed to a fast run. Side by side they rode all over the prairie land and among the cattle.

Calvin turned south when they entered the forest land, but Molly went west. He saw her and turned back, but she hid behind some persimmon trees. As he rode by, she spurred Prince into a run.

When she passed him, she laughed and yelled, "Catch me if you can." Off they ran again. Finally, they slowed their horses to a walk, and holding hands, they rode side by side to her home. They knew this had been a day to remember.

"Molly Anderson, I love you," he said when he held her close and said goodbye. He mounted his horse to ride away. She smiled, reached up, and kissed him again.

January of 1847, Jacob came home, looking thin and weary.

"Maw, I'm happy to be home," he said. "Ranger McCulloch led us and we took the general's command all the way to Monterrey in Mexico. We were supposed to only guide the men, but things became so bad we had to fight. There were so many killings that I could not eat or sleep at night."

"Did any of the Rangers die? Did a bullet hit you?" Molly wanted to know.

"No, we were lucky. After the fighting was over, our sergeant said our mission was finished. That was when some of us asked to go home to see our families. So, the next morning Commander McCulloch granted us a month leave."

"My son, I am happy you are home; so are the others," Molly said. Her heart ached, for her oldest son had become a man before he should have.

"Maw, I saw and learned the horrors of war. I saw men dying for no reason. I hope Willy and George will never have to fight in a war. I didn't join the Texas Rangers to kill without mercy and serve in a senseless war. I joined to protect people from renegades and thieves."

"Son, I wish I could erase this from your mind. I can only say that I'm proud of you. I know your father would have been, too."

"Maw, that's the reason I'll go back and serve the rest of my tour of duty." Then his voice became more cheerful. "This time we're going west."

"Wars are brutal and senseless, but I'm afraid they'll never cease as long as nations disagree," Molly said.

The first of the month, classes at the school began. And a new teacher would be teaching, a twenty-two-year-old young lady, all the way from near San Felipe. To be sure, all the parents wanted to see the new "school marm," so they brought the children that first day.

The students quietly sat on the benches, but the parents and other visitors stood against the wall. The door opened and a hush fell over the room. A pretty lady entered. She hung her coat and hat behind the door and quietly walked to the front of the room.

"Good morning, everyone. My name is Elizabeth Wood. I will be your teacher this school term," she said in a soft, clear voice. "If you like me and are good, maybe I'll stay the next term. But enough of that—our classes must begin. I thank all of the parents for bringing the students here. I'll later meet each one," that same quiet voice continued. "Thank you again for coming. Please, would the gentleman at the back, open the door so you all may go home?"

Jacob awkwardly stood there. He could not take his eyes off that beautiful person. At once, Molly reached over and whispered, "Jacob, Miss Wood is speaking to you."

Jacob returned to his scout duty for the United States Army. Only this time he did go west.

Molly had become accustomed to the mules, so she did a lot of the plowing in the cleared land. Although more cotton needed

to be planted, with Jacob away, they found little time to clear the
land. She knew it was important to plant more cotton. Also, she
wanted to raise some sorghum grains, as Calvin said seed could be
bought in Austin.

"Jacob is away with the army someplace west," Willy told their
friend Pablo Estrada when he came. "We need to clear more land
but with Jacob gone, we don't have the time."

"Señora Molly, I'll help you clear the land," Pablo said when
Molly came out to greet him. "You see, Alfredo, he don't go up in
the hill to catch the mares and wild horses. The government, they
won't buy them. Señora, we are now what you say 'United States
citizens.'"

Pablo did stay. They cleared more land and planted the crops.
In the early fall they harvested a good corn crop and George took
some to the mill to be made into cornmeal.

"I believe we'll have the best cotton ever this year. And I know
you helped us," Molly said to Pablo. "Just look at it, so fluffy and
white. I think we should start picking next week."

By dusk that evening a tropical storm blew in from the Gulf
of Mexico. Sometimes the wind exceeded seventy miles an hour.
Many tall trees bent, splintered, and fell to the ground. Next came
thunder, lightning, rain, and hail.

Fortunately, the house withstood the storm. But the cattle
stampeded and sought shelter down by the creek. The winds passed
over. But the rain continued to fall as if in sheets. Even above the
falling rain, they heard the roaring of the rising water in the creek.
They knew the cattle could be washed downstream. So, they put
on their slickers and, without saddles, rode quickly to drive the cattle to higher ground.

Strangely, the next morning the sun shone bright and clear.
Yet, a haunting stillness hovered over the land. Molly walked out-
side. She looked around. Even the swine were huddled together.
The chickens seemed disoriented and loose feathers lay everywhere.

She walked on to the cotton field. She stopped and gasped.

Cotton had been blown out of the bolls and beaten to the ground by the wind and hail. She felt sick inside and turned to walk back to the house. Then she saw Willy and Pablo behind her.

"Señora, do not worry. We will get some of the cotton when it is dry. It will be brown. The gin man, he will buy it, but he will not give you many pesos. I know. I see thees many times. Señora, there is good in everything, si?" Then he laughed and said, "Tomorrow we weel not have to pull the cotton out of the bolls."

"Pablo, I'm glad you came here," Molly said. "I know I should not fret. After all, we are alive and so are the cattle." Then she laughed and repeated Pablo's remark. "Tomorrow, we won't have to pick much cotton."

Not long after the storm, Calvin came. It distressed him to see the cotton on the ground. "Texans never give up," he said. "When I came by the Taylors, they were preparing for a dance. They want everybody to come to their house Saturday night. I have to go to Bucksnort, but I'll be back. Would you bring George and go to the dance with me?"

"Yes, Calvin, I'll be happy to go with you," she answered.

The sun had not gone down on Saturday evening when people began to arrive at the Taylor house. Some came in wagons, others rode horses. Or, in the case of Pablo Estrada; he came in a two-wheel cart pulled by one mule. No matter how they came, their children came with them, if there were children.

Flares, made from pine boughs, hung on the trees all around the house. They flashed unsteadily, creating a festive atmosphere. The Taylor twins, Eli and Elias, constantly turned the deer and pork meat roasting above the deep pit. The room stood vacant as all the furniture was removed and a fire burned low in the fireplace.

Around dusk, the intriguing sound of Oran Taylor rosining up his fiddle bow lured the people inside. He twisted the pegs until they were in perfect tune and the clink of the strings started toes to tapping. He hit one or two notes and the sound of "Turkey in the Straw" echoed loud and clear.

In rushed Jericho and Ramona Springer. Jericho reached into his pocket and pulled out his "Jew's Harp." He held the lyre to his mouth as his fingers beat out the rhythm, and he patted his feet in perfect time with the fiddle. Everyone chose partners and around they went dancing to the music. Suddenly, Oran changed to a faster beat.

"Grab your partner!" Jess Wheeler yelled out. "Everybody Sashay—do-si-do—promenade your fair maiden!"

"I know you'll need to rest. So Lacy, my wife, will play and sing you a song," Oran announced when the music stopped. "Matt, will you bring your maw a bench to sit on?"

Lacy gracefully walked across the room. She sat down on the bench, and holding the dulcimer on her lap, she plucked a few notes. Then in a melancholy voice she began to sing the ballad of "Barbara Allen" as she strummed on the instrument. When she finished, the people all clapped and whistled. She bowed and smiled. She knew she did well.

Long after midnight, the last waltz was danced. The people all said goodbye and went to their homes. They had spent a time of joy and laughter that helped to erase the daily worries.

Calvin left early the next morning to go back to Austin. Molly walked with him to his horse. They stood there a long time, talking of the pleasure of dancing through the night and of their future together. He kissed her and mounted his horse.

"I love you," he said as he bent down and kissed her again.

"Why, Calvin Hill. I'm happy you do," she answered. "Don't you see I love you, too?"

The following days she went about her work. But a strange thought kept coming to her mind. *When I dance with Calvin, it seems as if I am dancing with David. Am I losing my sanity? I know I love Calvin. Why can't I think only of him? Other times I look into his eyes and wonder, is it my face he sees or is it the face of beautiful, gentle Laquana?*

On February 2, 1848, at last peace came to Texas. The United

States and Mexico signed a treaty at Guadalupe Hidalgo in Mexico. It proclaimed the Rio Grande River to be the permanent boundary between Mexico and the new state of Texas.

"Molly, the Mexicans could not go against the powerful army of the United States," Calvin told Molly when he rushed to tell her the good news. "They just kept pushing back across the Rio Grande River. Finally, they surrendered at a little town near Mexico City."

"Maybe now we can start building schools, churches, and roads," Molly said.

"Already there is talk of building county courthouses. To be sure, that will cause towns to form and flourish. Many people are coming to Texas from other countries by boat loads," Calvin told her.

"Yes, Calvin, I think things are getting better. I believe we're on our way to a prosperous and peaceful year," Molly said.

"Maw, I'm home. And this time I want to stay—that is, unless more cattle rustling begins," Jacob said when he returned from his scout duty. "Oh! By the way, is Elizabeth Wood still teaching at the school?"

"Jacob, you hardly asked about things here before you mentioned Elizabeth," laughing, Molly chided him. "I think I know why. She's a pretty young lady and a very kind and good one, I must add. Would you like to bring her here for dinner some time? I would love to have her come."

"You bet I would," he answered. "If I don't, I'm afraid Eli Taylor will win her over."

Saturday, the day before Jacob brought Elizabeth for dinner, was a warm sunny day. It created the illusion that winter had gone. However, that night, as if in the throes of death, winter revived. A cold wind from the north came in and then swept on south. After that, came a shower of snow that covered the ground.

The next day when Jacob brought Elizabeth for dinner, the clouds had vanished, and the sunlight glistened on the fresh snow.

Like children they all began to throw snowballs at one another as they romped in the snow. Once Elizabeth fell and Jacob reached down to help her up. Their eyes met. Quickly, he gently kissed her on the cheek.

When Jacob came from taking Elizabeth to the Taylor house where she boarded, Molly said nothing to him. She simply smiled and acknowledged her oldest son was in love. Now she would, at last, have a daughter.

With Jacob and Pablo to help, Molly's work lessened. She even had time to work on the spinning wheel, a task she thoroughly enjoyed. Somehow, to her, it became a work of art. But, most important, it provided time to plan for her sons and her life with Calvin. Often she did not understand her feelings or her actions. Once the idea entered her mind, *perhaps I'm simply a frivolous, lonesome old woman beginning to realize I am getting old.* At that, she laughed at herself and went about her work.

"I've been thinking lately," she said one day as they ate the evening meal, "that we should build a dog-run on our house."

"But Maw, Ring and Rover run where they want to. We don't need a dog-run," George answered.

"George, don't chuckle. You're old enough to help. I'm not talking about a place for the hounds to run," laughing, she told George. "We'll build two more rooms. That way we'll have a porch between the two houses. That's what we called a 'dog-run' in Tennessee. We could walk from one house to the other under a roof."

As usual when the neighbors learned the Andersons would build more rooms, they hurriedly came to help. They measured off eight feet parallel to the older building. Finally, they suspended a roof between the buildings creating the dog-run.

This time Molly did not have to wait for windows.

"Molly, in Goliad there is a place where windows, doors, and building supplies are sold. It is, maybe, seventy miles from here," Calvin said when he came.

At once, she helped Willy harness the mules and hitch them to the wagon. Without hesitating, she sent him and Matt Taylor off to purchase the windowpanes and even a keg of nails.

The rooms were finished and the men prepared to go to their homes. "I think we should celebrate," Molly called out. "The rooms are finished so before the boys move their beds in, I'm inviting everybody to a dance this Saturday night."

Even before the sun went down on Saturday, people began to arrive at the Anderson home. One man rode a horse, all the way from west of the Brazos River, carrying his banjo.

"Howdy, I'm Bud Snow," the man politely said. "I saw Oran Taylor at Bucksnort and he told me about the dance. I'd sure like to help make the music with my banjo. If it is all right with the Missus."

"Welcome, everybody, I want you to know Bud Snow. He brought his banjo and is going to play with Oran and Jericho. So, let's get started," Jacob said as he waved his hand, whistled, and the music began.

Sometime after midnight Oran Taylor said, "I want to thank Mr. Snow for being here. Now maybe we should all go home. We will play our last waltz and say goodnight."

Just then the last waltz began, but Jacob let out a shrill whistle, raised his hand to stop the music, and called out. "Ladies and gentlemen, our schoolteacher and me have an announcement to make. We're getting married!"

Whistles, yells, and laughter almost shook the house. Instead of playing a waltz, Oran, Jericho, and Mr. Snow played a fast "foot-stomping" tune.

"Come on! Let's celebrate!" Jess Wheeler shouted. "Everybody, grab your partner. Sashay—do-si-do and promenade your fair maiden around the room."

Without stopping, the musicians began to play "Over the Waves," a slow waltz tune. Everyone stopped dancing and stood against the wall. Jacob put his arms around Elizabeth and they waltzed across the room. Calvin and Molly came behind, followed by all the other couples.

The announcement did not surprise Molly, even though she had not expected it that night. Yet, it pleased her.

"Jacob became a man early in his life. He has always tried to take David's place in the family. I am sure he wished his father was here tonight." At once she regretted making the remark. She knew Calvin had tried to be a father to her sons since they first knew him.

"Molly, I truly understand," Calvin said. "At one time you told me one could love the living and the dead, but in a different manner. My dear, I learned to do that. You and I, we have a special bond, one not known or appreciated by many people."

That summer passed quickly. Perhaps the arrival of new people in the country and new towns springing up gave Molly an unfair expectation that her life would remain peaceful.

To be sure, things did begin to change. Jericho Springer closed the trading post and the gristmill at Bucksnort and moved to a new location. The log house that housed the Land Office stood vacant, as well as the one-room cabin where Calvin once lived. The buildings remained, but there were no signs of inhabitants. The village of Bucksnort became a ghost town.

On December 1, 1849, Jacob and Elizabeth stopped the mule-drawn wagon loaded with Elizabeth's possessions at the front gate. Jacob helped Elizabeth from the wagon, and holding hands, they walked to the front door and he called out, "Hello, is anybody here? We're home."

Molly looked up. To her astonishment there was lovely Elizabeth standing proudly by Jacob.

"Maw, we got married three days ago at her uncle's house. A Methodist preacher happened to come by. So we asked him to marry us."

"Oh! I'm happy for you. Although I would loved to have been there," Molly, a little envious, said.

"Yes, I wish you could have been there. Elizabeth looked so pretty. You see, she has lived with her aunt and uncle since her parents died when she was only a small child. So, Elizabeth wanted them to be at her wedding," Jacob said.

"Elizabeth, I am glad they were with you. Welcome to your new home," Molly truly said. "Jacob, I knew we had a reason to build those new rooms. Your marriage must have been the reason. Just like King Solomon wrote in the Bible, 'there's a time to be happy.' I believe this is the time."

The population of the new state of Texas began to grow so rapidly that Congress divided it into counties. The portion, east of the Brazos River where Molly and her sons lived, was designated as Robertson County. Shortly, the location for a small village was selected to house the county courthouse.

Jericho Springer claimed the honor of being one of the first residents to move to this new place called Wheelock. He moved his gristmill and built a store where he and Ramona lived. Although he still traded merchandise for cattle, swine, and produce, he did not call it a trading post. Instead, above the entrance hung a big sign that read: Springer General Store.

To Molly's delight, Jericho sold calico and big balls of cotton sewing thread. Perhaps the most desired articles were the ladies' hats and feather plumes.

"Times are surely changing," Molly said one night as they ate supper. "It is hard to keep up with all the new ways. Still, one thing keeps coming to my mind. Home, government buildings, and stores appear almost over night. But, what about churches? Why can't we start church meetings in the School Creek schoolhouse?"

"You are right, Maw," Willy said. "So many people have moved into Texas, but there are no church buildings. I think we should hold meetings in the schoolhouse."

After that, Molly and Willy went from farm to farm inviting the people to worship. Some were of the Methodist belief. Some were of the Baptist denomination. The Mendez family was of the

Catholic Church. Some were of the Presbyterian faith. Then there were those who had no church preference. Still, they all agreed to come to the meetings.

The last house where they stopped happened to be the home of the Wheelers.

"I think an angel guided you all here," Jess Wheeler said when Molly and Willy entered the Wheeler home. "Brother Levett, a preacher from Tennessee, stayed with us last night. This is his first time in Texas, so Marion took him bear hunting this morning. I believe he would be glad to preach this Sunday. I will ask him when he gets back from his hunt."

On Sunday morning, November 3, 1850, Brother Levett did preach at the schoolhouse with its floor swept clean and a fire burning low in the fireplace. Probably thirty men, women, and children sat quietly on the hewn log benches as Brother Levett preached the sermon that lasted until after the noon hour. Nevertheless, no person complained. They all brought baskets of freshly cooked food which they shared with one another. Along about midafternoon they went to their homes, promising to come again.

Brother Levett soon left to go to other places. After that, the news about the church meetings at School Creek valley immediately spread through the settlements. This encouraged other ministers from different denominations to preach on different Sundays. Sometimes they stayed in the homes of the settlers for as much as a week before they went to another place.

One time, a Brother Webb became interested in Willy as he sensed in him the potential of becoming a minister. On his way north, he stopped by the Andersons.

"Mrs. Anderson," he said to Molly, "I thought you might be interested to know about the Baylor College at Independence, west of the Brazos River. I visited it once. I believe it is one of the best colleges in our land. It is a school of strict discipline and thorough instruction of philosophy, language, and interpretation of the Bible."

"I would like for Willy to attend that school. That is, if he wants to," Molly answered with great anticipation. "He reads the Bible very well, but he needs someone to help him understand. I try when I have time. But I need a teacher myself. I sure do thank you for telling me about this wonderful place."

By New Year's of 1851, the cotton was picked and hauled to the gin. Molly bundled up Willy's clothes and fixed a bedroll to put behind the saddle. He mounted Peppy and rode west to the one-street village of Independence and the highly honored Baylor College.

To Willy's discomfort, the fourteen young students were dressed as if they were attending a worship service. However, they greeted him well and showed him the stable where he could keep his horse. They took him to the one-room dormitory where he would sleep on a small cot with the other students. Perhaps, the biggest surprise was that of the professor. He spoke almost in a monotone voice, yet he proved to be a compassionate, remarkable person—an interesting and humble man whom Willy would never forget.

Molly missed Willy and so did George. Yet, she knew this to be the opportunity she wished for her son, with such a desire to serve. Even as a young lad, he wanted to be a minister like his friend, Jim Mason.

Too, she wished Jacob could have had a better education. Yet, she saw him happy, honest, and respected. She knew he possessed wisdom he did not learn in the classroom. Considering all things, she decided she should deed him a portion of the land. It truly belonged to him.

"Jacob, I need to say something to you and Elizabeth. I think it is time you claim a quarter of the First Class Headright land," she said. "But first, I want you and Elizabeth to ride over the land together. That way you can decide where you want to build a house and live. Maybe, in time to come, you will raise a family there."

Jacob and Elizabeth did ride over the land. They chose land north of Walnut Creek. Then, in the fall of 1851, they moved into their new home.

Calvin rode the almost one hundred miles from Austin to see

Molly that year. Those were happy hours they spent together. They rode recklessly over the land. Or other times they walked quietly among the live oak and tall, sturdy walnut trees. They talked of the days when they would be married and always be together. Still, unexpected reasons to wait to take their wedding vows always interrupted their plans.

"Señora Molly," Pablo said one day, "I want to go see my brother Alfredo and Francisca and their children. I promise I will come back to pick the cotton."

"Why, Pablo," Molly said, "I've been very selfish to keep you here. By all means, go see Alfredo and his family. Be sure to give Francisca my regards. I'll never forget how she cared for Jacob when he was wounded. Now, he's well and strong."

Molly never seemed happier than in the summer of 1851. True, Willy was away at the Baylor College. But she knew he was doing well and would be home in a short while.

Often, in the cool of the evenings, she walked down to Walnut Creek. She simply enjoyed the sound of the bubbling water as it forever flowed toward the big Brazos River. Once she kept walking, following the stream. She looked over the edge of a cliff at deep pools of transparent water. It almost seemed to be standing still. She could see untold numbers of little fish swimming back and forth as if they were playing games in the stream.

Without thinking further, she unlaced her shoes and took off her stockings. She hung her dress and petticoat on a bush. She lifted her arms and dived into the water. As she leisurely floated on her back, she looked up to the azure blue sky and listened to a turtledove calling to his mate. At that very moment, she decided to marry Calvin in the spring.

Afterward, she swam downstream perhaps a quarter of a mile. Shaking her head to get the water off her hair, she turned and walked back to the ledge where she left her clothes. She put on her petticoat and dress, and holding her shoes and stockings, she walked barefoot to her home on the hilltop.

"Maw, see what I have," George said that evening as he came through the room carrying a cub bear he had wrapped in his shirt.

"Where did you get that animal? You be careful, he could hurt you," Molly said, not believing what she saw.

"Maw, this little cub is too weak to walk," George said. "When I came through the forest, I saw a mother bear somebody shot. I don't know why anybody would kill the mother. They didn't even skin her. Maybe a big papa bear scared them so they ran away. I don't know. Two cubs were there. But one was already dead. He could have starved to death. I picked this one up. He is too weak to even walk. Can we give him some milk?" George asked.

The cub, George named Bud, became so accustomed to his new home that he followed George like a puppy. However, when he got larger, George put a chain on him and tied him to a stump. Bud seemed to enjoy that stump. When he heard the sound of the hounds or a strange person, he dropped one ear and then the other, signaling George to come.

Soon, Bud grew so large Molly thought he might accidentally harm some child. "George, I know you like Bud, but I think he needs to be with other bears," Molly said. "I think he would be happier in the woods."

Two days later, George and Molly led Bud into the forest. George took the chain from Bud's neck and let him go. Bud smelled around on the ground, then quickly wobbled out of sight.

Willy came home from college in the fall. The happy-go-lucky boy appeared very mature. Still, Molly sensed he had been extremely homesick. That night they sat alone on the dog-run. "Maw, I'm proud to be home," he told her. "I'm glad I spent that time at the college. But, it's not like home. I learned a lot. But somehow I don't want to go back. Maw, can I just stay here with you and Jacob and George?"

"My dear son," she said, "I'm glad you had a chance to study under such an educated schoolmaster. But if you don't want to go back, that is your choice. Of course, I welcome you home. There's always mission work to be done. Especially since so many new people are coming into Texas. You know, we might even have to build onto the schoolhouse and make better benches."

She did not say, but she felt disappointed he did not return to the college. Yet, in many ways she always understood him better than the other boys. He was so like her—up on a mountaintop, or down in a valley.

That fall they pulled the corn, cut the stalks, and piled them to be used as fodder in the winter. Only one more wagon of cotton remained when Pablo came back. This time he drove two mules hitched to a much larger cart. There, right beside him, sat a beautiful, dark-skin lady with a bright-red rose in her hair.

"My friends," he called to the family, "this is my Rosa. She is Francisca's sister. Now she is my wife. We went to the mission and the priest married us. Then we danced. Now we are here. Señora Molly, I did not pick the cotton. I could not leave my Rosa."

"Pablo, you did not tell us about Rosa," Molly said, "but we are happy she is here. Welcome, Rosa! I'm Molly. This is Willy and over there is George. That is Jacob and Elizabeth coming up the path. They only married a while back."

"Señora, you are as pretty as Pablo told me," Rosa said in fluent English. "I know Jacob. He was at my sister's when he was wounded. We talked many times. He told me his horse died from the bullet intended for him. We played many times with Francisca's children. Oh, there he is now." And she ran to meet Jacob.

"Take Rosa's things into the new room," Molly told Pablo. "Then after the last wagon of cotton is taken to the gin, we will build you a house."

"Señora, maybe you do not want Rosa and me to stay. I come so you could see my Rosa. I want to stay, but we go if you say we go."

"Pablo, I'm happy you and Rosa married," Jacob said. "Didn't you hear Maw say we wanted you to stay and that we will build you a house? Enough has been said about that. Now, I want Rosa to meet Elizabeth."

Afterward, Molly and Rosa sat on the bench in the dog-run.

"Rosa, Pablo has been a good friend many years. He helped us when David was killed, and when little John died of that terrible disease. Rosa, you have a good husband. He is like a son to me. I couldn't be happier to have you two here. Besides, now I have two women here," Molly told Rosa.

Shortly, work began on a house for Pablo and Rosa about fifty yards from the house with the dog-run. But the weather became cold and the building stopped. The cattle had to be driven down to the forest land where more shelter would be provided for them.

Frequently, calves strayed from their mothers and were lost among the brush and trees. Sometimes George and Pablo had to hunt them until dark. Otherwise, they could have wandered off and died in the cold.

Then, in the fourth week of December, it seemed snow fell most days—not wet or icy snow, nor did it freeze when it fell to the ground. It was merely gentle, large flakes that danced around and finally nestled in big mounds.

"Molly, is the coffee hot?" Calvin called out as he shook the snow from his jacket.

"Calvin, I wished all day you would come," Molly, recognizing his familiar voice, rushed to open the door. "Now I know we will have a good Christmas Day."

"You are lucky, Calvin," George said. "Pablo and Willy killed a big tom turkey up in the prairie land. Besides that, Maw baked an apple pie."

"Calvin, I made it from the apples I gathered from the little trees we planted. Of course, there were only enough for one pie. Anyway, I gathered them and hid them in the root cellar. So this morning, I made our first apple pie. I hope you like it."

"Molly, I believe I smelled that apple pie all the way from the Taylor farm," Calvin said.

On the afternoon of Christmas Day, only a few white clouds drifted across the blue sky. Molly and Calvin saddled their horses and crossed Walnut Creek at the shoals. They rode over the prairie land looking for the cattle, but they had wandered into the forest.

Riding through the oak and walnut trees, snow fell on them at the slightest movement of the tree limbs.

Quickly, they laughed, reached over, and brushed it off each other. Shortly, they found the cattle bedded down, so they rode on to the plowed land.

Sometimes they silently stopped and looked around as if they were engraving on their minds the beauty of it all. They talked little of their plans to marry and their future together. It was simply a time to enjoy and cherish a special day.

Even before the sun rose the following morning, Calvin mounted his horse and rode back to Austin. Soon the snow began to melt in the bright sunlight. So work resumed on building a house for Pablo and Rosa. In ten days the work was completed and the couple moved in. Yet, Rosa continued to help Molly take the soiled clothes to the creek to wash and hang them on bushes to dry.

Crops were good in 1852. Perhaps the gentle winter rains, and snow contributed to this. On the other hand, with Pablo to help, the annoying big rocks were hauled away and the soil tilled deeper, permitting the seed to germinate and break through the soil.

One day in early July, Jacob ran to Molly shouting, "Maw, me and Elizabeth, we're goin' to have a baby. Our own little baby!"

"A baby!" George stood stunned. "We've never had a baby before. I know it's goin' to be a baby boy."

"George, I don't care. A girl or a boy, either one is fine with me. Now, Jacob, you be sure Elizabeth eats a lot of greens. We want that child to be healthy," Molly cautioned Jacob.

However, only about three weeks later, Molly heard Jacob calling, "Maw, come quick. Elizabeth fell down the stairs. She's crying and hurting bad."

Elizabeth did fall down the stairs and as a result she experienced the loss of her unborn child. To be sure, the entire family sensed sadness and grief for their loss.

In early December, Calvin unexpectedly came to see Molly. At once she sensed it was not one of the delightful visits.

"Molly, let's walk down by the creek. I have something I want to talk to you about," he calmly said.

This surely disturbed her, but she said nothing. Holding hands, they walked down the hill and sat under their tall tree.

"Do you remember when we sat under this same tree and I told you for the first time that I loved you? Well, I still do. Maybe more now than then. You see, I needed to say that again as I may be leaving in a few days."

Hearing that, her heart began to beat so fast that to her it seemed an eternity. Then it appeared to almost stop beating. Nevertheless, she said nothing as Calvin continued. "I've been offered a job to go north and work with some Indians tribes in a recently developed reservation. It's where a little stream, called the Clear Fork, empties into the Brazos River. I haven't accepted this offer. Nor will I, unless you agree."

"Calvin, how can I say no?" Molly replied. "You've wished a long time to help the Indians. Maybe this is your chance. I will miss you. But I'll still love you and wait for you to come back."

"Molly, you're right. I do want to see that the Indians are treated fairly. I think they will accept and listen to what I say. The officials promised this tour of duty would last only one year."

"Go, my dear Calvin. And if George were older, I would go with you. I only ask one thing. Come back to me."

"I swear, my love," he quickly answered. After that they felt a unique closeness and talked of trivial things until almost midnight. He kissed her goodbye and left.

"Calvin will be gone for a year," she told the family. "He'll be an Indian agent north of here. I'm glad he will be helping the Indians. We'll be married when he gets back."

Afterward, she didn't mention Calvin to her sons, but many nights she cried because she missed him.

In the fall of 1853, Willy heard that a plantation owner near Brazaria raised a new breed of swine.

"If we could breed our old sow with one of those hogs, we

would have better animals. Get the wagon ready and we'll go inspect this new breed of hogs," Molly said.

The next day they headed south to Brazaria. They had not expected to see such magnificent animals as those at the plantation.

"Maw, look how short their legs are and how wide their body is," Willy enthusiastically said. "Why! One ham on that hog would be worth two from our tall, lean sow or boar."

"Mrs. Anderson, I do not want to sell you one of my Berkshire sows. I keep them to breed," the man said, pointing to another pen. "But I will sell you that young boar, over there. He's from my best sow."

"When we came here, I didn't expect to get another sow, but I sure would like to have one of these you call a Berkshire."

"I can sell you one of the young sow pigs that'll breed in about six months. She's not from the same sow as the boar. She'll give you strong, healthy pigs," the man said. "If you keep these swine in a pen by themselves, in a year you'll have a litter of purebred Berkshire hogs."

Without discussing the matter further, Willy and George put the swine in the wagon. They tied the hind legs together and headed back home.

In 1854, small villages began to spring up here and there. Large two-story houses were built on some of the big plantations. To Molly all of this presented a good omen that finally life in Texas was merging into civilization. Yet one thing still bothered her. The plantation owners were bringing in black slaves.

"We'll not have slaves on our First Class Headright," Molly constantly declared. "Oh, I hear people say that Texans don't whip or mistreat their slaves. Maybe they don't, but I believe it's wrong to sell or buy a human being."

That summer the cotton crop suffered another setback. It was not the giant grasshoppers, but a little brown insect that did not completely destroy the crop. So, once more, only a few wagon loads of cotton were taken to the gin. But it proved to be a good year for corn.

"Maw, this year we have gathered more corn than any year," Jacob said. "Maybe eighty bushels to the acre."

"We don't need all that corn for the Berkshire hogs and the old sow and her pigs. I'll have George take some to Jericho's General Store and trade for wheat flour and maybe some calico. Then, I'll not have to work on the spinning wheel."

Christmas of 1854, Molly read the story of the Christ Child from the Holy Bible to her sons and the new members of the family. She appeared happy as she continually related earlier episodes of happy times to Rosa and Elizabeth. Still, she missed Calvin. Now a year had gone by, and he still had not returned. She tried to believe that tomorrow he would come home.

In early January of 1855, she heard a knock on the door. Without hesitating, she opened it, believing it to be a friend. Two young men dressed in military uniforms stood there. The thought came to her, *they, I am sure, are looking for Jacob.*

"Good morning, Mrs. Anderson," one young man said, "may we come in? We have a message for you from the governor."

"Please come in. I will pour you a cup of coffee," Molly said, attempting to be calm as now she sensed this was not a friendly visit.

"Thank you, our commander asked us to bring you this message. We are very sorry to tell you Agent Calvin Hill was accidentally killed two weeks ago."

Dazed, Molly did not answer at first. She only thought, Calvin is not dead; we are going to be married. In an attempt to force the horror of disbelief down her throat, she finally asked, "Can you tell me how he died? Where did he die?"

"Agent Hill was returning home from his duty at the Indian Reservation," the young sergeant said. "He and two other men were riding through hill country when his horse stepped on a prairie-dog den. His horse tumbled and fell, pinning Agent Hill under him. Mr. Hill's companions believed his neck to be broken, so they tied him to a travois and took him back to the Indian camp. He died there shortly without ever regaining consciousness."

"Did they bring his body back home? If they did, I would like to go to his grave," Molly simply said, although inside she felt her world tumbling into an unknown chasm.

"No, ma'am," the young soldier answered, "they buried him there beside two soldiers on the Indian Reservation."

"Mrs. Anderson, we were told the Indians mourned over him. He must have been a good man. Governor Pease sends his regards to you along with this," the young man said as he handed a small, crumbled piece of paper the men found in Calvin's shirt pocket.

"Thank you for coming," she said as she accepted the piece of paper. She shook the young soldiers' hands. However, she did not read the words on the paper. Turning around, the young men walked out and closed the door behind them.

She quietly sat down. Without hesitating, she carefully spread open the wrinkled paper. In a whispering voice she read: *No matter what may happen in our lives, we will always have that special bond. I love you, Molly Anderson.*

She felt numb all over. She slowly stood up and walked out the door. Her feet seemed so heavy that she sat down on the bench in the dog-run. Strange thoughts raced through her mind. Could Calvin have had a premonition of death? No. No. He was coming home to me. Not realizing it, she screamed out loud, then suddenly remained silent.

Hearing the cry, Pablo ran to see if Molly was all right. Close behind him came her three sons as the young soldiers had told them about the death of Calvin. Each person tried to comfort her. But she only looked at them, smiled, and said, "Go back to your work. I just need to be alone a little while. If Elizabeth and Rosa look for me, tell them I'm going to saddle Prince and go for a ride."

"Maw, I'm going with you. I will saddle Prince," George said, not understanding her reactions. But Jacob, Willy, and Pablo understood.

"Maw needs to be by herself just like when Papa died," Jacob explained to George. Afterward, each one kissed her tenderly and walked away.

Spurring Prince into a fast run, he almost jumped over the creek. With his tail in the air, she let him run back and forth across the prairie land, then down through the forest. Finally, she pulled up on the reins and stopped him. She dismounted, then rubbed his nose, and he in turn, as if he were smiling, gently pushed her to one side. She silently sat there attempting to accept her loss. Then, she thought she heard the bawl of a baby calf, so she followed the sound. Yes, a little calf had strayed from his mother and became lodged among the brush. When she released the calf, it ran to its mother. Knowing he would be safe now, she turned and walked back to where Prince was grazing.

Sometime after dark, as she came back from her ride, she saw a light shining in the kitchen window. Rosa and Elizabeth had cooked her supper. She took the saddle off Prince and hung it on the rack. She opened the kitchen door, brushed the dust off her shoes, and went in. She threw her bonnet on the floor and sat down at the one empty chair at the table.

"One of the calves lost his mother and got tangled up in the brush. I had a hard time getting the little rascal out," she kept talking, ignoring the others.

"I've been thinking we ought to build a shed onto the back of this old cabin. And, maybe an upstairs room," she rambled on. "We need a smokehouse, too. You know, we have good hams now that we have the Berkshire hogs."

All at once she quit talking and walked out the door without clearing the supper table—something she had never done before. She sat on a stump and gazed up at the sky and twinkling stars. She relived, in her mind, all the wonderful years she spent with Calvin, a man who entered her life a short, happy time and suddenly left, leaving her lonely and sad. She knew when Willy brought a quilt and placed it over her shoulders, although she pretended not to see him.

The family knew she alone could work out her grief.

Resolutely, each day, she went about her daily chores, desperately trying to erase the treasured years she spent with Calvin.

True, they did build the shed on the back room and stairs in the dog-run. Those led to a newly erected room with a glass window. This became Molly's hideaway. George and Pablo carried the big bed up the stairs. Next, came the spinning wheel and loom. Day after day, or often into the night, by candlelight, Molly paddled the wheel. Somehow this gave her courage to soothe the anger in her aching heart caused by the death of this man she learned to love so dearly. Slowly, she accepted the loss and began to look forward to the days ahead.

Constantly, talks of telegraphs, railroads, and new schools circulated through the country. Yet, many of the primary schools were still supported by communities—School Creek school being one of them. The school building was enlarged and now served as a worship service on Sunday morning.

Matt Taylor and Willy made a hitching post where people tied their horses. Too, Oran Taylor and Jess Wheeler hewed a pulpit for the preacher from seasoned walnut wood. Probably the church bell, made by the blacksmith in Franklin, became the outstanding attraction.

On Sunday morning Willy went early to the church. He had volunteered to come and ring the bell. After tying Peppy to the hitching post, he walked to the bell tower. There, standing tall and silent, he reached up with both hands and tugged vigorously on the leather bell pull. At once, the clear vibrant tone of the bell echoed down School Creek valley, summoning the people to worship.

By ten o'clock, people began to arrive. They greeted each other as they waited for the preacher. Still, no preacher rode up the path.

"Ertha and me need to talk to you," Marion whispered to Molly. "So many people have come to worship, but we have no preacher. We know Willy studied the Bible in the Baylor College. Do you think we should ask him to preach this morning?"

"You make me happy to think of this," Molly said. "You know he is very shy. But look over there, he's talking to that pretty young lady. Go on. Ask him anyway."

Willy did agree to speak. He stood proudly behind the pulpit and opened his Bible to the book of Psalms. He eloquently read one of the Psalms, but when he attempted to explain the verses, he could not speak. Sweat broke out on his forehead, even though it was wintertime. "Lord, I'm scared," he said. Then he looked around the crowded room and saw Rachel Stevens, the young lady to whom he had been talking. She looked directly at him, shook her head "yes," and smiled. Suddenly, his voice returned. That morning he did preach an inspiring message.

Two months later, Willy Anderson and Rachel Stevens were married.

"We need to go to the courthouse," Molly said to them one day. "I'm going to deed you both one-fourth of our land. But first, I want you to ride over all of it and choose a place, except where Jacob and Elizabeth live, where you want to raise a family."

"Maw, Rachel and me already know where we want to live. We would like to have that land on the southwest corner of School Creek where the school and church stands."

As Molly rode Prince from the courthouse, she felt content. Willy was seeing his dream come true. Jacob and Elizabeth were happy and expecting a baby. George was attending the new public school in the newly organized town of Calvert, thirteen miles away. Yet, many thoughts came to her mind. *I know I should be happy, but I have no companion to share my joy. I miss David and little John. Nor can I ever forget Calvin, who always made me laugh.*

In the spring of 1859, an unusual amount of rain fell in Robertson County, causing the prairies and the creek bottomland to come alive with bluebonnets and Indian paintbrush flowers that covered the ground. Then traveling along the tree stumps were the wild rambling roses. When she looked out the window of her upstairs room, she marveled at the beauty around her. From that, she finally accepted the loss of Calvin. Right then she felt a desire to enjoy life.

Hastily, she put on her best dress and harnessed Prince to her brand-new buggy. She slapped the reins gently on the rump of the horse, and he trotted down the soggy path to the main road and turned south toward Calvert, a town unknown to her. As she approached the village, she noticed a two-story boardinghouse. She stopped and looked in awe. It reminded her of the boardinghouse in Nashville, Tennessee. She tied Prince to a hitching post in front of a store. She stood still and stared at a red, ready-made dress hanging in a glass window. She hurriedly opened the door, with a sign that read "open" on the latch, and walked in.

"Good morning," a kind voice greeted her, "may I help you with a dress? You see, I make all the clothes myself right here in my store. Oh, I'm sorry. I don't believe I know you. My name is Hattie."

Molly reached out her hand and said, "I'm Molly Anderson. I'm pleased to meet you. I would like to buy a dress. I think I like that one hanging in the window."

"Perhaps you would like to see other dresses, also," Hattie answered.

"No, thank you. I would like the crimson red one, in the corner of the room," Molly answered. About that time, she noticed four black straw hats neatly placed on a table. Then, hanging above the hats were black, blue, and white calico bonnets. Molly barely looked at those. She simply could not take her eyes off the black straw hat with a bright red ribbon around the brim that supported the purple plume.

She could not resist trying on this beautiful hat. She put it on, looked in the mirror, and stood speechless. To her, she appeared so old and unkempt. At once, she began to remove the hatpin holding that gorgeous thing on her curly, black hair that showed a slight tinge of gray. She intended to thank the nice dressmaker and go back to her home and never return.

However, about that time, the door opened. In walked a tall

man dressed in taylor-made clothes. She timidly glanced at him then turned away.

"Good morning. May I be so bold as to say you look lovely in that hat," he said. "Oh! Excuse me, I did not intend to be so rude. I'm Reuben Stanford, a cattle buyer from Houston."

"Pleased to meet you, Mr. Stanford. I'm Molly Anderson," she politely said. Suddenly, she did not feel so old.

Molly returned home and hung the new dress behind the door. She looked around to be sure she was alone, then she put on the straw hat with the purple plume. She cautiously looked into the little mirror she had kept many years, and somehow she did not look as old and haggard as when she put the hat on at the dress shop. She smiled and carefully hung it with the red dress behind the door.

With quick, steady steps, she went down the stairs, sat down on the dog-run bench, and thought about the handsome man she saw in Calvert. Perhaps he, too, came from Tennessee. Surely he must be a very important man. How else would he be so well dressed?

"Elizabeth, will you and Rosa come upstairs?" Molly called to them. "I want you to see my new dress and hat." They eagerly ran up the stairs, since as to their knowledge, Molly had never had a store-bought dress.

"Do you think I should wear this Sunday?" she asked. "Do you think it is too bright a color?"

"You look beautiful in the hat. And, Molly, the red dress is just right for you. It will help you to not look so sad," Elizabeth truthfully said. "I'm sure your sons will be proud when you wear that beautiful dress and hat to church on Sunday."

"Molly, you look so pretty in them. May I try the hat on?" Rosa said as she pulled her black hair into a big knot and put the hat on her head. She held up her skirt and clicking her heels danced around the room.

"Rosa, you are so happy all the time. No wonder Pablo loves you," Molly said. But somehow she failed to mention the incredible tall stranger with the enchanting manner she saw in Calvert.

CHAPTER 8

Each Sunday Molly wore her crimson red dress and her straw hat with the red ribbon tied to the purple plume. Most of the time she sat on a pew with George. However, one Sunday she decided to sit on a bench near the entrance door. Hearing people enter, she turned to say "hello" to them when, to her surprise, in walked the interesting man she saw at the dress shop in Calvert. He nodded and smiled. She smiled back at him. Throughout the minister's sermon, she felt a little uncomfortable. She could almost see those dark-brown eyes peering at her from the back bench.

After the service, as always, she greeted each person, and at last, walked out the door. That handsome man seemed to be waiting for her.

"Why, Miss Molly Anderson, I'm very surprised to see you here," he politely said. "May I have the privilege of escorting you to your home?"

"Yes, Mr. Stanford, I'd be honored to have you come to my home," Molly said.

Tying his horse behind the buggy, he sat beside her as they went to her house. They spent the afternoon with her family, talking about the new towns and other events in Texas.

Yet, he said little about himself, except to say, "I work for a company in Houston. I buy and sell cattle. I'll not be in Calvert long. You see, I have to travel a lot. I understand you raise cattle. You must have a lot of land. Some time I would like to ride all over it."

After he left later in the day, everyone, except George, expressed the opinion that Mr. Reuben Stanford appeared to be an interesting and intelligent man.

"Maw, this man seems strange to me. Will he come back to see us?" George asked, then said no more.

"You're just afraid Maw will marry this man," Jacob said.

After that first visit, Reuben came often. Once he and Molly rode over the prairie land to see the cattle.

"My company will buy your cattle," he told Molly. "I will see you get a good price. How many do you want to sell?"

"I know we need to sell some of the older cows—maybe a few bulls. I talk to my sons about such matters. You see, this land, the cattle, and the crops belong to the family. I'll ask them," Molly truthfully answered.

Each week Reuben came to see Molly. And each week she anxiously waited to see that charming person ride up.

"Molly, I've never been attracted to a woman like I have to you," he said one day. "I think I've fallen in love for the first time. Molly, will you marry me?"

"I believe I love you, Reuben," she said, then added, "but I think we must wait until we know each other better. My sons like you. I know they want me to be happy. Of course, George may not want me to marry. He's my youngest son. Sometimes I know I pamper him a little. You see, I need to think about this further."

"I understand," he answered, "but unless you say yes, I have to leave Calvert soon. Please say 'yes' to me."

That night she thought Reuben's proposal over for a very long while. *My common sense tells me to wait. Yet my desire for happiness tells me to say yes.*

"Reuben asked me to marry him," she told the family. "I think I'll say 'yes.' I believe I would like to be married."

"Maw, if you are sure this is what you want, I wish you well," Jacob told her.

"I want you to be happy. If you are sure Reuben is a good man, do what you wish," Willy said and followed Jacob out the door.

George said nothing. He picked up his hat and walked out.

A couple of days later, Molly hitched Prince to the buggy and started to Calvert. She wanted to buy a brightly colored parasol to match the crimson red dress she planned to wear when she married Reuben. But even before she went into the dress shop, she saw him. He asked her to come to dinner with him at the dining room in the hotel.

They sat at a table with a linen tablecloth and lighted candles in shiny glass candlesticks. She looked around the crowded dining hall and it seemed as if everyone envied her sitting with such a distinguished man. She had forgotten such sophisticated culture existed.

Reuben smiled, reached over, took her hand, and softly said, "Molly, I'm asking you to marry me today. Will you? I will go to Houston and tell my company I will not travel. I will return tomorrow and we'll be together from now on. I wish you could go with me. But, your sons would worry if you did not come home. You know I would never want to cause them to worry."

Without considering her answer, she agreed. After finishing an elaborate dinner, they went to the office of the justice of the peace and were married. Holding hands they walked out the door and to Molly's buggy.

"I must leave for Houston now. When I return we will be together from then on. My home will be with you and your sons. I'll miss you every minute I'm away. Goodbye, Mrs. Molly Stanford, you beautiful bride. Wait for me." He kissed her on the cheek, mounted his horse, and rode south as she waved.

She felt utterly confused when he rode away. Why did she not wait until he came from Houston to marry her? How would she tell her sons she was no longer Molly Anderson? Then the idea came to her that perhaps she would remain Molly Anderson, as she, now, believed this whole affair should never have happened. Considering that, she decided not to tell her sons about her wedding.

The second night, trying to be fair, Molly waited until after midnight to see Reuben come in. The third night, he did not come.

However, around midnight on the fourth night, she heard him open the door and come in. She rushed down the stairs to welcome him home. But immediately, she detected the odor of whiskey, and from the way he walked she knew he was drunk.

"Molly, go cook me some of that good ham. I'm hungry. I'm your husband, so give me the deed to all this land." He reached for her purse and blurted out, "I want all the money in this satchel. Then come over here and sit on my lap and give me a great big kiss!" At that, he reached over and grabbed her by the arm.

"Get out of here and never come back. I'm not your wife and I'll never be. You have no right on my land. You can't live in my house. Get out! Leave! If you come near me, I'll shoot you." At that, she reached behind the open door. She grabbed the old rifle and pointed it at him.

"Oh, don't try to scare me. I know you're jest a silly ole women," he muttered and lunged toward her.

"I said leave! And don't come back," Molly warned him. Again, he ignored her warning and lunged toward her. He stood unsteady a moment than went toward her once more. The next move he made, Molly pulled the trigger of the gun. The bullet almost grazed his left shoulder.

"Stop, stop!" he yelled.

Then Molly aimed the gun at the floor. She pulled the trigger twice. Although the shot did not even go near him, he ran out the door, mounted his horse, and rode south.

Molly dropped the rifle. She sat down and began to tremble all over. How did she ever believe such a man loved her, or she loved him? Overcome with humiliation for having succumbed to the lies and false promises of a man like Reuben, she blamed herself. To be sure, she knew she enticed him. Nor did the fact that she felt lonely excuse her actions. What could she say to her sons?

"Señora Molly, I thought I heard you shoot your gun last night. Did you kill another fox in the chicken pen?" Pablo asked the next morning. "Maybe I'll set a trap in the pen, but then I might catch a chicken," he laughed at his own joke.

"Pablo, I didn't kill a fox, but I shot at a skunk." Without explaining, she answered, "No need to set a trap, the skunk is gone."

She knew she must not wait any longer to tell her sons about Reuben. Perhaps they already knew—especially George.

"You will not see Reuben Stanford around here any more," Molly candidly said. "I should never have believed the things he told me. I don't think my being lonely is why I made such a terrible mistake. The fact is, I'm just a foolish old woman just like Reuben said. I guess him saying the truth made me mad. I got the rifle and almost hit him on his shoulder. He came toward me again. That's when I got mad and I shot twice close to his feet. I didn't intend to kill him." She paused for a moment, then said, "Well, maybe I did."

Her sons looked at each other. They did not speak. They put on their hats and walked out, saddled their horses, and rode toward Calvert.

"Put out a warrant for Reuben Stanford," Jacob said to the sheriff. "This man claims to be a cattle buyer from Houston, but we don't believe this is true. He tried to take the deed to our land from our mother."

"Mr. Anderson, this man is not Reuben Stanford. He is Ralph Ford. He's a drifting gambler who has taken money from a lot of widow women. We have orders to arrest him when we find him. Only two days ago I learned he was in Calvert. He lost every penny he had in a poker game with a plantation owner. Afraid he would be arrested, if he were known, he promised the plantation owner a deed to some land in payment for his gambling debt. Now I know why he attacked your mother," the sheriff said.

"But, what bothers us is the fact that he married our mother," Willy told the sheriff.

"Oh! That's no problem. The marriage license is not valid," the sheriff said. "Tell your mother she is still Mrs. Molly Anderson."

Relieved somewhat, the three brothers went home. They told Molly about their visit to see the sheriff.

"Maw, don't feel too bad about believing this Reuben. You are not the only lady to be tricked by this man," Willy said. "The sad part is, he will not stop taking widows' money."

"I know you want to protect me," Molly answered, "but I'm sure I'll never see that man again. Just let it be! I guess I'm embarrassed about the whole thing."

"Maw, you're not foolish, I'm to blame for some of this. I saw Reuben go into the saloon. When I looked in, he was sitting there holding his cards. I know lots of men spend time gambling, but I didn't know they gambled for such high stakes, or cheated when they lost."

After that conversation, no one mentioned Reuben Stanford. Still, Molly believed she could have prevented the whole unpleasant incident. Often she rode Prince all over her land. Once she galloped down by Walnut Creek where she noticed the bluebonnets and Indian paintbrush blossoms were faded and had fallen to the ground.

She stopped Prince and sat quietly in the saddle. For some reason, unknown to her, she sat silently. She gazed at the land around her, then suddenly the thought came to her that these beautiful faded flowers were like her life. For a short time, there is wonderful, happy times, but so often the good times fade like the flowers. Sitting quietly admiring the beauty around her, she remembered that the bluebonnets and the Indian paintbrush would revive in the spring, and brilliant, gorgeous flowers would return. She shook her head to clear her thoughts, knowing her life could be like the bluebonnets and Indian paintbrush if she tried. Only she was responsible for her happiness.

"Tell Rosa we won't be going down to the creek to wash the clothes today," she called to Pablo. "I'm going to go see Ertha. I'll be back late this afternoon."

"I've been expecting you," Ertha said when she opened the door for Molly to enter. "Marion told me about Reuben Stanford. I would have loved to see him running away. Marion never told anybody else, nor will he. But he said Jacob did report this Reuben, or whoever he is, to the Rangers."

"Oh! Ertha, I feel so ashamed. Why did I do such a thing?" Molly asked.

"Now, don't you go and feel guilty about this. That man's a handsome devil," Ertha said. "When we get lonesome for a mate and realize we are getting older, women, especially, do many things without thinking. Why, if I didn't have Marion, I probably would have done just like you did."

"Ertha, I don't believe that, but I knew you would understand. I even promised to obey that man," Molly laughed and said. "But he obeyed me when he ran off."

Ertha did not reply, she merely changed the subject. "Do you know that plans for a new town is underway? I think Marion said it would be named Bremond after a railroad man. What next! A railroad running right through this county!"

"Sometimes I can't keep up with all the new things," Molly answered. "This seems like a different country than when we came to Texas from Tennessee. Some day this will be the biggest and richest state in the Union."

With the news of railroads and other improvements, talk of moving the county seat of Robertson County began to circulate as no hope remained of a railroad through Wheelock. Consequently, a courthouse was built in the new town of Franklin, causing it to flourish.

"Maw, I saw a lady today in Franklin I would like you to meet," George said to Molly one afternoon. "She came all the way from Germany across the Atlantic Ocean to Texas. She is a dressmaker and lives alone on the road just before you get into Franklin."

"I would like for you to bring her to dinner on Sunday. You know, I love to talk about sewing," Molly said.

"I knew you would say that. I've already asked her to come,"

George grinned and said. "I believe, you see, I have fallen in love."

On Sunday, George did bring his new friend home to dinner. "Maw, meet Wilheminia Volk," George proudly said, "but she tells me she is called Wela. I like that. Don't you?"

From that time on, George spent each Sunday with Wela. Once, he took her to School Creek in Molly's shiny-topped buggy to hear Willy preach.

"Maw, Wela and me are going to get married," George told Molly when he came home one night. "She wants to come see you soon. She wants you to learn more about her." He said nothing else and walked out the door.

A few days later, Wela did come. As they sat quietly drinking a cup of coffee, Wela said, "Did George tell you he asked me to marry him? Before I answered him, I told him about my life. Now I want you to hear it, too."

"George did tell me he asked you to marry him. That makes me very happy. He tends to be restless since his brothers married. I often think I dote on him too much. Did you know his father died before he was born?" Molly said to Wela.

Wela did not answer Molly. She merely looked around, smiled, and began. "I want you to know this even though it is hard for me tell you. I came from Germany with my parents, my brother, and my young sister who died and was buried at sea just before we landed at Galveston."

"Are your brother and your parents still living in Texas?" Molly asked. " I would like to meet them if they do."

"My brother lives near Franklin, but my parents do not," Wela quietly answered. "When our ship landed at Galveston, an epidemic of cholera spread throughout the town. Many people died and among them were our parents. We were not allowed to see them because of the cholera, so we believed they were robbed and killed. Neither my brother nor I could speak or understand English. We had no relatives, so we did not know what to do."

"Two young children alone in a strange country. I can't think of anything more frightful. What did you do?" Molly asked.

"One day some men took us to this house a long way from Galveston. They made us work hard day after day. Sometimes, they beat my brother when he refused to follow their orders. Once they tied me to the bed and held my brother while they whipped me, even as I cried and begged them to stop." Wela took a handkerchief from her pocket. She wiped the saliva from her mouth and continued. "One night the men all went into town so we found some iron pieces of metal and broke down the door. We hid down by the river where a kind man found us and took us home with him. His wife was a German woman so we trusted them. They both died last year."

"I am sorry. I know you miss them," Molly sincerely said.

"That was when I moved to Franklin and now make a living by sewing for wealthy people. Mrs. Anderson, I don't want to marry your son if you object because of those bad men," Wela said.

"Oh! Wela," Molly said, "I love you as if you were my own daughter. I know my son loves you, too. I could never have been as brave as you and your brother were. You were two young children, but you had courage to run away."

"That was a long time ago. Until I met George, I was afraid to be with people, especially men. George is kind and thoughtful. I trust him and am truly happy." Wela smiled, looked at Molly, and said, "May I call you Mother Anderson? I hope you understand I already love you."

Even with all the enthusiasm of new towns, railroads, telegraphs, and better roads, a declining sense of prosperity prevailed throughout the entire state. The thoughts of the people were on the action of the legislative body of the federal government.

The majority of Texans were not slave owners. Yet, most people became agitated when President Lincoln declared the slaves to be free. Perhaps it was not the slave question alone that concerned the southerners, as well as the Texans. Old wounds, going back to the beginning of the Union, continued to fester in the minds of the people from both the north and the south.

Perplexed by such rumors, Molly became deeply troubled. She

tried to believe those problems could be resolved. Particularly, now that Sam Houston was governor again. However, the things that frightened her most were the constant threat of secession from the Union and the approaching signs of war.

Even so, in the fall of 1860, Willy and Rachel prepared for a wedding. Their home was scrubbed clean and vases of fresh-cut flowers decorated each table. At Wela's request, only the family and Pablo and Rosa attended this quaint wedding as Willy performed the ceremony.

On Monday morning, Molly went with George and Wela to the courthouse in Franklin. With steady hands, Molly joyfully signed a deed to George and Wela Anderson consisting of one-fourth of the First Class Headright land grant. From this, Molly experienced a genuine feeling of accomplishment. Although she knew other hurdles would have to be crossed, at least one more was solved. Her three sons now owned land of their own.

A log house was erected for the bride and groom, and George moved Wela's possessions into her new home. Numerous exquisitely embroidered table linens, pillow shams, and counter-panes filled the room, tastefully displaying Wela's skills as a gifted seamstress.

By January of 1861, talk of seceding from the Union grew stronger and louder. Therefore, in February a vote was put to the qualified voters; over two-thirds proved to be eager to secede. As a result, the state of Texas became the seventh state to join the Confederate States of America.

Long into the night the family discussed the situation. Molly noticed mixed feelings among her sons, and this saddened her.

"I swore to obey the Mexican law when we came to Texas," Molly said, "and I did. Then Texas became a Republic. I whole-heartedly became a law-abiding citizen of the Republic. In 1846, I gladly swore allegiance to the United States. Now, this? Frankly, I just want to live like we are. Anyhow, we have no choice. So, I'll help the Confederacy if I can and abide by the rules. Somehow, I still feel like Sam Houston can put an end to any fighting."

"Maw, Houston refused to swear allegiance to the Confederacy. So yesterday, he was ousted from office," Jacob told Molly. "I thought we had a cause when we fought for independence from Mexico. But, I don't see any reason to secede from the Union. I couldn't sleep last night because of this." He paused, shook his head and continued. "If I volunteer to fight on either side, I could be killed. That would leave Elizabeth and young John Newton alone. I finally decided if I'm called to fight, I will do the best I can to end this senseless war."

"We have no choice except to follow the leaders of our new government. Texas is our home and this is our land. If it comes to war, we must fight to preserve our lives and our property. I, also, pray that President Lincoln and President Davis will somehow stop the bloodshed. Maybe we'll be spared the horror the southern states are suffering. From my point of view, most of the fighting will be done as the Federal soldiers move south," Willy wisely said.

"I don't want war, either," George said, "but I signed the conscription paper to volunteer in the Confederate army. Wela did not want me to volunteer until I told her how Texans fought for this land. How Jacob, although a young boy, did his share. I'm willing to fight as long as it is necessary."

"I'm a Texas-Mexican," Pablo spoke up. "I'll fight, but I'll be with what you say—Confederacy? Thees is my country and you are my people. Tomorrow I go."

"Maw, I believe this is the time to begin the fight, or the Federal army might come through Texas. If that happens, battles will be fought on our land," George said the following morning when he handed Molly the *State Gazette* newspaper. "The entrance to the Port of Galveston has been blocked by the Federal navy. Now, we can't ship our cotton to other countries. Another thing, we won't be able to get imported products such as manufactured goods."

Hearing that the Union navy entered Galveston, Jacob rode to Franklin. He believed it time to enroll in the service of the Confederate army, regardless of his personal feelings.

"I see from this information that you are a married man with one child, and forty-one years of age," the recruiting officer said. I've also been told you are a Texas Ranger. Is that correct, sir?"

"That is right," Jacob answered, "although I only work as a Texas Ranger on special assignments."

"According to my last orders, we're only accepting qualified men up to forty years of age. Sir, there is a great need for law enforcement officers here at home," the man said. "We have stealing and killings right here in our own county. But if things get worse, we may be forced to notify you to appear for service in the Confederate army."

Riding back home, Jacob felt guilty not to go fight. On the other hand, perhaps it would be better to stay home to protect the family and to farm the land.

One week later, Willy, George, and Pablo put on their big-brim black hats and their best store-bought pants. With their guns in their holsters and sharpest Bowie knives in their belts, they said goodbye to Molly, their wives, and little John Newton.

After riding directly southwest to Milligan in Brazos County, they walked into the military recruiter's office. One by one, they each answered the questions asked by the army commander.

The following morning, with other young recruits they were ordered to Camp Herd in Hempstead County where they were trained in military maneuvers.

"I'm glad Jacob didn't leave with the others. There is so much work to be done," Molly said. "The cotton is almost ready to be picked. It seems chores never cease. The corn must be gathered and the cattle looked after."

By dawn each morning, Rachel and Wela were up cleaning house and feeding the animals. Later in the morning, they walked to the cotton field and picked until the sun went down. Elizabeth, with young John Newton to care for, did her share of the work.

She cooked meals for the family. And most afternoons, if the weather remained warm, she sat little John Newton on her cotton sack and pulled him along as she picked the cotton.

Cattle rustlers continually stampeded the cattle and took most of them. Sometimes the cattle were returned to the owner. Other times they were not found. Too, renegades plundered homes of women whose husbands were fighting east of the Mississippi River with the Confederate army.

About a month after Willy, George, and Pablo left, Rachel received a letter. All the women gathered around and she read:

My dear Rachel,
   This is the first time I have had a chance to write. We were mustered in at Fort Herbert in Hempstead County. George and me are privates in Company F—Elmore's 20th Regiment of Texas Infantry of the Confederate States of America. We are at Galveston. Pablo was mustered into Santos Benevides Command. He is somewhere west on the Texas border. I have never seen this much water before. When the fighting is over, we will come here and swim in the salty sea. I can see the Federal ships from our camp. I can not tell you anything more. I love you and miss you. George sends his love to Wela. Tell Maw we miss her. We are well.

Your husband,

Willy

P.S. Tell Jacob to take care of everybody and kiss John Newton for us.

Only one day after Rachel received the letter from Willy, Jacob brought in the *State Gazette* newspaper. Molly unfolded the paper and on the front page she read that Galveston was now under the rule of the Federal navy. Her heart almost stopped beating. She knew that one or maybe both sons could have been wounded or killed.

Christmas of 1862 became a bitter, cold one, so it was hardly observed. Fear filled the hearts of the people—fear that Union soldiers would now sweep through the country and many inno-cent people would suffer or die.

Later, along about the middle of January 1863, Jacob brought good news when he came from Franklin.

"Today I saw Bob Bower. He is home on leave from Galveston. Shrapnel went through his right shoulder so he spent a few days in the hospital," Jacob said.

"Tell me, Jacob," Molly asked, "did he see Willy or George?"

"No, he hasn't seen them," Jacob replied, "but he feels sure they are all right. He told me bales of cotton were stacked on two small wood-burning riverboats to hide the Confederate soldiers. Early New Year's morning, they sailed around the Federal ships and began to fire their cannons. This gave the Confederates an oppor-tunity to cross over the railroad bridge and get to the island of Galveston."

"What will happen now that the Federal army captured Galveston? Do you think they will be able to come right through the state?" Molly asked.

"No, Maw, the Confederacy surprised them. Bower was not sure, but he believes that at least three hundred Federal soldiers were captured and are being held prisoners of war," Jacob told Molly. "When Bower left Galveston, it was still in the hands of the Confederacy."

"Sometimes I don't understand how all of this comes about. Maybe I just need to believe that some day it will end," Molly remarked.

"Bower told me many lives are saved by having a hospital near," Jacob said. "It is only an old hotel where the wounded are brought in and cared for by doctors and nurses. Sometimes they work all day and often into the night. He also told me that cloth is needed to make bandages for the wounded."

"We must do what we can to help. One way is to send ban-dages to the hospital. The weather is too cold and windy to work in the fields most days. But we can help at home," Molly told her daughters-in-law and Rosa.

The following days, Molly and Rosa rode from farm to farm, asking women to make bandages or to send cloth to the hospital. Once a week they collected the cloth. Soon very little could be found as women no longer used their spinning wheels when material could be bought in the mercantile stores. Neither could fabrics be shipped in from other factories as the ports were closed. In any case, Wela and Rachel washed every little piece of material they found. They stripped it into bandages making sure they were rolled into tight, neat balls.

By late 1863, people began to feel the impact of the war. Even though the Federals were stopped from entering Texas from the Gulf of Mexico, there yet remained trouble in the north portion of the state and unrest in the south. Supplies could not be brought in. This caused people to attempt to substitute things they were accustomed to.

"Shucks, we still have more than we did during the war with Mexico," Molly often told the newcomers to Texas. "One thing is better. Now, we have a place where the wounded men are cared for."

"Some women in Robertson County have become widows because of this war that never should have begun. I'm glad Willy, George, and Pablo were not sent east of the Mississippi River," Jacob informed Molly. "I have heard that homes are burned, cattle, horses, and even chickens are carried away to be used or eaten by the Yankees. Texas is much better off than the southern states where the powerful, well-trained northern soldiers march on south."

"We must have a Christmas celebration so the saddened and troubled folks will know we care," Molly told the family. "I'll ask Oran if he will send a letter to his twin sons, Eli and Elias. They're fighting somewhere in Georgia. That way, they'll know we think of them."

On Christmas Eve 1863, the School Creek building was filled to overflowing. Laughter and singing was heard as if no war existed. Shortly, everyone sat in reverence as Elizabeth read the story of the

Christ Child. Oran Taylor, holding a piece of chalk in his hand, walked to the blackboard.

"Would everyone who has a son, a brother, a husband, or a father fighting in the southern states, please raise your hand," he called out. As each person responded, he wrote the names on the blackboard. Finally, Oran wiped the tears from his eyes, coughed to clear his throat, and softly said, "I am sorry to say two of those brave young men will not return home—Waymon Britt and Clarence Green. In honor of them, we will stand and observe a moment of silence."

When the people went to their homes, each wondered who would be the next son, father, or husband to not return.

"There is no need to plant cotton this year," Jacob said in 1864, "because we can't ship it to New Orleans or other markets. The government wants us to plant more corn. So we'll use the cotton land for more corn. We're going to have to learn to do without things we were accustomed to before the war."

"One thing I find hard to do without is salt," Molly said. "Even in Viesca a long time ago, we could get salt at Ramon and Celita's store. But, we'll get by."

"Oran Taylor, two more men, and myself are going north to the Ledbetter Salt Works," Jacob told the family. "We may be gone a week or more. We hope to get a load of salt to divide among all the people. Just watch for cattle rustlers, but don't try to stop them. We'll take care of that when I get back home."

"I've heard of salt flats up north where you can get salt," Molly told Rosa. "Once I learned to use dried okra for coffee, but I never have found anything to use instead of salt."

To be sure, the Texans were coping well with the war. Women brought out their spinning wheels and again began to paddle the wheels and make clothes for their families. Then once, some man brought a wagonload of needed things across the Sabine River from New Orleans to Calvert. Without waiting, Wela and Rachel rushed to get material to make bandages for the soldiers at the hospital in Galveston.

"The store was crowded with people," Rachel told Molly and Elizabeth when they returned, "all of them wanting to buy muslin, calico, or other imported merchandise."

"We were lucky," Wela said. "A gentleman heard us say we wanted the muslin to make bandages for our fighting men. Right then that man demanded we be allowed to buy the full bolt of muslin. But, we had to pay a high price. Much more than what we paid before the war."

"Worse yet," Molly said, "the Confederate money is worth very little. Just like when we had to use Mexican pesos." At that, she laughed and said, "Maybe we're going back instead of stepping up in this world."

Texans did feel the unrest and pressure in the war between the north and south. So did the slaves. Many times their owners did not explain the emancipation proclamation to their slaves. On the other hand, those who could read or heard people talking, learned of their freedom. Some of the younger people ran away in an effort to reach the north. Sadly, many times they suffered more than on the plantations.

Once, far into the night, the continual sound of the hounds barking awoke Molly. She listened again. Sure enough, the baying of the hounds sounded loud and clear. She got out of bed, walked to the window, but she saw nothing unusual. Sitting on the edge of the bed, she decided to go back to sleep, but the barking did not stop. Still in her nightgown, she got the rifle and went down the stairway. With Ring and Rover leading her, she walked to the hay barn. She struck a match on the barn door and lit the lantern. Shining the light here and there, she saw the forms of two people covered with hay.

"Come out, I won't harm you," she said as she believed them to be runaway slaves.

"We wuz wore out frum running, ma'am. We jest wanted a

place to rest a while," a black man said as he and a black woman came from under the hay.

"I'm Molly Anderson," she said. "I think you're running away from a plantation owner. Don't worry, you'll be safe here. It's cold in the barn. Here, come with me."

Molly warmed some food and gave them milk to drink. She asked no questions, but when they finished eating she said, "I will not ask where you came from. I believe I know. My son tells me it is hard for a freed slave to go north. But, you have a choice. You can go on, or you can go back to the plantation until the war is over. Just stay here a couple of days and decide what you want to do. By that time, the men chasing you will be gone."

"Ma'am, we'll cause you trouble," the man said.

"Let me worry about that," Molly answered.

The following day the slaves stayed in the barn. Neither Molly nor the others said anything to them.

"Molly, where are you?" Rosa called out as she came through the door. "Tell the slaves to run fast. Two men came by and asked if I had seen a black man and woman. I know they're here, but I did not tell the men."

"Rosa, run to the barn and bring the couple here," Molly said.

Off Rosa ran to the barn as fast as she could go. After that, she ran to get Rachel, Wela, and Elizabeth with little John Newton.

"Come with me," Molly said when Rosa brought the slaves to the house. "I'll show you the upstairs. Both of you crawl under the big, high bed. That way the men will not know you are here."

Meanwhile, the women all sat around pretending to be sewing when they heard a knock on the door. Molly slightly opened it and said, "We are busy making bandages for the soldiers. What do you want?"

"Have you seen two niggers? A man and a woman," one of the men said. "They're runaway slaves. Their owner hired us to bring them back to the plantation."

"We don't have time to look for runaways. As you can see, we are the only ones in this room," Elizabeth said.

"We looked in the barn," the other man said. "We think they slept there last night. We saw where somebody had been in the hay."

"Oh," Rosa laughed and said, "I guess you think I'm a slave. I climb up and down that hay all the time. Did you see my little kid goat? Well, we played in the hay this morning."

"All right, but until we can look in the house, our boss won't pay us," the other man said.

"This is my room," Molly said when they went up the stairs, "and if you put one foot into that room, my son will arrest you and put you in jail."

"All we want to do is look under the bed," the man said.

"I work hard to get that counterpane straight on that bed. If you even touch it, you will be sorry." That was when she reached behind the door and got the shotgun.

"We meant no harm. We're just doing what we were paid to do." They said nothing else and walked outside and down the path.

"Come on down," Molly called to the slaves. "My son is here and wants to talk to you."

"Well, Mr. Jacob," the man said when he saw Jacob, "I don't believe you remember me. I wuz jest a young'un when yous took care of the soldiers at the plantation. I'm Amos and this here's Beulah."

"So, you are from the plantation where General Houston and his men stayed. Yes, I was there for a while. Maybe I saw you then, I don't recall. That seems like a long time ago," Jacob answered. "If you want to go on north, we'll give you what food you can carry. But you should know that will be risky. The farther north you go, the more you will be chased. On the other hand, if you want to go back to the plantation, I'll take you. I think this plantation owner is a good man."

"Our master wuz good to us most of the time," Moses said. "We jest wanted to be free, so we ran away. But last night we got to thinking we ought not to leave our folks. Like Miz Anderson told us, we're goin' to have to learn to be free."

Early the next morning, Amos and Beulah climbed into the wagon. Jacob took them south to their home at the plantation.

The winter of 1864 brought in chilling, bitter, cold winds that swept through east Texas. It seemed the winds triggered an epidemic of malaria, dysentery, and influenza. Although a doctor now practiced in Calvert and Franklin, he could not care for all the patients. So Molly often rode with the aging Dr. Fatheree and drove his one-horse buggy while he slept beside her as they went from farm to farm.

Those were busy days for Molly. She searched the hills for winter herbs to boil and make tea or poultices to use in combating the dreaded sickness. She stripped the outer bark from live oak limbs and boiled the inner bark to make a tea that provided a soothing effect to the intestines of the ill people.

Day after day, and sometimes into the night, she rode to the homes. Always, she desperately tried to persuade the people to allow fresh air into the rooms that seemed to emit the odor of an abandoned coal mine.

Through it all, perhaps the three days she spent with Ertha, caring for her dear friend, Mrs. Wheeler, now eighty-five years of age, was the saddest time. Regardless of all they did, Mrs. Wheeler died.

Nevertheless, through all the work and sorrow, Molly kept thinking, *the more I do, the sooner Willy, George, and Pablo will come home.*

At last the dismal, long days passed. Soon, the sound of the turtledove, the meadowlark, and the engrossing call of the whippoor-will echoed throughout the land. Next came the tantalizing, faint scent of the bluebonnets, the Indian paintbrush, and endless arrays of flowers that burst from the quiet, dormant soil. Spring had arrived! Without warning, Molly felt a flash of energy and hope race through her mind.

However, only a week later Rosa came into the house and said, "Rachel and Wela are sick. They have a high fever, but they feel cold. Wela is sitting by the fireplace with a quilt around her even though this is a nice day."

Molly instantly knew they were coming down with the flu. She, also, knew Dr. Fatheree had no more quinine to control the fever. Suddenly, an idea came to her. "Rosa, go hitch Prince to the buggy and we'll bring Wela and Rachel here and take care of them," Molly said. "But we must not let Elizabeth bring John Newton into the room."

"Here is some fresh goat milk for Rachel and Wela," Rosa said as she placed the pail on the table. "I had a hard time getting the nanny goat to give down her milk. Finally, I tied her hind legs so I could squat behind and reach her big tit. Francisca always said not to strain the goat milk, but to drink it before it gets cold."

Wela and Rachel were improving nicely from the fever, when one day a soldier knocked on the door. When Molly opened the door, the man politely said, "I'm on my way home on sick leave. I just came from the hospital in Galveston. There are lots of wounded soldiers there, but there are more sick and dying from fever and chills. One is George Anderson. He has a brother, Willy, who asked me to bring you this message. Willy was with me when the Federal navy overtook us. He helped carry me to safety behind a cliff until they took me to the hospital. I'm grateful to him and am sorry to bring you sad news," the soldier told Molly and Jacob. After a good night's sleep, he rode on north to his family.

"I'm going to Galveston in the morning," Molly told Jacob when the man rode away. "Wela and Rachel are much better and George needs me."

"Maw, you can't ride Prince alone all the way to Galveston. Renegades could attack you on the way. You stay here and I'll go look after George," Jacob said.

"You can just take me to Brazaria in the buggy, then I'll go by stagecoach to Galveston," Molly explained to Jacob. "It's far better you stay here with the family. Please, do not argue with me. Go get the buggy ready."

Two days later, Molly climbed into the stagecoach that carried the mail from Houston, by way of Brazaria, to Galveston. At first she felt a little uneasy since this was the first stagecoach she had ever ridden in. Perhaps the fact that she was the only lady sitting with three men frightened her more. She truly wished to be back at home in her feather bed.

The men were very polite and appeared to ignore her as they discussed the war, the lack of imported goods, and problems in Texas. She listened quietly and before long she decided they were honest men.

"Is your husband fighting with the Confederate army?" one of the men asked.

"Oh! No, sir," she answered, "I have two sons fighting at Galveston. One is in the hospital with the fever. I hope to be able to see him."

"I am W. F. Coleman, a reporter from the newspaper in Houston on my way to write about the fighting and the soldiers stationed at Galveston. I'll be happy to walk with you to the hospital. I want to talk to some of the wounded and sick soldiers," the reporter said.

"Thank you, I've never been to Galveston," Molly told him. Afterward, she felt at ease and dozed off now and then.

Sometime in the late afternoon, the stagecoach stopped at a one-room log building that served as a way-station where the stage driver deposited a long leather bag that held the mail sent to Galveston.

There Molly and the three men got into a small boat, and two Mexican men rowed them across the narrow bay and to the town of Galveston. The young reporter carried Molly's one small satchel, and they walked to the two-story hotel that now served as the only hospital for the Confederate soldiers stationed on the coast of Texas.

People were walking down the long street of this strange city on an island. Yet, Molly saw no Yankee soldiers as the ones captured were held prisoners in a small log house.

As Molly and Coleman started up the stairway, she turned and looked around. A short distance away she saw the outline of the Union navy ships in a semicircle around the island. Then, at last, she understood why cotton could not be shipped out or medical supplies brought in.

She stared for a few seconds at the vast ocean and listened to the never-ending sound of the waves splashing against the seashore. She marveled at the beauty of it all.

Immediately, she turned and followed the young reporter up the stairs. They entered a dimly lit room. At once the stench of death filled her nostrils. She wanted to walk away because she could hardly believe such a sad, horrible situation existed. But she did not turn back.

"Good evening, Sarah," she heard the reporter say. "Can you tell us which of these cots belong to George Anderson. This is his mother."

"Oh! Mrs. Anderson, I'm so glad you are here," the nurse said. "But I must tell you that your son is very sick, even to the point where he may not know you. He was not wounded. He's like many other soldiers—he is suffering from dysentery, chills, and fever. Please follow me."

The weary young nurse squeezed through endless rows of crowded, low-lying cots of the sick and wounded, tenderly touching each one. Farther on, over in a dark corner of the room, Molly saw George lying there with a cool cloth on his brow.

"George, this is your mother. She came to help take care of you," the nurse, Sarah, said. George did not reply.

Molly, with tears in her eyes, knew her son and many more young men might not survive. All night she sat on the floor by his cot. Still, he showed no sign that he knew she was there by him. She could plainly hear the moans and labored breathing of the men around her. Suddenly, she became torn between the desire to comfort the youthful soldiers, to hold them in her arms, and the anger toward the officials of the Union and the Confederate states. She did not know what would be the result of all the deaths and injuries of innocent people.

"Mrs. Anderson, I'm sure you are hungry," an older woman said as she lightly tapped Molly on her shoulder. "Sarah is going downstairs. Would you like to go with her to freshen up and eat breakfast?"

"Thank you," Molly answered. "I would like to freshen up. I apologize for drifting off. Do you think my son will recover?"

"We never know, but having you here will help, even though it seems he does not know you're here. We welcome anyone who will help. See that young man about ten cots down? He lost his leg two days ago. Perhaps a kind word to him would help relieve some of his fears," the lady said, then turned to listen to a faint, anguished cry.

"I'm coming with a fresh, cool drink of water," she said as she ran her hand through his light brown hair. She turned and walked away with a cheerful word as she passed each cot.

Molly walked down the stairs with Sarah. When they reached the bottom floor she looked around. Everything appeared so quiet and orderly.

"Mrs. Anderson, I'm going to wash up. I may sleep a little while before I go back to be with the soldiers. Would you like to freshen up and take a nap? In that room over there are a few cots and a basin of water," Sarah said as she pointed to a room with no door.

"Yes, I would like to wash my face and hands, but I don't think I can sleep. I'll go back upstairs and see George. Maybe I can help some other young man," Molly answered.

After she washed, she walked outside for a brief time just to breathe some fresh air. Three young soldiers were leaning against the wall. Each had only one leg extended. The other one having been amputated or blown off by a cannon blast.

They smiled at her and said, "Good morning, looks like we might have more rain today."

On the third day, she knew George was better. He reached over and grasped her hand. With tears of joy falling down her cheeks, she only said, "Rest, my son. I am here beside you."

He did not speak, but he closed his eyes and fell asleep again. She lovingly stroked his forehead and knew his fever was subsiding.

"I knew you would come," he smiled and said the following morning. "Where is Wela? Is she here with you?"

"Don't fret, George. Wela could not come," Molly told him. "She and Rachel had the fever. But they are better now. They send you their love."

Many days and most nights, Molly heard cannon balls whistling overhead. Sometimes they landed in the water or near the building. Somehow the Confederates managed to answer with blasts from their cannons.

Often times she wandered around the hospital grounds asking if anyone knew Willy. After a while she did learn that he had been sent to the Sabine Pass. That was where the soldiers guarded the Pass from another attack by the Yankee navy.

In two weeks, George was able to walk down the stairs. He sat along the wall with other recovering soldiers enjoying the warm sunshine. On the third week, he marched with his comrades to their position as guard to the city of Galveston.

Although Molly knew she would not see George or Willy, she stayed at the hospital helping care for the sick and wounded soldiers, always comforting and encouraging their recovery. Once she held a young soldier who thought she was his mother as he died peacefully by her side. She assured those whose bodies were broken or damaged by impact of shrapnel, that in time they would be able to go home to their families.

Probably the long hours spent at the bedside of the young soldiers became too tiresome, causing her to develop a fever. Sarah sensed this and one day told her, "Mrs. Anderson, I'm afraid you are coming down with this ailment. The doctor and I think you should take the first stage back to your home. We will miss you, and so will the soldiers. We wish you a quick recovery and a safe trip home."

Early the following morning, two young soldiers rowed the

little boat across the narrow bay to the way-station. Molly got on a stagecoach and started back to Robertson County and her family.

Having reached Brazaria some two days later, the driver could see Molly was faint and shaking with a fever. He held her hand as she staggered to a bench and sat down. She kept repeating, "I'll be all right. I only want to go home. Please, ask the livery stable owner if I can hire a buggy to take me to Robertson County. My son will pay him."

Bright and early the following morning, she managed to sit upright in the buggy that took her north to Robertson County and her home.

"Mother Anderson, you are sick with the fever. Come, rest on the bed and I'll go get Jacob and Rosa," Wela said when Molly arrived there.

"Now, don't worry, I'll be all right tomorrow," Molly answered. "Just get Jacob and tell him to pay the driver for bringing me home."

Shortly, she lay down and went to sleep. She felt better the next day, but she yet shook with chills and a fever. So Jacob brought Dr. Fatheree out to see about her.

"Doctor, why did you come? I'm all right, just a touch of the flu. But I'm glad you came. I want to tell you about the hospital for our soldiers in Galveston." Without the doctor replying, Molly began to tell him all about her experience in Galveston.

"Your mother will be fine," the doctor said smiling at Jacob as he went out the door. "She just needs to rest a while."

"I never dreamed I would ever see the ocean. It's a beautiful sight. But, it's also a frightening sight. One can't see the end," Molly later told the family. Yet she never spoke of the wounded and sick soldiers, nor of the young man who died in her arms.

"Jacob, do you remember how, at one time, I wanted to take us and sail on a steamboat to Virginia?" she asked. "Well, now I believe I would be afraid, because I would not be able to see land.

We never know why things happen like they do. Still, I believe there is a reason."

In January of 1865, Molly rode Prince over her land. Much of the fields lay barren as there was no market for the crops and much work needed to be done. Of course, Jacob did what he could, but it seemed that he had to spend much of his time chasing cattle rustlers. Too, women whose husbands were fighting certainly needed help. She often wondered if the war would ever end. And if it did, would the malice of both the north and the south smolder in their hearts and minds? Or, would people be able to start anew and forget the horror? She knew only time would tell, and as always, she hated to have to wait. Right then she decided she must attempt to put the war behind her.

She harnessed the mules and hitched them to the plow. As in the past, she knew the harder she worked, the sooner she would rid her mind of all her doubts and fears. She continued to visit the lonely young women. Some had even received word their husbands died serving their country. Some had died from disease that ravaged the poorly clothed and underfed Confederate soldiers in the south. Others had died on the battlefields without being able to get help.

In mid-March as she roamed through the forest land looking for a strayed calf, she noticed the grass beginning to turn green. Too, buds on the redbud and dogwood trees were swelling. She knew that spring would soon be here. By April the bluebonnets, Indian paintbrush, and the rambling roses were coming alive. The sight brought hope of the return of Willy, George, and Pablo, along with the many tired and weary young soldiers.

Then sometime around the middle of April, a rider from Austin rode swiftly throughout the country, spurring his horse all the way. When he reached Franklin, he began yelling, "The war is over! The fighting has stopped!"

At that, others mounted their horses and hurried to tell all the people the news that the war was over.

Molly was plowing the field when she heard Rosa call, "Molly! Molly! Bring the mules and come home. Hurry!"

By dusk, people from all over Robertson County gathered in the dim light of a flickering torch in the one street of Franklin. Quickly, the county judge of Robertson County stood in the light and read the proclamation in a loud, clear voice. "General Lee surrendered the Confederate military forces in Virginia on April 2, 1865, to General Grant, Commander of the Union Army of the United States."

Four long horrendous years the north and south had fought that senseless war. Now it was over!

Molly felt relief the war was over. However, she detected a sadness in the eyes of the people—sadness for the young men wasted, and a devastating feeling of failure. The Texans, along with the south, had fought a useless war and knew little about the cause.

"I want only to put behind all the sadness. To wait patiently for Willy, George, and Pablo to come home to their wives and the land they love," Molly told Elizabeth.

The Confederate forces at Galveston surrendered their weapons and were marched to Houston. Then three weeks later, the Union officials released them and sent them home.

One bright, sunny day only a week later, with much enthusiasm Willy and George hurriedly walked up the path to the log house with the dog-run. They looked at each other, grinned, counted one-two-three, and fired their guns straight into the air twice. "We are home!" they shouted loud and clear.

The family rushed to meet them. Then Rosa asked, "Where is my Pablo? Is he hiding to tease me again?"

"No, Rosa," Willy told her, "he, I'm sure, will come soon. He was farther west of Galveston."

Rosa did not know it, neither did Willy and George, but Pablo kept fighting the war. He was with Benevides near Brownsville. But on May the thirteenth, a brigade of Yankee soldiers attempted to come into Texas by means of Brazos Island. When the small, rebel forces of Benevides saw them approaching, they captured some of the men. Only then did they learn the fighting was over. Benevides and his men fought the final battle of the war between the north and the south.

Each day Rosa waited for Pablo to come home, always smiling and saying, "Today my Pablo will come."

Three weeks later, she did see him coming up the path. She called out, "Come! Come, my Pablo is home."

Immediately, the family ran to greet him. When he got close, he threw his hat into the air. As it landed on the ground, Rosa drew her skirt up and, clicking her heels, danced around the hat. At once Pablo grabbed her and carried her to their house.

"Yes, the war is over," Molly said to the family that night, "but it may take a long time to forget. I feel a disturbing unrest is already clouding our minds."

CHAPTER 9

On June 19, 1865, under demand of President Johnson, a major general of the Union army landed at Galveston. He publicly proclaimed all slaves to be free and declared Texas to be under military rule.

On hearing this Molly and her sons gathered at her house to discuss this grave problem. The thought of being under military authority troubled them. Sitting on the benches in the dog-run, Molly was the first to express her opinion. "Rightfully, the slaves should have been freed a long time ago. But I don't think any Yankee should come into our state and set up their own government."

"I fully agree with you," Willy said. "Right now our officials have gone across the border into Mexico. Otherwise, they would have been held as prisoners; they had no choice. I can only see one way to regain control of our state. We have to vote for our own people in the next election." He scratched his head and added, "But it's possible there may not be an election."

"I'm glad Houston did not witness our defeat by the Union army. If we had listened to him, today we might not be under military rule," Jacob said.

"Although neither Willy nor Pablo thought we should secede from the Union," George said, "we all three fought with the Confederate army. Now we must try to restore the state to the Union." In an attempt to reason, he then added, "To my way of thinking, the slaves are not the question today. We must keep our own freedom. Right now the Federal government considers us as captives. Texans are proud people. They hate being punished like children who disobey their parents."

"We can't think of what should have been done. We must think of tomorrow," Molly wisely told her sons. "Look at all the barren fields. We must at once begin to till the soil and plant crops again. I saved enough good corn seed to plant this year. Of course, we have cottonseed since we didn't plant last year. This year we are going to do better."

The Texans knew that in order to recover imported merchandise and export goods to other markets, they had to cooperate with the military command. At times this became a far greater task than they thought it could ever be. Under the authority of the Union military, slowly most of the existing Texas officials were being ousted from office.

"We're beginning to lose the battle against lawlessness," Jacob told Molly when he came through the kitchen where she was baking. "Most of the officers are black men appointed by the military. They're not to blame. They only do as they are told."

"I believe the black people are as troubled over the results of the war as we are," Molly said. "I have seen hundreds of slaves roaming the country, looking for a place to live. I believe some will go back to the plantations, especially the older ones. The first thing we must do is open schools for them. I'm afraid a lot of them don't know how to read or write." She paused a second as if she dared say more, but then did say more. "I wonder, sometimes, if President Johnson isn't hoodwinked as bad as we are by the military rule."

"Maw, we have another problem," Willy announced one day when he sat watching Molly wash dish after dish, dry them, and put them in the cupboard, "people from the east whose homes were destroyed by the Union army are flooding Robertson County. They hope to find cheap land, a place to live, and a way to make a living. The worst thing is that thieves and even murderers are roaming the country, plundering homes and stealing cattle."

Regardless of the turmoil in the government, most Texans returned to a normal way of life in 1867. They planted their crops and reaped a good harvest.

In 1869, talk of the new town of Bremond resurfaced. Money was offered to railroad companies to bring trains north from Houston through Bremond.

"George told me people are buying town lots and building houses. A railroad will run right through the town," Wela said when the ladies sat resting in the dog-run. "Just think, we will only have to go no farther than fifteen miles to buy things we need. Already one clothing store is being built."

"Last week in the Calvert newspaper I saw an advertisement where people could buy lots for homes and businesses in this new town," Elizabeth said. "Many times people stop by on their way to look over the lots. Why! One lady even told me the seller would loan them money to build the house and buy the lot."

"Well, I guess that's fine for some folks. But, I don't ever want to borrow money to buy anything. If I can't pay for it myself, I'll just do without," Molly remarked. "And I hope I taught my sons to do the same."

"I believe this town will be good for Robertson County," Rachel said. "Willy says locations for a school and church have been laid out. Then the School Creek school will be closed."

One morning Molly was gathering eggs from the chicken pen when Pablo and Rosa came by. She called to them, "I saw some spring flowers this morning as I was riding Prince down by the creek. I don't know why, but for some reason wildflowers and budding trees cause me to feel better and have hope. Right now, I have a feeling that the military rule we are under is going to be done away with." At that she laughed and said, "Then, we can live like we once did. Not just like po' white folks."

"Maw, put on your best dress and the hat with the plume," Jacob yelled to Molly as he rode by. "The train is coming to town and we are all going to meet it."

"No, Pablo, we're not going to drive the mules," George told Pablo, as they prepared for this special occasion. "We'll put that new harness, we got before the war and never used, on the two horses and hitch them to the surrey Maw and Rosa polished yesterday. This is, indeed, a celebration and we are going in style."

Jacob, with Elizabeth and John Newton, led the way in their shiny black buggy. Next came Willy and Rachel in a buggy with a tasseled top that shook in the breeze. At the end came George and Pablo driving the horses, and in the back seat sat Wela, Rosa, and Molly.

The train was scheduled to arrive at two o'clock in the afternoon. Nevertheless, by one o'clock people were crowding the street, even near the train depot, in anticipation of this great event. Talk of crops, schools, and everyday occasions could be heard among the anxiously awaiting group of neighbors and friends. Around one forty-five, a silence fell over the crowd. At once, a man wearing a strange-looking black cap, pants, and jacket with bright, shiny buttons came from the door of the depot. He gazed at the solid gold watch in his hand and began to swing a lantern back and forth. A distant sound could barely be heard. At once it became louder and louder. A whistle blew two short, shrill sounds. A bell began to ring. All the time the man continued to swing his lantern back and forth. Slowly, the wheels of the train began to creak on the iron tracks of the rails. Gradually, it came to a stop. At once, the people began to cheer and young boys threw their caps in the air.

This was the first train many of the settlers had ever seen. Truly, it did create an exciting event. It turned the people's thoughts to good times and assurance that Texas would be honored again.

After the first appearance of the train, the town did begin to flourish. A two-story hotel stood near the train depot. In the fall a school opened. Stores sold furniture, medicine, and clothing for men, women, and children. One even sold kitchenware and farming equipment. A blacksmith shop and a stable hung signs above their doors to entice the patrons. Indeed, the town of Bremond surely came into existence overnight in a troubled period of time during the reconstruction era after the war between the North and South.

The winter of 1871 proved to be a repeat of 1837. North winds rattled the windows and doors of the ill-constructed houses. People hovered near fireplaces and wood stoves to keep warm.

"Mother Anderson, I thought about you being all alone last night. I wondered if you slept warm," Elizabeth said one morning.

"Yes, Elizabeth," Molly answered, "I went down by the creek and found a big rock. I just heated one of the old quilts and wrapped it around the rock and put it in my bed. I was just as snug as a bug with that warm rock by my feet."

"These cold winds are driving the wolves and mountain lions down from the hills. I found where they killed one of our best calves," Jacob said when he and Pablo came into Molly's kitchen to warm their hands. "Even though we brought the cattle down from the prairie to the forest for protection from the cold, they still look gaunt. The calves are not strong enough to fight the wolves. Of course, even cows can't fight them sometimes. Pablo, let's go down and set some traps. We might get some hides to sell."

Little snow fell during that good winter. Neither did the spring rains come as they usually did. As a result, Molly and her sons had no hope of a good harvest in the fall. Still, they planted the seeds and enough moisture fell for a short harvest. The corn did better than the cotton and sorghum grain. After all, that was the most important thing, since the prairie was now wilted and very short.

In spite of the shortage of the cotton crops, newcomers continued to move into the county. They came mainly from the war-torn states east of the Mississippi River. Some bought land and began to farm. Many settled in the bald prairie lands which most farmers did not consider good farming land.

"George told me some of the new people are from Poland, across the Atlantic Ocean," Wela told Molly. "One family bought land from Oran Taylor and built a house. I told George I must go welcome the family. I was only a young child when I came to Texas, so I learned to be happy and call this my home. I got to thinking: if a person is older, they would have many memories of their old home. They might even become lonely. Maybe they would like a visit from people here. Molly, would you like to go with me to see them?"

"Sure, Wela, I would like to go. But do you think they speak the same language we do? I know, I'll take them some fresh churned butter. That'll make them feel welcome," Molly said.

That proved to be a delightful time where a friendship was formed that lasted many years.

Some time later, Willy went to see Molly. He opened the door and called to her, "Maw, I have good news. Rachel and me are going to have a wedding at our house. She's already scrubbing things from top to bottom, getting ready."

"Who's getting married? Do I know the couple? Any more, I never know who is who," Molly chuckled and said.

"After all this time, it's Matt Taylor," Willy told her. "He's marrying Vicie Poloski, that pretty Polish girl. Vicie wanted to be married in a Catholic Church. But, as you know, there is no Catholic Church here, nor is there a priest. So, Matt asked me to perform the civil ceremony. After that, they'll go south to a Catholic Church where a priest will perform the religious ceremony. Pablo and Rosa are going with them."

Around ten o'clock Saturday morning, the Poloskis, the Taylors, and the Andersons arrived at the home of Willy and Rachel. Standing proudly in front of the fireplace, decorated with fresh flowers emitting the aroma of spring, were Matt and Vicie. At once everyone quit talking and sat quietly. Willy, holding the Holy Bible, and a small note concerning the ceremony, pronounced them man and wife.

Unexpectedly, the elder Mr. Poloski grabbed his wife and began to dance around the room, singing a Polish song. Then came the Texans dancing closely behind them.

"Come. Come with us," Mr. Poloski called out. "We must a have a toast and a feast at our house. Now, not only do I have a Texas son, now I have Texas friends."

In the winter of 1872 an abundant amount of snow fell. Then

in the springtime, once more, wildflowers appeared and came alive all over the hillsides and in the Walnut Creek valley. To Molly it appeared there were more than she remembered seeing before. Rains came, not in hard violent outbursts, but in slow, gentle showers that replenished the dry, thirsty ground.

Texans learned to put behind them the trauma of the defeat in the war between the North and the South. Seeds were planted, and with the rains came the renewal of the prairie grass. This caused the cows to produce good, healthy calves. Now, even the danger of mountain lions and wolves seemed to have vanished.

However, in early 1873, children began to be plagued with an illness not known before.

"Today I heard one woman say that the newcomers and the freed slaves brought this terrible disease into the country," Elizabeth told Molly.

"Jacob told me what that woman said. Right then I knew that rumor had to be stopped," Molly replied. "I went straight to see Dr. Fatheree in Franklin. I told him how John Newton came down with a rash. I just plainly asked him, 'Could he have the measles?' He agreed with me. Then he told me this is different from the other sickness. Elizabeth, he said for you to keep John Newton in the bed a couple of days." Pushing her hair back she added, "Don't let Rachel come into the room. Cassie always said if a woman, with child, gets the measles, the baby would be born blind. I didn't ask Dr. Fatheree about that, but Cassie was very wise, so I believe her."

The same year, another disease that the young Dr. Adcock in Bremond called typhoid fever appeared in different parts of the country. He rode out to see Wela when she came down with the same symptoms.

"George, your wife is very sick and may be down with this typhoid fever quite some time. She will need constant care. We have not found how this germ gets into our bodies. But we're still trying. Hopefully, some day we will find the answer," Dr. Adcock told George.

"Maw, please stay with Wela. I love her so much I can not think of living without her," George said.

"My dear son, don't worry. Wela will be fine. But you must do exactly as I say. Every spoon she eats from must be boiled for at least one-half hour. Scrub your hands any time you touch her. Above all, do not let anyone into the room with her. I believe this is catching," Molly told George.

"Maw, what can I do to help?" George asked.

"Just let her know you love her. Go about your work," Molly answered. "Here, take this bright-colored cloth and hang it on the gate post of the front yard. That'll warn people to not come into the house."

"Wela is very weak. But she must not eat hard food, and only a few sips at a time of clear broth," Dr. Adcock told Molly when he came again.

"Doctor, what if I gave her some egg whites beaten until they stand up fluffy and light?" Molly asked. "I believe that would soothe her stomach. I think it is tender."

"Perhaps you might try that, a little bit at a time. I have not found that method in my books," the doctor replied. "We need to find a way to fight this disease. I'm willing to try anything not harmful to the patient. We need to find the source of the germs. Maybe then we can find a cure."

Often Willy and Jacob came home and told of deaths caused by this devastating illness. First, a ten-year-old boy died. Only a week later a young lady and then a sixty-five-year-old man both died. Mrs. Radcliff, wife of the merchandise storeowner, also developed the fever. She was a frail woman so she died within three weeks. This unknown source of danger was not limited to any age, class of people, or location.

"Mrs. Anderson, I think you should go home. If you don't rest and get some sleep, you may get sick, too. George told me he wanted you to rest," the doctor told Molly.

Some time later in the afternoon, Molly heard a knock on the door. "You can't come in," she called out. "Wela is very sick and you could get the disease."

"Molly, this is Rosa. I'm coming in to help care for Wela," Rosa said and walked in. Looking right at Molly she said, "You go take a nap. I'll sit here beside Wela. Soon, she will be well. In fact, I believe she is better even now. See, she knows I'm here."

Exhausted, Molly walked out of the room, sat down on a chair, and fell asleep.

Wela did begin to recover, and Rosa continued to stay with her. She fluffed her pillows and let in fresh air from the open window. She sang songs in her Spanish language. Sometimes, they were songs of conflict and daring adventure, but mostly they were songs of love and happiness.

A month later, George carried Wela outside. They sat on the front porch. She looked thin, but still he knew she would be all right. He held her close as they watched the evening sun go down beyond the western horizon.

In early March, Molly saddled Prince and rode toward Walnut Creek. She let the reins fall loose as Prince knew the way. She headed north to the forest land, looking for stray cattle. Riding peacefully along, her thoughts went back to the years she spent with David. *With him, I always felt loved and secure. Too, he gave me four sons. Although one is no longer with me, he remains in my heart.* As if from out of the sky, Calvin's face came into focus in her mind and she thought, *he brought laughter into my life and taught me to accept the loss of little John. I do not understand all of this, nor the fact the two men are forever in my heart.*

Only one brief moment did the thought of Reuben Stanford come to her. When it did, she spurred Prince into a fast run and swiftly rode to the prairie land where she could see far away in every direction. At seventy-three years of age the thought of him yet caused her to judge herself to be "a silly old woman," just like Reuben said.

The year 1873, indeed, tried the spirit and hope of the Texans.

The drought and sickness hovered over the people. Yet, another problem remained—the radical military government plagued the Texans.

"I'll ride to every town or farm in Robertson County to encourage men to vote in the upcoming election. I'll even beg them," Jacob said when the family all sat around discussing their problems. "We must defeat Davis and elect Coke. That is the only way we will ever regain our freedom from the military rule."

"I agree with you, Jacob," Willy, who abhorred all fraud and deceit, answered, "but I don't think it is right to try to persuade the colored men not to vote. They are free now and have the same right as we do."

"But, Willy, that other party is threatening to jail the freed slaves if they do vote our ticket. Limestone County is right now declared under military law. Of course, the citizens became outraged when a colored man killed a white man," George said. He quickly added, "That was when I knew we must do something to stop all of this unrest. Whether we do it by hook or crook, it must be done."

"The freed slaves are suffering as much now as before the war," Jacob said. "In many ways they are slaves to the military law."

"I understand the pride the young freed men must feel when they arrest a white man," Molly said. "We must teach them to live an independent life. Above all, we must accept them as free citizens of our great state."

"As usual, you are right, Maw," Willy said. "These people are used to further the purpose in the dispute between the power-hungry men. They are not the cause of the dispute."

Coke did win over Davis in the election. Little by little the state began to recover from the horrors of war. The monitory loss, also, began to gain more trust by the citizens. Texas, once more, with all her boundless lands, looked forward to the future.

However, one minor problem cropped up—that of the buffalo hunters and the Indians. After the slaughter that all but destroyed the buffalo herds, the animals went west. Trailing close behind came the buffalo hunters, but the Indians attempted to drive the hunters back east.

"I read in the paper today that there is Indian trouble again, but this time it's out west," Molly told the family. "The buffalo hunters are evil men. They have no respect for animal lives—not even human lives." Instantly, she said no more. A long time ago, she vowed not to repeat the incident of David's death to her sons. Especially, not to George, who was deprived of ever seeing his father.

"If the buffalo are completely killed out, the Indians will all have to live on the reservations. There is no other means," George said. "I even heard one man from Washington say he would like to see all the buffalo gone. That way they could raise more cattle."

"The Indians were in Texas before us Anglos came. Actually, they are treated worse than the slaves," George said.

"I think of Running Wolf often. I wonder where he and the mixed tribe of Cherokee and Caddo Indians are today," Jacob said. "Sometimes I wonder if we will ever see him again."

"Running Wolf said he would come back. He always kept a promise," Willy said to himself more than to the family.

That fall they gathered the corn and cut down the stalks. They piled them in stacks where the cattle could graze in the winter months. Only the cotton harvest remained before they began to till the soil for the next crop.

Willy was busy sharpening a plowshare when he thought he heard a faint sound. He put down the sledgehammer, turned his head to one side, and listened again. Sure enough, he heard Rachel calling, "Willy, where are you? Please come. Help me. I think I am going to have our baby."

Without thinking further, Willy jumped onto his horse and rode bareback. He raced by Molly, but he did not stop as he yelled, "Maw, hurry! Run get Rosa, then stay with Rachel, I'm going for the doctor. Maw, Rachel's time has come."

Sometime around three o'clock in the afternoon, Rachel gave birth to a healthy baby boy they named James. Laughter and happiness radiated in the Anderson family that night. Yet, among all the merry-making, Molly sensed sadness in the eyes of Jacob and Elizabeth. Only two weeks before, Elizabeth experienced the loss of another unborn child.

Soon the cotton bolls burst open and the white, fluffy cotton was now ready to be picked. Pablo and George were repairing the wagon in which to put the cotton when it was picked, when a black man and woman with two children came up the path.

Many freed slaves walked the roads looking for food or a place to sleep causing Molly to think nothing of the incident. She opened the gate and called out, "Ring. Rover. Come here. Sit." Holding the dogs by the leash, she turned toward the people, "Don't be afraid of the hounds. I won't let them harm you."

"Good day, Miz Anderson," the man said, "I declare, I believe you've plum forgot us. We're Amos and Beulah that stayed in your barn. That was when we started to run away during the war. Course, we didn't have any chillens then. This is Luke, our boy, and Nelly, our little girl. We want to talk to Mr. Jacob. Is he home?"

"Oh, you're right, I didn't recognize you," Molly said. "That seems such a long time ago. I'm sure Jacob will be here soon. He lives in that house over there," Molly said as she turned and pointed to the house across the creek. "He and Elizabeth have a little boy named John Newton. I'll ask Rosa to ride over there and tell him you are here. Do you remember the pretty woman with the goats?"

"Yes'um, Miz Anderson. She was a pretty one," Beulah said. "Not long ago I told Luke how we run from the slave catchers. And how Miz Rosa said the goats played in the hay."

"So, we meet again. Maybe we're not supposed to forget each other," Jacob said as he laughed and shook hands with Amos. "Are you going north? How are the folks at the plantation?"

"Well, Mr. Jacob, that's why we come here. The old folks, they mostly live in the cabins," Amos said. "They work for the plantation owner. He pays them for the work but tain't hardly enough to buy vittles."

"Some of the ole folks can't work hard like they used to,"

Beulah spoke for the first time. "So they don't make much money. Some of the young ones went on north, but some come on back. Hit ain't no better there."

"Me and Beulah, we got to thinking we ought to go work for you. That is, if you want us to," Amos said. "I see you got a pretty good cotton crop. Me and Beulah, we can pick cotton. So can Luke. We could sleep in the barn. Now, we wouldn't set fire to it or anything, " Amos honestly said.

"Well, Amos, I never dreamed you wanted to pick cotton for us. Pablo will be happy to hear that," Molly said.

"We need help in picking the cotton," Jacob told Amos. "Rachel and Willy have a young son, so Rachel can't pick. Neither can Wela—she and George are expecting a child in December. Of course, Elizabeth picks some in the afternoons. Rosa and Maw help when they can. But this year we made a bumper crop and need more pickers. When can you start?"

"We shore do thank yous. We wuz 'fraid you wouldn't want us to stay. That's why we left our clothes and cookin' vessels down by the front gate," Amos said.

"Amos, you and Beulah go back and get your things," Molly said. Holding Luke's and Nelly's hands, she started toward the kitchen. Thinking again, she turned and said, "I've got plenty of chicken and dumplings on the stove. You all can eat here tonight."

Jacob seated them at the table, and Molly put the big bowl of chicken and dumplings before them. She said, "I guess you can sleep in the barn. That is, until the boys put you up a log house. If you want to stay and work for us, we will give you a house to live in, just like we did for Pablo and Rosa."

"We've got sweet potatoes under the hills and salt pork and ham in the smokehouse," Jacob told Amos and Beulah.

"Something else, if you will milk the cow for me, you can have milk to drink. That is, until you get paid for picking the cotton. But, from that time on, you will raise or buy your own food," Molly calmly said and looked away.

"But, Maw, they are freed slaves. You know some store owners won't sell to them," Willy later admonished Molly.

"Willy, I know that, but they must learn to live on their own," Molly said. "I simply want to encourage them. Besides, if a merchant refuses to sell to them, I will not buy in that store and I'll ask other people not to. We must all learn to live together peacefully."

Not long after Amos, Beulah, and their two children came to see Jacob, a log house was built near the big house and the freed slaves moved in. So it was that Molly added four more people to her First Class Headright land grant.

That fall the School Creek school did not open. All the money allotted to the education department was spent on the new school in Bremond. In many ways Molly felt sad. Sincere friendships were formed among the parents of the students.

However, one day Molly hurried to open their front door when she heard a knock. What a pleasant surprise! There stood Oran and Lacy Taylor.

"Come on in. Lacy, I'm glad to see you looking so well after that terrible typhoid fever. Sit right over here in this soft rocking chair. Oran, I'll go warm you a cup of coffee," Molly said, happy to see her friends.

"Molly, you know we are of the Methodist faith and we know there's a new church in Bremond. But that's a long way to go when a person is not well. Lacy and me got to talking that since the school on School Creek is closed, we should all pitch in and buy that land from you. We could have a church for all denominations in the old school building. Will you sell that land?"

"Oran, you know full well I would give you that land for a church. But you see, I gave Willy and Rachel their part of the grant and they chose that land. I know he will give it to you. Ask him." Molly grinned, and said, "And don't tell him I told you to ask."

Oran did ask Willy to sell the land and he did not hesitate.

"I will be happy to give you the land, but first we must hold a meeting and elect a presiding elder. Then I will have a deed written and given to the church. We must have a name and somebody to keep all records of any money given by the people," Willy said to Oran.

A meeting was called and interested people from all over the county came. Oran Taylor stood at the front of the building and declared, "This meeting is called to discuss organizing a church. Marion Wheeler, we all agree, should be declared the presiding elder. He is well trained by his father, Jess Wheeler, who suffered a stroke last week and is now partially paralyzed." At that, every hand was raised. "If you all agree, I will volunteer to be treasurer," Oran offered, and everyone else called out, "Yes."

"It is imperative we keep a true record of the church meetings," Willy said. "If there are no objections, I would like to ask Elizabeth to serve as secretary." Quickly, words of approval went out over the room.

At last, time came to select a name. At that time people stood up all over the room, suggesting name after name. Still, no specific name was selected by everyone. Finally, Oran Taylor yelled, "Please, let's have order. We must all agree. I heard the name 'Free Will Church' from someone on the back row. Does everyone agree on that name?" Oran called out loud and clear.

At once everybody raised their right hand and, laughing, yelled, "Yes." Therefore, it was on September 10, 1875, that the Free Will Church on School Creek was organized.

In a month the church building was repaired. The little school benches, with no backs, were removed. New split pine lumber benches, rubbed to a shine, were placed side by side in perfectly shaped rows.

At last the iron bell was raised to the top of the bell tower. Benito Mendez timidly handed Willy a sign he made and inscribed with a branding iron the words "Free Will Church." Willy held it up and yelled, "Look what Benito made!" He gave it back to Benito and asked, "Will you hang it over the door for us?" A look of pride and joy gleaned from Benito's eyes as he climbed up the ladder and nailed the sign securely above the door.

The following Saturday, Molly, Beulah, and Rosa swept the floor of the church. Beulah scrupulously arranged an embroidered tablecloth that Wela had made on the pulpit. Then Molly sat a glass water pitcher and tumbler that Lacy Taylor contributed to the church on the right edge of the pulpit.

"Is this the Holy Water?" Rosa asked. "I thought the priests have a silver bowl for the Holy Water."

"No, Rosa, this is not Holy Water," Molly replied. "Sometimes the preachers preach so long that they become thirsty. So they pour themselves a drink of water."

Just after sunrise on Sunday morning, Willy rode to the church and rang the church bell. It was a quiet, cloudless morning and the sound of the church bell drifted down School Creek valley. By ten o'clock, the people in their best Sunday clothes began to arrive. There were wagons filled with more than one family with children playfully following behind. Not only wagons, but there were carts, buggies, and horseback riders.

That day was the appointed day to dedicate the newly organized Free Will Church. A preacher from the town of Marlin came the seventeen miles to preach the sermon that first worship service. Molly smiled proudly when Willy introduced the minister. Then he spoke loud as he announced, "This morning we will pass the plates for our offerings. I know you will give freely so we can continue the services."

Marion Wheeler and Jacob went from row to row with the plates and instantly the sound of coins falling into the plates was heard all over the room.

After that Rachel began to pump the organ that Oran Taylor had brought all the way from Houston. Oran stood up and said, "Turn to page seventy-eight in your hymn book and stand as we sing."

The melodic sound of the hymn rang out:

Brethren, we have met to worship and adore his Holy Name.
Brethren, pray and Holy Manna will be showered all around.
Sisters, will you join and help us; Moses' sisters helped him, too.
Let us pray and Holy Manna will be showered all around.

It was in December of 1875 when Wela gave birth to a baby girl. It was the first of Molly's granddaughters. Naturally, the family all rushed to see the new baby.

"A little baby girl," Rosa said, peeping over the pretty pink blanket Wela made. "What is her name?"

"We thought about Rachel Elizabeth. But she looks so much like Maw, we decided we would just call her Molly," Wela smiled and answered.

Late in the fall after the cotton was picked and sent to the gin, Molly told Rosa one afternoon, "I think it is time we all gather and talk about the crops and cattle. Would you go tell everyone to be at my house after supper? That includes you and Pablo and, of course, Amos and Beulah."

"We made a good crop this year," Molly began when everyone was seated that evening. "So, I thought we should divide the money we made when we sold the bales. I want to be fair. We all worked together, and each person did his share. Actually, the way I see it, we should split the profit four ways. I have never given Pablo and Rosa any land, but he and Rosa did most of my work. Because of that I want them to have half of what I made. Now, Amos, you and Beulah will be paid for every pound of cotton you picked that Jacob weighed on the cotton scales. That includes what Luke and Nelly picked, too."

"But, Miz Molly," Amos interrupted, "we got to pay fur our vittles. We don't have no more money. So yous jest keep what we made picking cotton."

"Amos, you didn't understand me," Molly said. "You keep the money this year. But next year you will farm the forty acres east of where you now live. Pablo has agreed to get two more mules and a plow for you to use. Then in the fall when the cotton is ginned, you will get half of the money from selling the bales. Of course, you'll keep half of the corn and grain. That way, I might even quit work. I sure get tired most days."

"Miz Molly, me and Beulah, we never thought that some day we would be sharecroppers. Yous a saint! We'll work real hard," Amos said.

During the war years, no cattle were sold causing the herd to increase, even with the loss of calves by wolves and mountain lions. This caused the prairie land to be over-grazed.

"We need to separate some of our older cows and the heifers who do not breed and sell them," Jacob said. "I'm not sure farmers around here will buy them. Besides, I hear the market in New Orleans is mighty risky."

"I hear talk of cattle drives going north to the railroad towns," George told Jacob. "There the cattle are loaded on train cars and shipped to eastern markets. I've been told a cow would sell for twice or more than what we get here."

"It sure would take a long time to drive a hundred head of cattle that far. I don't think it would pay," Molly said.

"But, Maw," Jacob answered, "this is different. More than one herd is driven at the same time. Each owner sends drovers that work together. There's a wagon that travels behind, or maybe they might go ahead, to carry the food and a man to cook."

"Some of the big cattle ranchers are already getting ready to send herds north even now. They are going up by way of Waco and Fort Worth and into the Indian Territory, all the way to the railroad town of Abilene in the state of Kansas," Willy said. "They'll be coming near us in a couple of weeks."

"I believe this is what we should do. If you all agree, I'll volunteer to drive our herd with the others all the way to Kansas. But, first, we must brand the cattle," George told the family.

At the beginning of the venture, Molly was opposed to the plan, but later she saw the advantage. She helped round up the cattle and stayed close to help keep them from stampeding.

A lengthy discussion began when they chose a formation and

name of the brand, as each person had their own suggestion. Eventually, in the end, they agreed on the one Molly suggested—Triple AAA.

Pablo heated a strip of iron until it sizzled and turned red. He twisted and turned it into the form AAA. Quickly, he slapped it on a piece of rawhide and watched it sizzle until it became a replica of the AAA brand of Anderson Cattle Company.

Molly and Rosa rode to the courthouse in Franklin. They gave the cowhide to the clerk, who registered it under the name:

Anderson Cattle Company—Triple AAA—Brand #1657

Finally, they finished the branding and cut out one hundred and fifty cows, bulls, and young heifers. They drove them to the outskirts of Waco where as many as one thousand head of cattle continually bawled and milled about. One man, Joe Broon, had been hired as trail boss. He greeted George and as they went from animal to animal inspecting the brands, he told George, "We are waiting for another wrangler. The man who was supposed to have taken the job sent word his horse fell and has a broken leg. We sure need another man today."

"Joe, I may be able to help you. Wait right here, I'll be back," George told the man and walked to where he saw Amos leaning against a tree.

"Amos, I see you know how to handle horses. This trail boss is looking for a good wrangler to take care of our horses. Would you like to sign up for the job?" George asked. "We'll be going through rough country. I've been told that rustlers and even Indians at times try to steal the cattle. Too, the cattle often stampede, especially when the weather is bad. This can be dangerous work. But the wrangler is paid a good wage. If you want to go with us, Jacob will explain to Beulah. Maw will see that your family is taken care of."

"Mr. George, I jest been dreaming 'bout that. I even talked to Beulah. But she didn't think a man would hire a Negro," Amos anxiously replied. "Yes, sir, I'll be a good wrangler. I'll take real good care of the horses. I still recollect how Mr. Jacob and the others took care of the soldiers' horses at General Houston's camp at the plantation. Tell Beulah I'll be home in the spring to plant the cotton."

Two days later the cattle drive started north. The weather remained fairly nice, so the days went well. They angled around the fort called Fort Worth. From there they continued north and west until they were to cross the Red River into Indian Territory. A storm came in and the cattle began to be restless and mill around. George and the other drovers spent the entire night herding the cattle into a valley in an attempt to prevent a stampede. Even the wranglers mounted horses and helped. They were stranded there four days. On the fifth day they continued north and things seemed to be better.

That is, until they started through Palo Duro Canyon. A band of Indians on the edge of the canyon stood anxiously watching down below with their bows and arrows aimed directly at the cattle.

The drovers grabbed their guns from their holsters and prepared to shoot. About that time, Amos's companion, another black man, yelled, "Wait. Don't shoot! Can't you see the hill is covered with Indians? Put your guns away and we will be all right. The Indians are only asking for cattle to feed their people. I have been through here before. I know all the buffalo have been killed or driven west leaving no means for food for the Indians."

On hearing that, George and the others cut out some cows and drove them back to the entrance of the canyon. At once the Indians raced swiftly down the canyon and drove the cattle away.

From the canyon the cattle drive went directly north and saw no more Indians. Six weeks later they bedded the cattle down west of Abilene in Kansas. The following day a cattle buyer handed George the money due the Anderson Cattle Company. He strapped it in his saddlebag. Saying goodbye, he and Amos started back to Robertson County in Texas.

In early June, news that the train would come through Bremond again created more excitement. Hurriedly, Molly and her family prepared to go watch it come in.

"Beulah, aren't you and Amos going to come with us so Luke and Nelly can see the train?" Molly asked.

"No, ma'am, we ain't welcome in Bremond. So, we jest stay away," Beulah said.

"Now, Beulah, you know we will be with you. If you and Amos won't go, can we take Luke and Nelly?" Molly asked again.

"No, ma'am, like I said, we ain't goin'," Beulah replied.

Nothing else was said and the family rode into Bremond. They walked to the train station and stood patiently among all the people to see the approaching engine. At last they heard the train whistle in the distance. Then, with the wheels screeching on the train tracks, the engine came to a stop.

A man placed a wooden step at the door of the train car. He swished a feather duster over it. Two young ladies came out and waved to another lady. The last to come down the step was a straight-shouldered gentleman wearing a big black hat and clothes that resembled a banker's suit.

Willy stood speechless. He gazed intently at the man. He yelled, "Running Wolf, is that really you?"

Rachel, holding young James in her arms, did not know who that handsome person could be, nor why Willy became so excited.

"Rachel, this is Running Wolf, my dear friend I have not seen in such a long time. Running Wolf, this is Rachel. She is my wife and this is our little boy. We named him James after our good friend who died at the Alamo. Come with us to our house. I want you to tell us about your family."

"Where is the little white-eye boy whose toes I used to count?" Running Wolf asked as he smiled and looked at George.

"Many years have passed since that time. But Maw has told me about the days you spent with the family. You must tell us where you live. Is it a good land?" George asked.

That night the entire family met to hear Running Wolf tell

about the mixed tribe of Cherokee and Caddo Indians. As Molly quietly sat and looked around her, she felt as if another son had come home. As a result, she wiped tears from her face—tears of joy.

"As you can tell, I went to the white man's school for Indian children," Running Wolf said. "I learned to talk and dress like them."

"Is your father still with you? Where did the soldiers take you when they drove you from Cow Creek?" Molly asked.

"The soldiers put my people in a wagon when they drove us from Cow Creek. They took us across the river with the red water. That was when they left us and we walked until we found an Indian camp where many white soldiers stay. White people call this Oklahoma. My father did not want to stay there. He tried to run away but the white soldiers shot him," Running Wolf said with no emotion in his voice. Nevertheless, Molly saw anger and grief in his eyes.

"Running Wolf, you seem to have done well," Jacob said. "Are your people happy?"

"The white people make many laws. We were not born to follow laws, but I learned to accept them. The old men have no desire to abide by them or to learn to love the land. They sit side by side waiting for the night. Many will die before they should. I can not help them. Maybe I can help the young ones who never knew our ways in the good land. They do not know the thrill of the hunt. Now, they do not know the reason for the birth of our maidens and warriors."

"I want to know about you. Do you have a wife and children?" Willy asked. "I hope you are as happy as I am."

"Yes, I am married," Running Wolf replied. "I have a beautiful wife called Winona. She teaches the young children to read and write."

"We would like to know her. Maybe she will come with you to see us when you come again," Willy said.

"Perhaps I will come again and she will come with me. I have told her many times how we walked together, and how I learned that all white people are not evil," Running Wolf said.

"I must go back to my people," Running Wolf said two days later. "I told you I would come. So I have. I wanted you to know I am helping my people. Now I am happy. Maybe I will tell Winona we need a baby like Willy and Rachel."

"Goodbye, my friend," Willy said. They shook hands, and Running Wolf, preferring to walk alone, started down the path to the train station in Bremond. Willy wanted to take him in the buggy, but he respected Running Wolf's wish. He simply turned to harness the mule in order to plow the sod.

Molly said nothing to Willy. She knew that guiding the mules and making a straight furrow in the soil would ease his troubled mind. She could feel the concern he had for the older people of the mixed tribe of Cherokee and Caddo Indians. Without a doubt, he knew they would soon disappear among the larger tribes and utterly be forgotten.

That night, when Molly thought her sons were sleeping, the door opened and Willy came in. "Maw, I couldn't sleep and I knew you could not either," he said. "I came to tell you I am happy. Running Wolf is doing what he vowed to accomplish. Now I believe the dreams we had as young boys are coming true. Maw, I know it is you who helped Running Wolf." He affectionately kissed her on the cheek and walked out the door.

To Molly, 1877 passed quickly as many good things came to her. To be sure, among those was the visit from Running Wolf. Too, the cattle George and Amos took to Kansas brought more money than the bales of cotton they ginned. Molly even hired a man to drill a well in the back yard of her house, and Amos installed a hand pump.

"Now, Miz Molly, yous jest don't worry," Amos told her. "I recollect how my pa done this for our master. First thing you know, you'll have water right by yore back door."

When Amos finished his task, Molly handed him money for

his labor. He put his hands behind his back and said, "No, ma'am, I don't want no pay. Yous already give us too much."

"Amos, listen to me. Come help me catch one of the Berkshire sows and a boar," Molly scolded him. "You drag them home with you and build them a pen. Before you know it, you will have hams and jowls all year."

Molly thoroughly enjoyed washing the clothes by the house and pumping the water. She even found time to spend with her grandchildren and with Luke and Nelly. She taught them how to make a kite and to fly it when the wind began to blow. Other times she told them Bible stories or stories she had told her sons when they were young. Once she told them about little John. When they asked why he did not stay with her, she calmly said, "He went to heaven to live with God."

In 1878, snow fell most of the winter in big flakes. Molly saddled Prince and rode over the prairie land. She let Prince rest as she looked in every direction. She thought, this is such a beautiful land in the winter. The snowflakes are like big, sparkling diamonds in the sunlight without a breeze to disturb them when they fall.

She sat for some time easily reflecting on the past. True, the long road ahead had often become hard to travel. She smiled, reached over and rubbed Prince between his ears, and said out loud, "Now, I am happy. My three sons, yet with me, have families and land to call their own. I will, shortly, be seventy-eight years of age. Still, I can ride Prince over my land and enjoy life. What else can I ask for?" Instantly, she whipped Prince into a fast run smiling and singing, *"Oh, ye take the high road and I'll take the low road. And I'll be in Scotland afore ye. But me and my true love will never meet again on the bonny, bonny, banks of Loch Lomond."*

That winter passed and preparation for planting another crop began. Indeed, things looked mighty good in the state of Texas.

Early in the spring, Molly once again rode Prince, but this time she crossed Walnut Creek. She followed the lazy water flowing south in search of jimson-weeds to make a poultice to put on one of the mule's irritated shoulder. Spring flowers were blooming all over. She smiled as she passed by the bluebonnets and Indian paintbrush in bloom. To her, they stood out above the others.

Riding back across the prairie land, somehow Prince stumbled. Molly bent over to see what happened. Suddenly, she became very dizzy and abruptly dropped downward. This startled Prince. The horse began to run, dragging Molly on the ground.

Later that afternoon Prince trotted up to the stall, the girth of the saddle hung loose and dangled to one side. Seeing that, the family knew something, probably very severe, had happened to Molly. Without waiting, they all rushed to look for her.

Jacob led the hounds a short distance, took the leash off, and yelled, "Go boys! Go find Maw."

After about a half hour, the hounds began to bay. Everybody ran fast and found the faithful hounds standing over Molly. Pablo, at once, knew either her hip or leg was broken. Amos and Willy ran to get the two-wheel cart. George mounted his horse and ran at a fast pace to get Dr. Adcock in Bremond.

When Willy and Amos came with the cart, Jacob and Pablo gently moved Molly onto a tarp and then onto the cart. She began to regain consciousness by the time they reached the house. But she appeared disoriented.

"Don't take her from the tarp," Rosa calmly said, "just slowly lift her onto the bed."

"Her hip is broken but the only thing we can do is to keep it steady," Dr. Adcock said when he arrived with George. "Be sure she doesn't try to set up or walk until it begins to knit together. That will probably take a month or more. Rosa, you stay with her. Give her some of this laudanum at night. It will relieve the pain so she can sleep. I'll be back tomorrow to see how she is doing."

"There is no need to worry. I'll be fine in a short time and able to take care of myself," Molly said. "The only thing I need is for my sons to take down a door and lay me on it. That way they can carry me up the stairs. I want to be in my own room and on my high bed. There I can look out the window."

Until September, Molly did lie on her high bed and look out

the window. She counted the birds as they flew by, always laughing and saying, "I fooled that mockingbird. He tried to answer me and he flew straight into my window."

Other times she asked her grandchildren to bring Luke and Nelly. She wanted all of them to tell her about Rosa's little goats. However, she never failed to ask if they watered her apple trees. Yet, she never told them the trees were special because Calvin gave them to her.

More often, she lay quietly or pretended to be sleeping. That was when Dr. Adcock asked Rosa to tell the family he needed to talk to them.

"Molly is not getting better and I'm fearful she had some small strokes. Sometimes people recover. But, if Molly does, it is doubtful she will ever walk again. Continue to put her in her chair at least once a day. Then when she gets stronger, I will send to Houston for a chair she can move around in. I'll be back in a few days," the doctor said when he walked out the door.

"Mother Anderson, here is a cup of coffee, brewed strong just the way you like it," Wela said one morning.

"Thank you, Wela. You are a good daughter-in-law," Molly said. "So are Rachel and Elizabeth. Everybody cares for me as if I am a child. Rosa is like a daughter and Beulah even helps in the house."

"Rosa, will you put me in my chair?" Molly asked some time later. "This seems like such a nice day. Will you, please, move my chair closer to the window so I can look outside?"

"Is this better?" Rosa asked as she pushed the chair closer to the window. "I will spread this quilt over your feet."

"Yes, I can see the bluebonnets are fading and the pedals are falling to the ground. But they'll bloom again in the spring. After that, more flowers will blossom. Perhaps we are like the flowers. We need to rest sometimes." Molly smiled, then continued, "Could you please give me a little sip of cool water? And go tell all the family to come upstairs. We have some things to discuss and business to attend to."

Rosa raced down the stairs. She rang the dinner bell, not once but repeatedly. She sensed Molly knew the time had come when she could not live as she once did.

"Now, don't tell me to be still or to be quiet. We need to talk about a few things," she resolutely said when the family came in. "Here, wait a minute, Pablo, you come back. And I want you girls to listen. I'm seventy-seven years of age and Doc Adcock says I may never walk again. But, remember one thing, I'm still boss of the Anderson Cattle Company with its Triple AAA brand. But after today, I'm turning it all over to you."

"Jacob, Willy, George, I gave you all land when you married," Molly said. "Now, I want Pablo and Rosa to have some, too. I believe they should have half of my portion of land and the big house goes with it. That is, if Rosa keeps taking care of me. Then, there is Amos and Beulah, I want you to sell them the forty acres where they live. Don't charge them very much and let them pay it out bit by bit after each harvest."

"Maw, I think we need to wait until tomorrow to finish this," George said as tears came to his eyes.

"I don't want any land to worry about, so give what is left to my grandchildren," Molly continued, ignoring George's remarks. "Don't ever forget that Texas is your home and this is your land. So, I hope you will never sell any of it to a stranger." Finally, she smiled and said, "Maybe you should all go and let me rest a little while."

Silence filled the room. Each person lovingly kissed her and walked out. Sorrow all but controlled their being. They knew that if nothing changed, she would never recover. Or, if she did, she would never walk down the stairs she loved.

George and Wela sat by her bed that night. She appeared to be sleeping soundly. Nevertheless, when they attempted to awaken her, she did not respond. They knew, immediately, that she had died peacefully in her sleep.

The sun was peeping out from behind the eastern horizon when Marion and Ertha arrived the next morning. Pablo had ridden from farm to farm. He made sure the people knew of Molly's "going."

Once again her sons took down a door. They carried it up the stairs, braced it on two chairs, and placed Molly's withered body on it. They quietly walked out of the room, and Ertha closed the door.

"We must find a pretty black dress for Molly," Ertha said.

"Oh! Ertha, not a black dress," Rosa said. "Let's put the crimson red dress on her. Molly must not look sad." Then she carefully placed the purple plume in Molly's hands.

Around noon the Taylor family came. In the back of their wagon was a hickory-lumber casket. Oran and the Taylor boys had worked during the night to make it. They lined it with a soft cotton cloth, showing just a slight tinge of blue, that Wela gave them.

It was three o'clock in the afternoon when friends and neighbors gathered to give their last respects to this person, who in her own way, also conquered Texas.

The people slowly walked behind as Molly's body was carried to the newly made grave that Marion, Pablo, and Amos had dug in the early morning light. There, Molly was laid to rest on the hill that stood above the clear blue water of Walnut Creek. They knew that the bluebonnets, the Indian paintbrush, and the rambling rose would blossom in the spring, just like Molly always said.